Praise for Banquet

"A thrilling mystery with delicious romance."
Fresh Fiction

"A fine treat."
RT Book Reviews

"This book is pure reading pleasure! "
Historical Novel Society

Praise for The Emperor's Conspiracy

"Diener (Keeper of the King's Secrets) delivers a rousing read . . ."
Publisher's Weekly

"This riveting spy thriller pits two people against Napoleon, with England's gold as the prize."
Fresh Fiction

The fast pace, twists and fleshed out characters immediately swept me up and kept me entranced.
The Caffeinated Reviewer

Historical Fiction Titles by Michelle Diener

Susanna Hornenbout & John Parker series:
In a Treacherous Court
Keeper of the King's Secrets
In Defense of the Queen

Regency London series:
The Emperor's Conspiracy
Banquet of Lies
A Dangerous Madness

Other historical novels:
Daughter of the Sky

Fantasy Titles by Michelle Diener

Mistress of the Wind
The Golden Apple
The Silver Pear

A Dangerous Madness

MICHELLE DIENER

ISBN: 0-9874176-9-X
ISBN-13: 978-0-9874176-9-5

ACKNOWLEDGMENTS

A big thank you to everyone who helped make this story the best it could be. To beta readers Julia, Jo, Lorna and Celeste, thank you for your great feedback! To my critique partner Edie, your suggestions were much appreciated. Thanks to Amy at AEMS for the technical side, and Croco Designs for the amazing cover.

This book is dedicated to Grant and Chiara. I was working on the final proofs of this book while visiting them for their wedding. May true love always be with you.

Chapter One

Sunday, 10 May, 1812

Phoebe stood next to the portrait of Sir Harold Fitzpatrick as instructed, the note the footman had given her crumpled in her fist.

She hadn't seen Sheldrake all evening, had had to endure hours on her own of being either snubbed or fawned over, but he must have seen her—the note was evidence of that. Just one more odd instance in a string of them.

A waving motion caught her eye and she turned slightly to see a hand reach out from behind aquamarine velvet curtains. A man's hand.

He grabbed her sleeve and pulled her into an enclosed nook that by day was a perfectly innocent bay window. Phoebe blinked, trying to adjust to the sudden dark after the well-lit gallery.

"Sheldrake?" She peered at the man taking up most of the small space.

"Good grief, keep it down, would you?"

Phoebe's betrothed's forceful whisper was as loud as her soft-spoken question, but she bit her tongue.

She wondered what her tongue would look like after they'd spent a lifetime together. Maybe one day she'd bite it in half.

"Look, dear thing, I needed to speak to you in private, without anyone seeing me here." Even in the dark, Phoebe could see Sheldrake plucking at his lapels.

"Well, this is very private." She waited patiently for him to enlighten her, and there was an uncomfortable silence. For the first time since she'd been jerked into the dark, into what would be considered a scandalous rendezvous, Phoebe felt the gentle hand of trepidation caress the back of her neck.

"My dear, dear thing. I . . . that is to say . . ." She saw the shadowy outline of his hand coming up to his head and realized he was mopping his brow with his kerchief, even though the Halliford's house was made of such thick stone, it never truly got warm.

A buzzing started in her ears.

"I can't marry you, Pheebs. I know that's going to make things difficult for you and I want to go through with it, of course I do, it would solve a number of problems, but I don't have the time for it, you understand?"

"You don't . . . have the *time* for it?" Her words seemed to be coming from far, far away.

"No. I'm . . . well, soon I'll be in a bit of bother, m'dear. Or I think I will. And I'm going to have to make a run for it. I thought I could hold out until I got my hands on your money, but it looks like I was a bit too optimistic." He gave a sigh.

Phoebe wanted to shriek at him like a woman she'd

once seen in the marketplace had shrieked at her husband.

Like a fishwife.

"You owe money?" She bit back the scream, forcing it down like too many pillows stuffed into a wooden kist. She'd had plenty of practice. Her voice didn't even wobble.

"'Fraid so. But that's not why I'm running."

"Then why were you hoping to get my money early?" She tried to be calm and logical.

"Living in exile is more comfortable when you have funds." He tugged at his kerchief as if he meant to tear it in half. "I already asked your father's lawyers if your dowry could be made available before the wedding, but it appears not." He sighed again. "And your trustees control it anyway. It's not as if you could help me. They'd have to approve, and I know for a fact they won't because I already asked one of them."

Phoebe stared at him.

"Well. That's that, then. Don't say anything, will you, until tomorrow? About my jilting you and taking off. I'm due to catch a boat to the Continent from Dover tomorrow or the day after, and I'd like to have a clear run."

"You're leaving London tonight?" Phoebe's voice came out lower than usual.

"Yes. The whole thing is coming to a head. If I don't run now, I risk being closed in." He shrugged. "You can put it about later that I was on my skids. Better a bankrupt, money-grubbing cad than a . . . " He jerked his waistcoat. "Well, never mind what."

"Sheldrake, I have no idea what you're talking about."

"No. You wouldn't." He patted her arm, in the way

he'd done countless times before. A way that made her want to jerk her arm viciously away and do him some bodily harm.

She drew in a deep, deep breath. Pulled her arm very gently from under his grasp.

Oblivious to her fury, he lifted his pocket watch to the thin stream of light coming into the alcove through a gap in the drapes, and turned it this way and that until he could read the time. He gave a grunt.

"My coach will be waiting." He twisted his lips in a grimace. "Sorry, dear thing. Sometimes the best plans turn to ash and well . . . Don't believe everything you might hear about me if this comes out. I was doing something. Taking action. But it's all gone to the dogs. Our puppet has lost his nerve. I'm afraid he'll crack or botch it, and it will all come out. I refuse to be sacrificed." He rubbed his forehead one last time and pushed his kerchief into his pocket. "Be careful for the next few days, eh? Watch your step."

With a last pat, he cocked his head, listening for any sign of someone nearby, and then opened the curtains to step out. Hesitated.

"You should be safe enough." With a little nod of his head, he slipped out between the heavy curtains, leaving nothing behind but the sharp scent of his pomade and his sweat.

Phoebe collapsed onto the deep window seat, her fingers clutching at the thin cushions beneath her.

Her betrothal was over. And from the way Sheldrake had spoken, he was involved in something illegal, or at least immoral. He was running from the authorities.

She lifted a hand and rubbed it over her heart. She touched her face, but the tears she expected weren't there.

After some time had passed, she couldn't say how long, she stood and parted the curtains. Walked slowly back to the light and sound of the ballroom.

Her world, her future as she had thought it would be, was gone.

All she could feel was relief.

Chapter Two

Monday, 11 May, 1812

"My lord! His Grace is in his bath. You can't . . ." James heard the unusual sound of his valet in full panic moments before the door to his dressing room was wrenched open and Lord Dervish stepped, grim and breathless, into the room.

"It's all right, Towers. Lord Dervish is welcome." James said nothing more, and neither did Dervish until Towers had closed his mouth with a snap, closed the door, and retreated to wherever aggrieved valets go.

He was almost finished with his bath, but James lay back and raised his brows as Dervish continued to stand quite still, head cocked, as if to hear if Towers or anyone else may be trying to listen in.

They probably were.

"Move the water in your bath about so it's harder for anyone to hear." Dervish stepped closer, something stealthy in the move. He hummed with suppressed energy and adrenalin.

"What is it?" James didn't deign to follow his instructions. Their voices were low enough to make listening at the door impossible.

"The Prime Minister has just been assassinated." Dervish ran a hand over his stark, sharp face, and James could see it shook.

He sat up suddenly, and water slopped over the side with a splash. "You're not joking."

Dervish never joked, but James wondered if he could have made a mistake.

"I wish I were." Dervish walked over to the window and looked out on the garden at the back of the house, his tall, wiry frame barely able to stay still.

James rose from the still-warm water and wrapped a towel around his waist, took up another and began to dry himself in quick, economical movements.

"Who did it?"

"Some fellow called Bellingham. Put the gun right against Perceval's chest as he came through the lobby to the Lower House, pulled the trigger and then went and sat down on a bench nearby. Didn't try to run, just sat, waiting."

"Part of a group? Some conspiracy?"

Dervish turned as James pulled a fresh shirt over his head. "It's the most likely explanation." He turned back to the window, shook his head. "I know a lot of people hated Perceval's politics, and with this current inquiry into the Orders in Council, they've been more front and center than usual, but when the word spread, when it got out that he'd been killed . . ." Dervish ran a hand through thick, dark hair winged with silver at the temples. "I had to fight through cheering, celebrating crowds to get here. They were all but dancing in the street. Calling for the Prince Regent to be next."

James pulled his trousers on and considered things. He'd despised Perceval. It hadn't been difficult to pretend to be a malcontent these last few years, because the sheer pomposity and self-righteousness of the prime minister had been everything he disliked in politics. In life in general.

But rioting in the streets and calling for the death of the regent? How could it end well? "What have you done with the killer?"

"They tried to take him to Newgate, but the crowds were too strong, too wild. Everyone was cheering him, trying to shake his hand. They had to take him back inside, wait for the guards to clear the crowds."

For the first time, James noticed a small bruise high on Dervish's cheek. Realized he'd been speaking literally when he'd said he'd had to fight the crowds.

"What do you want of me?" He'd already pulled on his boots, and was shrugging his way into a coat.

"The problem is, so many people wished Perceval ill. The slave traders. The manufacturers. The Luddites. The shipping industry. Bellingham claims he did it on his own, that it was for personal reasons. But I can't bring myself to believe that. It's too good to be true."

"Yes." James slung his cravat around his neck and started to tie it. His valet would be surprised to see how well he was able to accomplish the task. "A lone man with a grudge would certainly be the most convenient explanation. Leave no one with a cause to take up." He pulled his shirt straight and began to button his jacket.

"We want you to focus on your area of specialization, Wittaker. There are plenty of noblemen who were being ruined by Perceval's Orders in Council and he had such a grip on government—hell, he almost single-handedly *was* government—that some might have seen assassination as the only way to dislodge him."

"I haven't heard even a whisper about something like that." James leaned back against his dresser and crossed his arms over his chest.

Dervish glanced at him sharply. "Yes, but you haven't been hanging around your usual haunts for the past month and more."

No. James had to admit he hadn't.

The lustre had gone off his old lifestyle. Not that there was much lustre to begin with, though he'd felt he was helping in some way. But there was only so long you could wallow in the mire before the mud started to stick.

He shrugged. Let the silence draw out.

Dervish looked away. "Your help was always much appreciated. I know it wasn't said enough." He cleared his throat. "It's not likely, but there are enough idiots in both the Upper and the Lower House who may have thought they were doing England and their family fortunes a favour by taking Perceval out of the running."

"Even more manufacturers, exporters, and slavers who were being ruined." James tapped his lips. "What are Bellingham's connections?"

"He's from Liverpool, apparently. Involved in the shipping trade to Russia."

"Hmm." James and Dervish exchanged a look. "So looking into the young hot-bloods is really just being thorough. If he's from Liverpool—"

"He's most likely working for the slavers or the shipping trade." Dervish gave a nod of agreement. "But it's almost too obvious."

"Sometimes," James opened the door to Dervish and waited for him to step out the room, "a thing is exactly what it seems."

***

"I have heard the most unbelievable news from Mrs. Jenkins." Aunt Dorothy stripped off her gloves with hands that trembled, and Phoebe paused in the act of pulling the tea tray toward her and looked up at her aunt.

"Something bad, I take it?" She looked down at her hands, suddenly unable to pick up the teapot in case she dropped it. Someone must have found out about Sheldrake and told her aunt.

"The worst news I've ever heard. The Prime Minister has been shot."

Phoebe lifted her head to stare at her aunt's angular, beautiful face for a long moment. "When?"

"No more than a few hours ago. Shot down like a dog in the lobby of the Houses of Parliament."

"Surely that can't be right?" Harriet picked the pot up at last and poured them both a cup of tea with steady hands.

She should have told her aunt right away about Sheldrake's abandonment of the engagement that had been both their fathers' dying wish. But the shame of it, the humiliation, still stung; an inflamed, pulsing bite out of her pride.

"It's right, all right. Mr. Jenkins was there. Still is there, by the sounds of it. He got a note out to his wife, but as a witness, he's had to stay on while they charge the assassin." Aunt Dorothy lifted the delicate cup to her lips and took a deep gulp.

"They have someone in custody? It wasn't an accident or something?" Phoebe couldn't imagine anyone actually shooting the diminutive, cherub-faced man.

Dorothy shrugged. "So Mrs. Jenkins understood from her husband's note. The details will no doubt come out soon. Something about him being like a puppet with its strings cut after he did the deed. Just collapsed onto a bench and waited for the inevitable."

"That's terrible. Who would shoot a man in cold blood?" She didn't know why she was suddenly thinking about what Sheldrake had said last night, each word burned into her memory in charred, ugly letters.

The word 'puppet', that was it.

An icy drop of unease snaked down her back and made her shiver.

"More than one person of my acquaintance has threatened to do away with him," her aunt said, eyes avid. "Ruining the country, my dear husband says, almost every morning when he reads the paper. Single-handedly ruining the country." She settled back in her chair and took a piece of Madeira cake. "It's been one of the few things I've not missed about him, being in Town with you for a few weeks. What does dear Sheldrake say about it?"

"Sheldrake?" Phoebe had to force herself to breathe so

her voice wouldn't squeak. "He's never seemed to have much of an opinion when it comes to politics."

"Lucky you. Mr. Patterson drives me almost 'round the bend going on about how Mr. Perceval is trying to throw England into a pit of economic ruin and despair."

"Not any more," Phoebe said, and gripped her teacup a little tighter. "By the sounds of it, not any more."

Chapter Three

"Haven't seen you before, luv." An arm came around James's waist, and a soft, well-endowed body pressed up against his back and rubbed. He smelled rose water and powder, with just a musky hint of old sex.

James turned slightly and stepped away, removing the woman's arm as he did.

Behind him, a room full of well-dressed men shouted and laughed as they played Hazard. The pungent aroma of cigar smoke, along with the sharp-sweet stink of spilled drinks, layered over with sweat, washed over him.

He hadn't missed this.

It amazed him that at one time, he hadn't even noticed the smell.

"I can keep you company, if you like." The woman gave him a saucy wink.

He looked her over. She was dressed in a peacock blue dress, cut so low her nipples were just visible above the neckline. It was nipped in tight at her waist, and she had a peacock feather dressed into her up-swept hair.

"You must be new here." She looked no more than eighteen or nineteen, but he couldn't accuse Jillie Bellows of breaking her deal with him. Her new girl was of age—just—and did not seem to be coerced or afraid.

Of course, coercion was a tricky line to walk. How many of these girls really felt they had a choice in entering this life?

"Your Grace." Jillie stepped into the hall from her little office, the old parlor, James guessed, from when this smart West End house had been a family home, rather than The Scarlet Rose, one of the most profitable gaming hells and brothels in London.

"Madame Rouge." James gave a nod. He called her the name she went by here, although she was well aware he knew all there was to know about her.

"Bessie, don't bother the Duke. He's here strictly for the gaming." Her voice was sharp, gilded with a little fear, and Bessie blushed, curtseyed, and fled down the passage and through a white and gold door.

"A little harsh. She couldn't have known my . . . rules."

"No. You haven't been by for more than a month, and she's only been here two weeks." Her tone was almost as fierce with him as it had been with Bessie, and she looked away, her shoulders stiff.

He didn't respond. He wasn't prepared to answer to her.

"Well, nice to have you back." On that lie, she gave a nod, still not meeting his eyes, and stepped back into her office.

Jillie Bellows hadn't been pleased to see him since the day he'd threatened to close her down for selling a child into sexual slavery, and that had been two years ago.

Since then they'd reached a strange truce. She didn't send any of her girls out to him, and swore never to deal in children again, and he, by the cachet that came with being a duke, lent her establishment an air of high-class sin.

It appeared to be doing quite well without him, though, if the crowd in the gaming room was anything to go by.

"Wittaker. There you are! Thought you'd abandoned this place. I even started enquiring where you'd moved on to." Banford was slumped in a chair near the door, his face flushed with the close heat of the room and the whisky in his glass.

So that was the reason behind Jillie's sharp tongue. She sensed the sheep were getting ready to follow him to what they thought were greener pastures.

"Busy with other things, is all," he said to Banford, slurring his words just a little. He wondered if he'd ever get drunk again—risk actually sounding like this.

Somehow, he doubted it.

"Oh?" Banford sat a little straighter, his eyes lighting at the possibility of something even more dissolute than what was on offer at The Scarlet Rose.

Wittaker didn't hide his contempt at Banford's reaction, flicking him a look before turning his attention to the room without making a reply.

It made him even more popular, even more respected among this lot, he'd found. The more contemptuous, the more dismissive he was of them, the more they tried to please him and follow his style.

"Like that, eh? Keeping all the best secrets for yourself." Banford narrowed his eyes. "What's a fellow got to do to get an invitation?"

James looked back at him. "You hear about Perceval?"

"You'd have to be living under a rock not to hear." Banford got unsteadily to his feet. "Damn disgrace. Shot down in the one place he should have been safe." He tipped slightly to one side and stumbled a little as he steadied himself on the chair.

"Worried about your own neck next time you're at Westminster?" James didn't look at him as he spoke, his eyes on the raucous game of Hazard happening in the middle of the room.

Banford laughed. "Not in the House often enough for that to be likely. Still, some places should be sacred."

James gave him a cool look. "As you say."

It was a hard line to walk. To play aggrieved enough by Perceval's policies to let a possible conspirator know he would lend a sympathetic ear, but also suitably outraged enough that a man, any man, had lost his life by murder.

Almost as hard a line as to know how he genuinely felt about the prime minister. He'd approved of Perceval's practical support of the abolition of the slave trade, but found the man himself objectionable. When facing off against his political opponents, Perceval attacked the individual, not their policies, leading James to think he didn't have the intelligence to argue against them.

Perceval used his obviously genuine love for his family and the Church to garner himself more support, and further his political agenda, thereby sullying any moral high ground he would otherwise have had.

Perceval was a thorny problem of a man.

Unbending, unable to see any opinion other than his own, wholly annoying, and yet, no matter what, he did not deserve to be killed.

James rubbed the back of his neck.

He was on a wild goose chase here.

No one would say anything different to Banford. Certainly not a few hours after the murder itself had been done.

The breech of the sanctity of the Houses of Parliament, the way murder had slipped into a place where all thought they were safe but for a tongue-lashing from a political opponent—that would shock all of them, no matter if they hated Perceval or not.

Nevertheless . . .

He stepped toward the Hazard table, and was surprised to find himself tensing, as if for a blow.

It wasn't so far off.

Forcing a sardonic smile on his face, he waded into the crowd, listening for anything unusual.

By the time he waded back out again, 2000 pounds richer, he had a name.

Sheldrake.

Chapter Four

Tuesday, 12 May, 1812

Everyone with any sense was at home this morning. Phoebe had the paper open in front of her, but her eyes were on the street. Empty in a way she'd never seen it before. The only person in sight was a gardener in Portman Square's fenced park, raking a bed.

According to the news, Bellingham had been moved to Newgate prison sometime in the night, after the crowds outside parliament had been dispersed. There had still been some people waiting for him outside the prison entrance, though, to cheer and wave him on.

She folded the paper with a snap and pushed it aside, stared down at the letter lying beside her plate, delivered early this morning.

Sheldrake's unkempt script scrawled across the front. She wondered if she would even be able to make out what the note said. She rarely could.

It had been the cause of a number of missed engagements, and more than a few arguments between them.

Only, they weren't arguments, as such. More teeth-gritting conversations with no satisfactory conclusion.

Relief at never having to have such conversations again made her a trifle light-headed. Her mother had often talked about silver linings. The silver lining on the storm cloud of Sheldrake's betrayal was . . . Sheldrake's betrayal.

She smiled, the first one she'd been capable of since Sunday evening, and lifted the note, brushing the paper with her fingertips. It was expensive and smooth, and she marveled that he'd remembered to pack his stationary when he took to the road.

She wouldn't have expected that of him.

She lifted her letter opener, slid the blade carefully into the flap and gave a vicious upward swipe to break the seal.

A thick letter fell out, landing on the table.

Phoebe lifted it, and saw it was an official document, a petition for compensation, addressed to the Prince Regent and dated 21 January.

There was nothing else inside but a piece of notepaper, on which was written what looked like an address, an inn called The King's Arms in Kent. She could barely make it out.

But she recognized the hand who had written it. No one could scrawl as illegibly as Sheldrake.

She looked at the document he had enclosed again. A petition for compensation for 8,000 pounds for loss of income resulting from the failure of the British government to aid a British citizen in the Russian port of Archangel. The language was formal and careful, and she was sure drawn up by a lawyer.

She wondered why on earth Sheldrake had sent her this.

And then her gaze fell on the name of the claimant, and a terrible chill stole over her, freezing her in place.

John Bellingham.

The man who had just assassinated the prime minister.

***

"His lordship is not at home." The butler who answered Sheldrake's door had wary eyes and held the door mostly closed, for ease of slamming it in his face, James realized.

"He will be at home for me." He gave a smile, and handed the man his card. The late spring afternoon sun warmed the back of his neck, and he angled his body to get a little more of it.

The butler looked down at the card and straightened. Opened the door wider.

"My apologies, Your Grace, but Lord Sheldrake is not actually here. He left for a hunting party on Sunday evening, and I only expect him back in two weeks' time."

"Where did he go?" James leaned against the door-jamb, and the butler opened the door wider still and took a step back.

"He didn't say." The man pursed his lips.

"That's very disappointing." There was something about this situation that was off. James could almost smell the rot in the air.

The butler seemed to be struggling with something.

He opened his mouth to speak, closed it, then looked down at his shoes. "You might ask his betrothed, Miss Hillier. She may know where he's gone. She lives in Portman Square."

James felt a stir of excitement. "I will. Thank you."

The butler looked up, and there was something calculating in his expression. "Her address is Home House."

James tipped his hat and took his leave. He felt the butler's eyes on him until he turned the corner and was no longer in sight.

Miss Hillier's address was only a fifteen minute walk away, and James spent it trying to remember if he'd ever met her.

Sheldrake, he knew; from his club and from places like The Scarlet Rose, but he hadn't attended a ball or polite dinner for many years.

Home House, on Portman Square, was large, and spoke of money and taste. And when the butler admitted him and he stepped into the hall, even he, with one of the finest houses in London, stood entranced by the staircase.

It was golden and bright, rising up to midway and then splitting to curve right and left, and frame the pale gold marble and white of the classically rendered wall behind it.

The butler cleared his throat and brought James back to himself. He followed him into a warm, sun-filled drawing room in pale gold and cream. While he waited, he looked out the window to the gardens of Portman Square, and wondered if he would be able to buy this place.

The door opened, and a woman stepped through. She was in her early twenties, five years or more past her coming out.

Her hair was the color of moonlight, almost silver it was so blonde, and she was slight and fair-skinned. Her eyes were a dark blue and her cheeks were flushed, as if she'd been out in the garden in the warm sun.

He smelled fresh-cut rosemary and the clean green scent of crushed leaves as she stopped in front of him, and guessed that was exactly where she had been.

"Your Grace." She curtseyed and flicked a nervous look at the open door. "I'm afraid my aunt is out, and she is my only companion. I'm not sure . . ."

James saw her quandary. She was alone in the house but for her servants, and propriety demanded a chaperone.

"My apologies, Miss Hillier. I would have made an appointment, but I urgently need to speak to your betrothed, Lord Sheldrake, and his staff directed me here, as they don't know where he is. If you could give me his current address, I will be immediately on my way."

Her reaction was not what he was expecting.

She took a step back and lifted an ungloved hand to her lips, pressing her fingers against them.

His eyes jerked to hers, and they stood, staring at each other for a long beat.

Then she turned away, her arms tight across her chest, and walked to the small arrangement of chairs at the center of the room.

She half-turned to him, checked herself, and then braced both hands on the back of an armchair, her head bowed. "I am uncomfortable telling you this, but it will be common knowledge soon enough." She straightened and finally turned to him again, her face composed, although

James could see her cheeks were no longer flushed and pink. "Sheldrake broke our betrothal on Sunday. His plan was to leave England. He left London for Dover on Sunday evening, and his intention was to take a boat to the Continent,." She hunched her body. "That he hasn't told his staff is despicable, even for him. They will wait for him in vain, and with no salary. I will have to make it right."

She sounded so desolate, he took a step toward her and then had to force himself to stop when her eyes widened. He cleared his throat. "Do you know why he left?"

She shook her head.

He read genuine frustration in her face, but there was something else there, as well.

"All he told me was that he was in debt and couldn't get his hands on my dowry in time to save himself from his creditors."

"Did you believe him?"

She started. "What do you mean?"

"Did you believe that was why he was leaving? His debts?"

"What else could it be?" Her voice wavered, and she turned away again.

"Have you had any word from him since he left?"

James watched her closely, and she went very still at the question. Seemed to take longer than necessary to answer.

"I received a quick note from him, from an inn called The King's Arms in Kent."

He knew it. It was a popular staging post for the mail coaches and travelling coaches heading for the coast.

"What did it say?"

She looked up, and now he could see anger sparking in those blue eyes. "I don't mean to be rude, Your Grace, but why do you want to know the contents of my private correspondence with my former betrothed? What is your interest in Sheldrake?"

She stared boldly at him, and again they stood, looking into each other's eyes for longer than was polite.

"I'm afraid I can't disclose that." James shrugged. "It's a private matter."

She kept her gaze on his face for another beat, and then looked away. "Well, I don't suppose it makes a difference. Sheldrake said nothing in that note." She looked down at her hands, and unclenched them. "Absolutely nothing."

"What do you mean by nothing?"

"I mean he wrote the address of the inn, and nothing more." She crossed her arms under her breasts again, and drew his attention to her pale blue dress with sprigs of green posies embroidered on its scoop-necked bodice.

It seemed incredible that Sheldrake would have done something like that. Sent a blank letter. But James could not doubt her genuine anger at it.

"Thank you. My apologies for disturbing you." He moved to the door, and when he looked at her again, her face was more composed. "I'm sorry to hear that your engagement is broken and I look forward to meeting you again under more pleasant circumstances."

She gave a nod and another curtsey, and the butler was suddenly there to show him out, as if he'd been waiting nearby. Even though it annoyed him to be watched, James was glad for the man's protective instincts.

As he stepped through the gleaming black door and down the stairs, he reflected both Miss Hillier and he had done little but lie to each other for the last five minutes.

Miss Hillier was hiding something, and he, well, he wasn't sorry Sheldrake was no longer her betrothed. Not at all.

Chapter Five

He was dangerous. Phoebe watched the Duke of Wittaker walk down her front path and turn in the direction of Grosvenor Square.

She wondered where his coach was. The Duke of Wittaker didn't have to make his way on foot anywhere, but the way he strode down the street told her that he not only enjoyed it, but did it often.

When Sheldrake said people would be looking for him, she'd imagined rough-edged Bow Street runners, or hard-eyed businessmen with IOUs. Not the Duke of Wittaker, with his beautifully cut clothes, and his dark, sartorial looks.

He was at least head and shoulders taller than Sheldrake, with a long, lean body and a way of moving that suggested if he wanted to, he could be very, very fast.

She'd heard whispers about him. That he was a rake and gambler, a disaffected nobleman with a grudge against the government.

Just the sort of person Sheldrake would be in league with, if he were involved in the death of the prime minister —

She didn't want to even touch the thought. Wanted it out of her mind. But it was too late.

And when she'd been looking, too long and too deep, into the Duke of Wittaker's dark gray eyes, she'd had the uncomfortable sense that he had seen too much. Had picked up on her disquiet.

And yet she hadn't looked away. She was still trying to work out why.

She pulled back from the window.

The duke was long gone, had turned the corner and was no doubt already on his way home in his carriage. But Phoebe knew he'd be back.

There was a steely certainty about him.

Yes. He was most certainly dangerous.

She walked out of the room, to the small withdrawing room containing her writing desk, and removed the petition Sheldrake had sent her, still folded within his strange, blank letter.

She should burn it.

She rolled it up into a tight cylinder, and tapped it against her open palm.

There was no question that it was better to be rid of it.

But, better for who?

For herself, certainly.

She'd never thought herself a coward, or selfish. Sheldrake had sent this to her for a reason, and while she no longer cared about what was safe and good for him, perhaps she owed the family and friends of Spencer Perceval the respect of preserving it.

Just for a while.

Until she could work out what was going on.

***

James stepped from the upstairs landing of the exclusive St. James club into the common room. It was only the fifth time he'd been here, although he'd been a member since his father signed him up at seventeen, ten years ago.

He hadn't come originally because it was his father's domain, and then later because it hadn't suited the image of himself he'd needed to portray.

Over the last few weeks he'd made up for that, though, and the few servants in attendance recognized him and bowed as he made his way to the isolated grouping of chairs at the far end of the room.

Dervish had invited him to meet here, but he wasn't alone. James slowed his steps as he saw Durnham and Aldridge with him. He knew them both, and had occasion earlier in the year to get to know them a little better.

He'd had a sense then that they were more than just friends. Now he had his answer.

The way they sat, talking quietly, was more than a meeting. It had the whiff of a council of war about it.

This early in the afternoon, the club was relatively quiet and as James approached the group, they looked up from their conversation and Dervish indicated the fourth chair for him.

"Afternoon, gentlemen." James was struck by the easy way they sat together, none trying to show his superiority or assert himself as leader.

It was calming.

He lowered himself into the chair with less tension

than he would usually feel, but it made no sense to completely drop his guard.

Dervish waited until he was seated. "You must be acquainted with Aldridge and Durnham?"

James inclined his head. "Yes. And I count Aldridge's betrothed, Miss Barrington, to be a friend."

Dervish gave him a quick, hard look, and a frown, then tugged a little on his bright blue cravat, an item of clothing that seemed incongruous with his personality, yet suited him perfectly. "I thought we could discuss our findings together, in case there's an overlap. Aldridge?"

Aldridge had been watching James intently, but now he was all business, and gave a shake of his head. "I can't find any evidence of an organized group of former soldiers beyond the smallish groups that put themselves out as watchmen or laborers. Some of them are living rough, or in such squalid circumstance, I wouldn't blame them if they had got it into their heads to kill Perceval off, but if they had a hand in it, they've kept it very quiet. More quiet than I think they're capable of, given what a diverse and ragtag bunch they are."

Dervish steepled his fingers. "Durnham?"

Durnham leaned forward. "My contacts among the Luddites tell me they're getting more organized, and more violent, but they know killing Perceval isn't going to change things. The switch to more machinery in factories is being pushed in by the business owners, not the government, although the government is certainly taking the businessmen's side."

"And the Catholics?"

Durnham grimaced. "Perceval is loathed by the Catholics, especially in Northern Ireland, but they also know killing him won't change anything. Things were bad enough before he got in to power, and they won't change if he's removed. And if they were found to be behind it, things would get even worse for them. They can barely manage as it is. I don't think they would have risked this."

"That still leaves a very large field of suspects." James tapped his fingers on the smooth, glossy oak armrest of his chair.

"I know." Dervish rubbed his temple, looked across at James with eyes that were blood-shot and dark-ringed. He hesitated a moment, and then looked at Durnham. "And your wife?"

Durnham's face hardened. "She's still making enquiries."

James was surprised at how he'd gone from amenable to stone cold in a moment. Whatever Dervish was asking of him, asking him to confirm, was something he would rather not discuss.

He slid a glance at Aldridge and saw him frowning, and then the frown cleared, as if he had worked out what was going on. "The common agitators, you mean?"

Durnham gave a stiff nod. "The radicals. Some of them have the resources, and enough of a grudge, to pull this off."

James wondered how Lady Durnham's name had come into this. Surely she did not have connections in that world . . .

"When will she know?" Dervish asked, but he was

clearly uncomfortable now, as if he regretted bringing the matter up.

"I think you can take it as not having come from that quarter, unless she informs me otherwise. But she thinks not. Bracken . . . Bracken is still away, and no one else has the intelligence, the means, and the axe to grind that he does. Not that his people aren't happy about this turn of events. They were probably the ones dancing in the street outside Parliament House."

Luke Bracken. James had heard that name. Read it, he remembered now, in Dervish's report into gold guineas being smuggled out of England. He lifted his gaze and caught Durnham's eye, but the man just stared back, calm and closed off. A mystery he might one day have the answer to, if he was invited to stay in this tight circle of men.

"I've been busy looking into the traders up in Liverpool, seeing as that's were Bellingham is from, and the profession he used to be involved in." Dervish rubbed his face. "Most of them are terrified that Perceval's Orders in Council are going to start a war with America. In fact, they say it's a certainty. The Orders are interfering with the Americans' trade, and the fact that Perceval was shot on his way to defend the Orders in Council in Parliament might be a message on its own. The problem is there are so many different trading interests, and all of them are bitterly opposed to Perceval's policies. They were sure Perceval wouldn't abolish the Orders, and that a war with America as well as Napoleon will cripple us."

"And did you find anything?" James wondered how he could have done, given the distance to Liverpool, and the hundreds of suspects in that area of enquiry.

Dervish shook his head. "How did you get on?"

"I've got a name." James noticed they all turned their focus on him immediately. "What it means, I don't know. And why I was given it at all is an interesting puzzle in itself."

"You don't trust it?" Aldridge was watching him again. He had been an officer in the Peninsula Campaign, before his brother died and he inherited the family title. A man of action and intelligence. There was a challenge in his stare, as if waiting for James to prove himself, one way or the other.

Or it may be because Aldridge's betrothed had been to visit James just two days ago. Or rather, James's chef, but she always came and said hello to James as well while she was there.

James didn't blame Aldridge for his annoyance. He wouldn't like his future wife visiting a duke of ill-repute on a regular basis either. He was simply glad Giselle Barrington had the strength of personality to insist on visiting whomever she chose, and Aldridge for respecting her enough to say nothing about it.

James raised his brows. "I don't know that I don't trust it. But it felt too easy. Too pat."

"Who is it, first of all?" Dervish sat straighter.

"Lord Sheldrake." He watched their reactions and gave a nod of acknowledgement. "I see you share my misgivings. I was being as subtle as I could be in a crowd of drunken gamblers with half-dressed women squirming on their laps, fishing for anything I could get on anti-Perceval sentiment. Sheldrake's name came up. I challenged it, because the few times I've run into Sheldrake he's never said a word about politics."

"I don't think he's ever set foot in the House of Lords," Durnham said, his mouth twisting up in a wry grin. "Don't know much about him."

"He was engaged to a Miss Hillier." James didn't know why he was suddenly uncomfortable—the broken betrothal would no doubt be common knowledge soon enough and Miss Hillier had not sworn him to secrecy—but he felt oddly reluctant to talk about her.

"Was?" Aldridge asked.

"Yes. Broke it off with her on Sunday evening, and took off for the Continent via Dover. Debt dodging."

"Miss Hillier?" Dervish tapped his lips. "Daughter of Sir Blanbury, although he's passed on. I seem to remember she's extremely well-off. If he was engaged to her, surely Sheldrake could have invoked his upcoming wedding as surety against any claim?"

"I wondered that, too. She claims he told her the debts couldn't wait, and he couldn't delay payment any longer."

"Why didn't he ask her for a loan?" Durnham's tone said more than words could how distasteful such an occurrence would be, but he was right to ask it. James hadn't thought of it.

"Perhaps her money is in trust?" That was more likely. It could well be Miss Hillier couldn't have lent him the money, because she personally didn't control it.

"You said 'she claims'. You don't think she's telling the truth?" Aldridge propped his elbows on his thighs and steepled his fingers.

"No. She's hiding something. But aside from that, it's interesting that the one name I was given was for a man who's run for the coast and a fast ship."

"You think he's been set up to take the blame, whether he's involved or not?"

"Well, it would be convenient if the only suspect was no longer in the country."

"And suspect, how, exactly?" Dervish shook his head. "What was Sheldrake supposed to have done? Paid Bellingham to assassinate Perceval? I struggle to imagine Sheldrake stirring himself to something like that. And his family fortune is long gone. He wasn't being ruined by the government. There was nothing left to ruin."

James leaned back in his chair and kept his face impassive, although he sensed he was on the trail of something that was worth following and didn't want Dervish to rein him in. "You're right, which only makes his name coming up more interesting. What I'd like to do is interview Bellingham. See what he has to say."

Dervish met his gaze. "You and almost every one of Perceval's close friends. They want to understand why Bellingham murdered him. They're going to be furious when they learn Gibbs is hearing his case on Friday."

James blinked. "Friday? How has anyone had time to gather evidence? Perceval hasn't been dead twenty-four hours yet."

"The wheels of Justice can turn quickly when they want to, especially when justice is not what they are trying to achieve." Durnham's voice was dry.

"They want Bellingham tried and hanged as fast as possible, to make an example of him and get him out of the public eye?" Aldridge leaned forward in dismay. "But if he's part of a conspiracy, we could lose the chance to find out who's behind it."

"Vinegar Gibbs doesn't want any hint of a conspiracy to come out, you can be sure of that." James thought of the Attorney General. Sir Vicary Gibbs hadn't come by the nickname Vinegar Gibbs for his sweet nature. "If Bellingham has made a statement that he was acting alone, you can bet Gibbs will do everything he can to keep him from changing that tune, and have him hanged before anyone thinks to dig deeper."

"*I* want to know if there is a conspiracy, though." Dervish spoke quietly, and James wondered, not for the first time, the extent of the power Dervish wielded within Whitehall. He wouldn't be surprised to find it was considerable.

"Even if we can't prove it definitively?" Aldridge asked.

Dervish sighed. "I'd rather know the players than not. Even if I can't move against them." He and Durnham exchanged a look, and James wondered what other investigation had yielded that outcome.

Perhaps one day he would be established enough in this small group to ask.

"Can you arrange for me to speak to Bellingham, then?" The question was a courtesy only. James could get into Newgate on the strength of his title alone and Dervish knew it.

Dervish gave a nod. "I'll organize it for later this afternoon. I've had mixed accounts of the suspect. Some are sure he is mad, but many others have found him to be perfectly sane. I'd like your opinion."

"If it's a conspiracy, then he's sane enough." Aldridge spoke quietly.

"Bellingham says he killed Perceval to obtain justice for himself, as the government had turned down all his requests for compensation for something that happened to him in Russia seven years ago. He's spoken to his Member of Parliament, all the relevant departments, there's even a petition for compensation he submitted to the Prince Regent himself."

"Killing the head of state because you didn't get compensation is hardly the act of a sane man." James raised his brows.

"Perhaps," said Durnham, "Gibbs merely hopes he's sane, so that he can, in fact, be hanged."

Because a hanged man couldn't talk, and certainly couldn't stir up the crowds.

Chapter Six

This was most likely a mistake.

Phoebe stood on the busy pavement covered by her oldest cloak and looked up at the high walls of Newgate Prison. The blank, windowless stone rose up, frightening in its grim indifference.

Around her, people went about their business, although she caught a tension in the faces of the people passing her by. A small crowd had gathered to one side, the men dressed like laborers, and Phoebe was willing to guess they were there to support John Bellingham.

They were being watched by guards standing in front of the prison, but neither group approached the other.

Now that she was here, she realized getting in to see the man accused of killing the prime minister would be impossible. She'd seen two men turned away already as she'd hesitated, gripped by indecision and nerves. And she had slipped out without her aunt, without a chaperone.

They would not let her in.

In a stroke of luck—because it certainly hadn't been planning—the sharp wind blowing down the street made the raised hood of her cloak all too natural, but she had no explanation for her presence. No excuse to see the prisoner that would be believed.

And what would she ask Bellingham anyway? If he knew Sheldrake? If Sheldrake had helped him carry out his plan?

She turned to look for her carriage.

There had been nowhere to stop on the crowded road outside the prison, and the driver had dropped her and told her he'd find a place further up Newgate Street to pull in.

She could see it up ahead, and took a hesitant step toward it. She had not thought this through as she usually would before putting a plan into action, and as a result, she'd wasted her time.

And yet . . . She turned back. The hard, stubborn knot in her chest that had driven her here would not loosen.

She accepted she had no hope of seeing Bellingham, but she could watch the comings and goings of the prison and hope one of the men or women entering or leaving the narrow entrance would be familiar to her. Would offer her some lead.

She had known Sheldrake since they were children, his father and hers had been first cousins.

The two families had come together often, although she hadn't understood as a child why her mother had not liked them, why their frequent visits caused arguments behind closed doors between her parents.

With the benefit of hindsight and maturity, she could see how it would have grated on her mother's nerves to be looked down on by Lady Sheldrake and her drunken, gambling-addicted husband, while they foisted their son under Phoebe's nose and made unsubtle enquiries into her mother's wealth.

Phoebe wondered what her choices would have been if her mother had been alive when her father's older brother had died and he'd become Sir Blanbury. Whether her mother would have ever allowed the betrothal her father had engineered to take place.

Sheldrake himself had been slightly offensive, innocuous and dull. Even when they were younger and had played together, he had an annoying habit of underestimating her and condescending to her, but that fault was hardly unique among the men she knew.

She had never, not once in all the years she had known him, suspected he had the nerve or the daring to get involved in something as huge as the assassination of the prime minister.

A snide bet in his club's books, or pushing a friend into a pond while out duck shooting, that was more his line.

It shook her that he could hide so much from her. It made her doubt herself more than his small put-downs and absent-minded arm patting ever had.

Frustration built in her.

She refused to let this pass.

She would get to the bottom of it, and she would understand what had driven the plump, selfish and self-centred man her father had manipulated her into accepting to involve himself in this affair.

From behind her, the bells of St. Paul's Cathedral tolled the hour, and she decided to give herself another half hour of watching. Any later, and her aunt would expect an explanation for her absence.

Phoebe moved a little closer to the prison entrance and found a spot where she could stand that was out of the way of pedestrians.

Then she settled in to watch.

***

John Bellingham sat calmly in his special cell, looking like a man taking his ease. That in itself set a bell ringing in James's head.

Bellingham's jailer, Newman, stepped back when the door was opened and bowed to James for the fifth time.

James fingered the guinea in his pocket as he gave the little man a nod in return.

Newman had quick, beady eyes that missed nothing and James would have a private chat with him after he was done with Bellingham. The jailer would know exactly who had come and gone since Bellingham was brought here.

"Good afternoon, sir." James stepped into the cell.

Bellingham rose from his chair, and gave a short bow. "Good afternoon." He looked expectantly at James, waiting for an introduction, and then indicated the other chair beside the small writing desk.

James sat and observed Bellingham, choosing to say nothing about who he was. He knew his title cowed some, made sycophants of others. He wanted Bellingham to treat him like any of the officials who must surely have seen him since he killed Perceval.

Bellingham's clothing was well-made, but ripped and torn in places, and James realized that he must be in the same clothes he'd worn when he shot Perceval yesterday afternoon. His handling on being taken into custody was obviously rough.

Bellingham looked down and ran a restless finger over some notepaper on the desk. He was dark-haired and had a long, thin face. "Do you have my papers, sir? Or can you get them? They were taken from me after . . . They were taken from me, and I need them back to argue my case."

James frowned. "What papers are these, Mr. Bellingham?"

"My notes. My petitions. The evidence to prove that I followed every step correctly. It will show the court can do nothing but acquit me, sir. Because I fulfilled every requirement, left no stone unturned. When there was no other recourse, I had to take the regrettable step of killing the prime minister, but there was not malice on my part in the act. It was purely justice. I had to administer justice for myself, because the government would not do it for me." He sounded so reasonable, the hair on James's neck rose.

"How was killing Mr. Perceval administering justice, Mr. Bellingham?"

Bellingham shook his head as if there was a bee buzzing about his ears. "It is simple. They would not compensate me for the most terrible dereliction of their duties, sir. The most terrible . . ." His finger moved faster and faster over the desk. "I have a family, I have to support them, and how could I when my business was ruined, and the government to blame for that?"

"So you received no help when you made known your troubles?"

"No help from anyone who held authority! Some

sympathetic ears from a few quarters these last few months, sir, but they could only give advice, no real help."

James leaned back in the uncomfortable wooden chair. "Sympathetic ears?"

Bellingham looked up and held his gaze for the first time. James suppressed a shiver at the dead calm in his eyes. "Just so. Sympathetic ears. That's all."

It didn't sound rehearsed, so much as learned.

Someone had repeated this to him, over and over again.

"Who did these sympathetic ears belong to?"

Bellingham slid his gaze away, and folded his hands over his stomach. "No one of import. Men in the coffee houses and taverns, is all. Men who know how hard it is for a man to make his way with the government against him."

"Mr. Bellingham, I need to ask you directly. Did you receive any help in carrying out the murder of Mr. Perceval?"

Bellingham stood suddenly, shaking with emotion. "It was not murder, sir! It was justice. Justice with no malice aforethought."

"My apologies, I misspoke." James kept his voice even.

Bellingham looked across at him, and seemed to be convinced. He sat again, relaxing back against the chair.

"There was no one. I have pursued this since I returned from Russia, with no help, no help at all."

There was no guile about him. Bellingham was telling the truth as he knew it.

James rose and gave a bow. "Thank you for your

time, Mr. Bellingham. I hope you enjoy the rest of your evening."

It should have been a ridiculous thing to say, but Bellingham gave a genuine smile and bowed back. "I'm sure I will, sir. Thank you for your company."

He was let out, and Newman led him through an office, his step light and cheerful, almost incongruous in the fetid, gloomy surroundings.

James fingered the guinea again. "Mr. Newman, what can you tell me about your prisoner?"

"Cool customer, Your Grace. Very cool. Calm as you please, he is, when you'd think he'd be pacing up and down and wringing his hands. But none of that." He smoothed a hand over his almost bald head and then rubbed the back of his neck.

"Who's been to see him?"

"Plenty, but only a few've been allowed in. Some what come had interesting tales to tell."

"Oh?"

"Chap round here today, name of Hokkirk, said Bellingham's father was mad. Committed to St. Luke's. For the barmy ones that go violent, St. Luke's is. Said the son has taken after the father." Newman leaned a little closer, and James caught the whiff of porter and beef stew on his breath. "That *British Press* journalist, Jerdan, he were right pleased to hear what the man had to say 'n all, seeing he believes the prisoner is mad as they come." He rocked back on his heels and tugged the grey wool of his waistcoat over his pot belly. "Be in the paper tomorrow, no doubt."

"No doubt." James wondered what effect an article

like that would have on the current mood of the country.

From the few minutes he'd spent in Bellingham's company, he had the sense of someone desperately trying to control himself and his situation. He had felt no hint of violence, except that one moment when he'd spoken the word 'murder' and Bellingham had stood.

Then again, Bellingham had killed a man—the ultimate violence.

It could well be he had inherited his father's madness.

"Do you agree with Jerdan, Mr. Newman?"

"Rubbish, is what I think. Never seen anyone so ordered and calm. He's not mad."

But mad didn't mean frantic. There was a disturbing earnestness to Bellingham, an inflexibility under the good manners and the good clothes.

"Why does Jerdan believe him to be mad?" It was curious that Jerdan was so convinced of his insanity he was visibly pleased to find evidence of it, when everyone else seemed to be looking for reasons to pronounce Bellingham sane.

"Jerdan were there. When it happened. He were standing right behind the prime minister when he were shot." Newman shrugged. "Suppose that affects the way he sees things."

James gave a nod in agreement. "Anyone else come to see him?"

Newman shrugged again. "Plenty. The magistrates, the Treasury solicitor, journalists." He smiled, a thin, wicked drawing up of his lips. "I only let the officials in, though."

James pulled the guinea from his pocket and held it

out to Newman, who took it in a smooth, practised move.

He gave another bow and James made his way to the entrance and stepped out, standing on the top step and looking out into the street.

Jerdan would be a good person to speak to next. Someone who'd witnessed what had happened.

He was trying to remember the address of the offices of the *British Press* when he caught a furtive movement from the corner of his eye.

He turned, and found himself staring, once more, into the dark blue eyes of Miss Hillier.

Chapter Seven

She hadn't seen him go in.

Phoebe wondered if it had happened when the crowds had gotten a little rowdy, and she had turned her attention to them for a time, or if he'd been inside already when she arrived.

It didn't matter.

He had seen her, and she knew that nothing but at least some of the truth would appease him now.

He strode toward her, his face stark and guarded, and she was surprised again to see none of the dissolution and decay she would have expected from someone with his reputation.

"Miss Hillier." He stopped in front of her, and his brows rose in question.

"Your Grace." She gave a flawless curtsy and as she rose again she caught his grimace as her actions attracted the attention of the crowds around them.

"This is a surprise. To see you here." His voice was low, neutral, but his eyes were anything but.

"Likewise." Phoebe matched his tone.

He stared at her, surprised, and then gave a short

laugh. "*Touché.*"

She couldn't help the smile his sudden humour brought to her own lips. She schooled her face to blank neutrality again, but the damage had been done.

"We will talk." It was not a request.

"Not here," she said, lifting a hand as the wind tugged at the hood of her cloak, threatening exposure.

"No." He looked around. "Where is your carriage?"

She pointed down the street and he offered his arm and walked her to it.

"You will go to the park, and I will meet you there." He gave her a smile that had enough steel behind it to cover a barn door.

"And then?" Surely he didn't mean to walk with her without a chaperone? Nothing would get the tongues of Mayfair wagging faster, cloak or no cloak.

"Then we'll ride in my phaeton, and we will talk."

"That will be a little unusual. As we are neither betrothed nor even acquaintances."

"I consider you an acquaintance, Miss Hillier. If that makes you feel better."

She gave a half-laugh. "When it is discovered that I am no longer betrothed to Sheldrake, and a few days later am out alone with the Duke of Wittaker, I can promise you, nothing will make me feel better. I will be ruined."

It was true. Completely true. But a lie, as well.

She ached to break the rules, to heave off the yoke of polite manners that kept her small and cowed and unable to follow her inclinations. But the cruel joke was she did not want to be alone, either. Did not want to be a social pariah.

So a half-truth, perhaps.

He considered her words carefully, watching her with those sharp gray eyes. "Very well. I'll meet you in your garden in ten minutes." He helped her into her carriage, and paused before closing the door, and she saw, for the first time, the hard, cold heart of him. "Be there, Miss Hillier. No games."

She opened her mouth to give him a hot retort, then thought better of it and gave a curt nod instead.

"Ten minutes," he repeated as he closed the door.

Phoebe glared at him, and tapped the roof of the carriage. As they pulled into the traffic she looked back and found him watching her.

They stared at each other until her carriage turned the corner.

Neither looked away.

***

Damned if he wasn't intrigued, when he should have been suspicious. Hot on the scent.

Or perhaps he was too hot on the scent, and it wasn't for a potential assassin.

James stood in the lane behind Miss Hillier's house, and tried the garden door.

Locked.

He'd said no games, but to be honest, he hadn't made it clear he would be coming in the back way, to completely shield her from any speculation.

With nothing for it, he made sure he was alone, and then pulled himself up the stone wall.

When he reached the top, he could see Miss Hillier

standing with her back to him, talking to someone within the house, her full concentration on the conversation.

"I feel like sitting in the garden, that's all. I was shopping and have a headache. I'll come in for tea in a little while."

He couldn't hear the response, but it clearly frustrated her. She gave a sigh.

He dropped lightly into her lush, colorful garden.

She turned at that moment, and gave a small squeak of surprise to find him standing in a flower bed.

"I tried the door," he said, brushing the dust of the wall off his knees. "It was locked."

"I wondered if you'd come in the back. I've only just managed to get into the garden myself." Her gaze moved beyond him to the wall. "That's quite an impressive climb."

She was stalling for time. Hoping the tea would come out, no doubt, and he would have to hide or go away.

He smiled as he tugged down his jacket sleeves. "What were you doing waiting outside Newgate Prison today?"

Her eyes narrowed. "I'm sorry if this sounds ungracious, Your . . . Grace . . . but what were *you* doing there?"

He stepped out of the flowerbed, wiped his boots on the perfectly green, springy lawn. "Why are you so loathe to tell me?"

She took a step back from him, turned and walked away, toward a filigree arch sent in a yew hedge.

"Miss Hillier." He could be harsh when he wanted to be. In fact, many people would swear that was his usual demeanor.

She didn't turn, didn't even acknowledge him. She stepped through the arch and disappeared from his sight.

She was forcing him to follow her. He didn't know if it was a deliberate move in what was becoming a battle of wills, or her way of avoiding his questions.

Avoiding him.

He grit his teeth and took the same path she had, stepped through the arch and into a small herb garden, enclosed on all sides, either by the garden wall or the hedge.

She was standing just within, on the narrow paving that ran around the outside of the garden.

"If my aunt comes out with the tea, she'll call me out to her, she won't come in here, and you can stay hidden," she said. She was looking at him without challenge, and he saw he'd misunderstood her. She'd only wanted them out of sight of the main house.

He didn't know if he was pleased about that or not. The notion of her complete disregard for his title and station was as refreshing as the cool green of her hidden garden.

He turned to look at it properly, and found it a wild, thick riot of parsley, fennel, rosemary, mint, thyme and many other herbs he didn't know the names of. There was an order to it, but the human touch on this place was light, guiding rather than regimented, free but not out of control.

He had a sudden, deep sense it reflected its creator. He turned to look at her, and saw she was watching him carefully. There was a defiance in the way she stood now, and his frustration at her attitude gripped him.

"Miss Hillier. One more time. What were you doing

outside Newgate Prison?"

"I don't want to tell you." She jerked her gaze from his face, leant down and snapped off a fennel stalk, twirled it in her fingers.

"I am well aware of that." He crowded her on the path. "But you will tell me anyway."

"Why should I?" The aniseed flavour of the fennel scented the air as she crushed the stalk and looked up at him.

She wasn't being coquettish. She wasn't being petulant, either. She was deadly serious.

He forced himself to consider her question. "You have no reason to, beyond that I am asking you." Usually, simply being a duke did it. Or his money. Or his influence.

None of those things seemed to motivate Miss Hillier.

And if he told her the real reason, the carefully built fiction of the dissolute nobleman with a grudge against the government would come unravelled.

He tried to ignore the temptation of that. Of finally heaving off the chains of what had started as a lark, and had ended up defining his life and his relationship with everyone around him.

He'd started taking the first tantalizing steps of setting himself free over the last month, but now was not the time for his secret to come out. Not with the prime minister dead and no answers.

"You aren't asking, you're demanding." She threw the now shredded fennel stalk into the garden and picked another one. "If you were to explain yourself to me, I would consider explaining myself to you."

"How about the other way around?"

She gave an indelicate snort. "You're the one who wants information from me. While I'll admit you've made me curious about you, I'm not as desperate for your story as you seem to be for mine."

She picked up a basket that lay near her feet, and began to work her way down the row, snipping sprigs of herbs.

Serene. Completely at ease while she waited for him to decide if he would explain to her or not.

He didn't have time for this.

"You drive a hard bargain, Miss Hillier."

She shook her head. "I just really don't want to tell you."

He choked back a laugh, and made his decision.

"Coo-ee. Phoebe, my dear. Tea's ready."

Miss Hillier looked toward the house, then slanted him a look. "You took too long to make up your mind. You'll have to come back tomorrow." She started walking back down the path.

"Tomorrow is too late." He reached out and clamped a hand around her arm, and she stopped. "What are you doing tonight?"

"I was going to a ball, but I think it's been turned into a sort of memorial to the prime minister."

"The Edgeware thing?"

She gave a nod.

"I'll see you there."

"Phoebe, do hurry, the tea's getting cold."

"I can't go off with you," she whispered. "The same

rules apply at the ball as would have done in the park."

"Well, then." James gave her a quick grin, relief at missing the Edgeware ball, no matter what the reason, a sweet fizz in his blood. "You'll have to keep having that headache, cry off, and meet me in this garden at nine o'clock tonight."

She drew in a sharp breath. "You assume a lot."

He huffed out a quiet laugh. "Miss Hillier, nothing about you so far has been in any way the normal run of things. It is far too late to pretend outrage now." He moved to the wall, reaching out with his hands to find the holds he needed to climb it, and looked over his shoulder. "I'll expect you tonight. Right here. Nine o'clock."

Chapter Eight

He could still smell the fragrance of Miss Hillier's garden on him. He must have crushed some lavender underfoot when he had been tramping through her flowerbeds, because the scent of it rose up as he navigated the traffic on Fleet Street.

Fortunately, the lady herself was not as fragile as her plants.

She had not wilted or even bent under his demands, and he couldn't understand why he did not feel frustrated by that. Instead, he was charmed. Intrigued.

An idiot.

He smiled at himself, and pushed open the door to the coffee house Jerdan's colleagues at the *British Press* told him the journalist would be.

He asked one of the servers, and she pointed out a large man sitting on his own, staring into a mug of coffee beneath the window facing out onto the street.

"William Jerdan?" James stood beside the table and Jerdan looked up, blinked, and then rose, lifting his bulky frame up with surprising dignity.

"Good afternoon, Your Grace."

James made a gesture with his hand for Jerdan to sit, and slid onto the bench opposite him. He'd hoped not be recognized, but Jerdan was a political correspondent, after all. He shouldn't be surprised the man knew who he was.

He hoped Jerdan wouldn't question his interest in Perceval's death. And if he did think it suspicious, he would not publish any speculation about a duke in his newspaper lightly.

There were also usually more interesting things to write about James in the papers than his interest in political assassination.

Like whose fortune he had won in a game of Hazard.

"I have some questions for you about the death of Mr. Perceval." He watched Jerdan think about that, and take a long sip of his coffee.

"What do you want to know?"

"Your impressions. I understand that you were there, that it happened in front of you."

Jerdan gave a tight nod. "I didn't hear the shot. I know it's incredible, but I didn't hear it. Been wondering ever since if there is something wrong with my hearing, although I've never had a problem before."

"Did the others there say it was loud?"

Jerdan shrugged. "Vincent Dowling, who's with the *Day*, was in the gallery, covering the Orders in Council inquiry, and he heard it. But he said most people ignored it. It was more the furore that happened in the wake of it that alerted the House and the gallery that something was wrong."

James hid his surprise at the mention of Dowling's

name. He knew it. He had read the man's reports on political radicals more than once as part of his duties on the committee he sat on for the Home Office. He hadn't realized the man worked as a reporter, as well as a government informer. "So Dowling was a witness?"

"Not of the shooting, he came down too late from the gallery for that, but he helped secure the assassin afterward." Jerdan paused. "Him and General Gascoyne."

There was something in the considering way he said Gascoyne's name that made James lean forward.

"You're talking about Gascoyne, the Member of Parliament for Liverpool? What about him?"

Jerdan pursed his lips. "I don't like him, so you can take what I'm about to say with that in mind. But he lied at the committal proceedings that were held straight after the murder. A bald-faced lie."

James tried not to let the eagerness in him show on his face.

Jerdan lifted his mug and wrapped both hands around it, even though the coffee house was more than warm enough. "The room where we were all gathered for the hearing was packed, and so hot, there was no air to breathe . . ." Jerdan lifted the mug to his lips and took a long gulp. "I was pressed against a wall, and I was in shock, I suppose. I'd just seen the prime minister shot down. I decided it was a lie in the heat of the moment, Gascoyne putting himself forward over-much. Taking the limelight, you know. He's the sort to do it."

James didn't know Gascoyne well enough to agree, but he knew enough to know he was a strong advocate of the slave trade and bitterly opposed to the Orders in Council. No friend, by any means, of Perceval and his policies.

He also represented Liverpool, which was where Bellingham was from.

"What did he lie about?"

"He said he grabbed the pistol from Bellingham, to prevent him from taking another shot." Jerdan set his mug down with a thump. "Thing is, he wasn't anywhere near the man when he shot Perceval. He came down with Dowling, from upstairs. By the time they got there, Perceval had been taken into a room off to the side. Bellingham was just sitting there, quite still, and the gun was on the bench next to him. Gascoyne did grab his hand, so hard Bellingham cried out in pain, but he didn't have anything in his hand at the time, and he was no threat by then."

"So you could be right. He was simply putting himself forward as a bigger hero than he had cause to claim."

Jerdan shook his head. "I've thought about it a lot since it happened. Gascoyne grabbed the man, and then later made a big production about recognizing him. Bellingham's from Liverpool, it seems, and Gascoyne's his parliamentary representative. He's been to see Gascoyne in the past about some petition for compensation he feels the government owes him. But it was suspicious. The way he behaved when he 'recognized' the man. It rang false."

"Where are you going with this, Jerdan?"

Jerdan sighed, and shook his head. "I don't know. Perhaps I'm wrong. It was an extraordinary day. Perhaps I mistook. But that doesn't change that Gascoyne lied. And that no one so far has nay-sayed him. Not even me. The trouble it would cause, and the offence he'd take at being contradicted." Jerdan shrugged. "Is it worth it?"

"Perhaps if you'd spoken up at the time, at the hearing." James spoke slowly. "But now, yes, it would be awkward for Gascoyne if someone contradicts him. Especially if there are others who would agree with you."

"Dowling was there. So were a number of others." Jerdan rubbed his cheek. "They may think it's worth setting the record straight. But I'm stirring up trouble for nothing, most likely. Gascoyne may not be asked to testify at the trial. Why should he, particularly?"

James gave a nod. "And what of the prisoner? Bellingham? His prison warden says you think he's mad?"

Jerdan looked him in the eye at that. "I do. If you had seen him after he shot Perceval . . ." He shuddered. "I've never seen a man so affected. He was hitting his chest, as if to get air into his lungs, and sweat ran down his face like he was standing in a spring shower. He was so pale, so very, very pale, and completely without animation."

"It wasn't just the shock of what he'd done?"

"Then why did he do it?" Jerdan's voice rang out too loud, and he shook his head in apology. "If he was a criminal, and had his wits about him, he could simply have walked out the door. No one understood what had happened for some minutes after the shot rang out. Someone called for the doors to be closed, but people were rushing in from outside, and they stayed open. He could have walked out unnoticed and no one would have even known who had done the deed. Not even me, and it happened right in front of me."

James thought about that. "What did he say, when he was confronted?"

"That is the strange thing. The very reason many think him sane is one of the strongest reasons I think him mad. Even though he was shaking, even though he was in obvious distress, he spoke calmly, at odds with his physical reactions. There is something wrong with him. He is not in his right mind."

James sat quietly for a few minutes, and Jerdan seemed unable to say any more. He sipped at his coffee, though by now it must surely be cold.

"Thank you for your honesty." James stood and gave the big man a bow. Jerdan had sunk back into the gloom he'd been in when James arrived and he gave a nod, but didn't reply.

James left him at the table, grateful that the journalist had been too preoccupied to ask why he was looking into the details of Perceval's assassination.

He stepped into the darkening street and realized it was too late to chase down Dowling. But he would. As he walked back to his coach, he wondered what the significance was of a Home Office informant being at the scene of the prime minister's assassination.

It would be interesting to find out.

But first, he had to get home for dinner, or his chef might think him unappreciative and leave him, and after that, he had an appointment with a lady in a garden.

Chapter Nine

Phoebe gripped the handles of the French doors leading to the back garden, pushed them slightly outward, and paused.

The night was fresh and fragrant, the air moving over her like a cool compress over hot skin. Usually she would step out into the garden on an evening like this with delight.

But tonight Wittaker was lurking out there, a dark shadow waiting for her to lay her secrets bare. She shivered, wanting nothing more than to close the doors and avoid him.

He would not stand for that. The steel beneath his genteel façade had come more to the surface as the day had progressed. This morning he'd been civil enough. Outside Newgate, his demeanor was less accommodating, and this afternoon in the garden she had seen the gleam and shine of the metal.

There would be no delay in their meeting, if he had to storm the barriers and search every room in the house to find her.

She straightened her spine and pushed the doors out completely, taking the shallow stairs down into the deep, lush greenery that was her haven.

She saw him immediately.

He was standing beside the trellis arch to the herb garden, all in black.

The moon was almost full, and the light shone down on him and lit one side of his face and body.

He was looking at her, and she lowered her gaze as if to watch her step as she made her way cautiously across to him.

She was afraid to look in his eyes again.

"Thank you for being on time." He kept his voice low, but that was still too loud for her.

She shook her head, lifting a finger to her lips, and walked past him into her little enclosed garden.

He followed her, his steps almost soundless.

When she stopped and turned, she found him closer than was comfortable. Was forced to look up at him.

"Might I remind you, you're here to explain yourself to me, in the hope I will do the same." Fear and dread gave her voice a sharper edge than usual. "Don't loom over me and try to intimidate me, Your Grace. It won't work."

He lifted his brows. "I wasn't aware I was intimidating you, Miss Hillier. My apologies." He stepped back a little, but there was a gleam in his eyes, of challenge and determination, that made her heart sink.

She would not get out of this garden without parting with at least some of what she knew.

He stared at her for another long moment, and she understood that he was as unwilling to share his secrets with her as she was with him.

"It's a fair trade, then," she said, and he went still, and then gave a quick nod of his head.

That she hadn't had to explain what she meant was as exciting as the fastest ride she'd had on horseback, and a feeling gripped her that was disturbingly like desire.

Not a physical desire, although he was well-built and handsome enough for her to notice him that way, but one to spend time in his company and not have to hold back or phrase what she said carefully.

The freedom of a companion like that was something she had long abandoned hope of experiencing.

She was forced to gulp in a breath of air.

"Can you tell me, before I lay my secrets at your feet, why it is you are unwilling to trust me with what you know?" His voice was slightly lower than it had been before, and she repressed a shiver.

"I know Sheldrake is mixed up in some bad business, and I'm afraid that you are one of the men he's mixed up with." She didn't know why she decided on the truth, but it was liberating.

His lips twisted up in a wry smile. "And you think I might be one of his cronies because . . .?"

"Your reputation is that of a dissolute rake. You're said to gamble and duel and spend your time in places of ill-repute. Sheldrake mentioned men would be looking for him, and not two days later, you arrive at my door doing just that." She gave a shrug.

"What if I told you that my reputation was somewhat of a fiction?" His face was very serious now, his gaze focused on her as he spoke.

"Why do you do nothing to change it, then?"

"At one time, there was a need for some information about a certain group of young noblemen. Men around my own age. I was asked by my father, who was heavily involved in government, to mingle with them. Listen to what they said and report back anything of interest. After the . . . assignment was over, it was thought best to continue to use me in that capacity—my reputation having already been established as a gambling wastrel, so to speak." He spoke lightly, but it was at odds with his face and his eyes.

"How long ago was that first assignment?" She wanted to reach out and touch his arm, but she gripped the skirts of her gown, instead.

"Too long ago." He gave a wry smile. "So now you know the answer to a mystery the more conservative members of the ton have long exclaimed over, namely why my father, straight-laced and upstanding as he was, tolerated my outrageous behavior without cutting me off or disinheriting me. And that contrary to general wisdom, I didn't send him to an early grave. My behavior was his idea, all along."

"He shouldn't have asked it of you. Not for so long."

She spoke without thinking, and he jerked at her words, shrugged them off.

"I'd recently made the decision to follow my own inclinations more, but then yesterday, the prime minister was shot and I was asked to . . . re-acquaint myself with my usual haunts, see what I could find out."

She closed her eyes. He wasn't in league with Sheldrake, but against him. She batted away the last few spider-web strands that held her loyal to her former betrothed, and was free. "What led you so quickly to Sheldrake's door?"

"That's an interesting question." He tipped his head to the side, as if to see her better in the moonlight. "More than one man gave me his name, but I don't know if they genuinely thought he might be involved, if they were laying a false trail, or just repeating something they'd heard."

She shook her head. "It isn't a false trail, but Sheldrake can only be involved in the most minor way."

"Why do you say that?"

She hunched her shoulders.

Months of forcing herself not to criticise Sheldrake was a hard habit to break, despite her new freedom. "Because he isn't capable of planning something like this. He'd have gotten involved because it made him feel important, or because he believed he was doing the right thing, but he isn't competent enough, or trustworthy enough, to be granted a major role."

He considered that for a long time before he spoke again, and she tried to stop herself cringing inwardly as she wondered how disloyal he thought her. He had wanted the truth, and she was giving it to him.

"What exactly did Sheldrake tell you?"

"Nothing." She realized she had spoken too loudly and lowered her voice. "He never mentioned the prime minister at all. He was giving his excuses for breaking our betrothal. All he told me was he'd gotten involved in something that was going wrong. That if they were discovered, they would get no help, that they would be left to face the consequences alone, and that he'd decided the only way to be safe was to leave the country."

He moved closer, now, and really did loom over her. "How did you tie what he said to the death of the prime minister then? Surely not simply the timing?"

"The puppet." She rubbed her arms and looked down at her feet.

"Puppet?" His hand came up, and he cupped the back of her head, tilting it so that her face was illuminated by the moonlight.

She stared at him, transfixed. Partly with shock at his boldness, but the feel of his hand and arm, the touch of skin on skin where his jacket sleeve rode up and his wrist and inner arm cradled her neck, made her heart beat faster than it had before.

She swallowed, and forced herself to take a step back. He released her reluctantly and with no apology.

"Sheldrake said . . ." She cleared her throat. "He said their puppet had lost his nerve, that it was going to the dogs." She wouldn't, couldn't look at him now, but could not turn her back on him, either. She had the sense she had to know where he was at all times.

"Bellingham."

She shrugged. "The assassin was described to me as a puppet with his strings cut shortly after the prime minister was shot. It worried me."

"But surely," he tapped a long, blunt finger against his lips, "surely that wasn't enough to have you waiting outside Newgate?"

She sighed. She hadn't decided whether she would

tell him about the petition for compensation Sheldrake had sent her or not. It was so tangible. A cord that bound Sheldrake to the assassin as tightly as if they had been seen together.

He waited for her to answer him, and in the long stretch of silence, they both heard the distinctive sound of someone climbing over the wall into the main part of the garden.

Chapter Ten

James lifted a finger to his lips and saw Miss Hillier nod in understanding.

She had led them deeper into the garden than they had been this afternoon, and by the time he reached the trellis arch a man in dark clothes, similar to his own, was walking quietly across the garden toward the open doors of the library.

James could see the intruder's surprise and indecision as he approached the house at seeing it so open.

A hand brushed his arm, and then Miss Hillier pressed herself against him, crowding next to him in the deep shadows, to see for herself what was happening.

The man slowed to a stop just beyond the pool of light spilling from the lamps in the room before him. It was quite clear the room was empty, but he only took one more step forward before he must have thought better of taking the chance of someone returning and discovering him.

He turned, sliding back into the shadows of the garden.

James watched the way he moved, sleek and competent. He did not head directly back to the wall, but seemed to be searching, perhaps for a hiding place.

James knew the moment the man spotted the trellis arch and swerved toward it.

Not good.

James didn't mind confronting an intruder, but the warm rub of Miss Hillier against his side was a stark reminder he was not alone.

Before the man got close enough to see into the shadows that concealed them, he stepped out, two long strides that put him squarely in the man's path.

"Perhaps you would like to state your business?" James could see the man's shock; his head jerked and he took a step back.

He didn't answer, he turned and ran for the wall he'd come over.

James ran after him.

The man half-leapt up the wall, scrabbling for purchase, but slipped and fell and with a curse ran to the right along the back wall until he was up against the hedge that enclosed the herb garden.

With nowhere else to go, he ran down the length of it, and James was left too far away as the intruder made for the opening into the herb garden and dived through it.

Straight at Miss Hillier.

As he sprinted across the smooth, springy lawn, James heard a cry of astonishment, a thump of bodies and when he burst through the arch, he saw the intruder rolling to his feet, and Miss Hillier doing the same, hampered by the skirts of her gown.

"You." The man hissed the word out, his eyes on Miss

Hillier, and he lifted his arm.

For the first time, with the moon shining down on them, James saw he carried a small pistol in his hand.

He didn't think, he moved, closing the distance between himself and Miss Hillier and scooping her up, swinging her around so that he stood between her and the gun. There was no other way to shield her. No other cover.

He turned and took up as much space as he could.

The gun wavered. The intruder stepped back, his eyes darting between them. He brought up his other hand to grip the pistol.

At that moment, Miss Hillier gave a shout. "Lewis! Lewis. In the garden."

James started, and he saw their intruder did, too.

The man muttered a curse and turned, ran for the back wall and scrabbled his way up.

James started after him.

"Miss Hillier?" A call from the open doors of the library. "Miss Hillier? Are you there?"

James turned to her as he reached the wall.

She gave him a wide-eyed look. "What are you doing?" Her whisper was fierce.

"Going after him." James could hear the man clambering down the other side of the wall and the sound spurred him up the rough grey stone.

"Are you mad? He has a gun." Her whisper wasn't very soft this time.

"Miss Hillier? Are you in the herb garden?" The butler's footsteps came closer and James reached the top of the wall.

He looked back at her one last time, saw her gaze fixed on him. She made a gesture with her hands, throwing them up in exasperation and incomprehension.

"I'll see you later." He called it low enough that hopefully the butler didn't hear.

As he dropped over the other side, he heard Miss Hillier call out. "I'm here, Lewis. I'm all right, but there was a man in the garden."

Chapter Eleven

Lewis made a fuss, but she had accepted that would happen when she called out to him.

A little fussing was far preferable to seeing the Duke of Wittaker shot dead in front of her. She'd watched the intruder's grip tighten on his pistol, and had seen no alternative.

A shiver racked her body, and she hunched her shoulders.

Lewis had insisted on steadying her with his arm as he walked her back to the house, and she found to her surprise that the thin, wiry strength of him was most welcome. More solid and comforting than she would have expected.

She could feel a tremble in her hands and gripped him a little tighter to make them stop.

His face was only slightly lined, but as they come within the glow of light spilling from the library, it creased in dismay. "Your dress. Did you fall?"

She stared down at the stains from her roll through her parsley patch.

"He pushed me out of the way in his haste to climb

back over the wall." Phoebe held the skirt of her gown out for a critical look. "My parsley is no doubt completely crushed."

"We must call the magistrate's office." Lewis escorted her back into the room and closed and locked the doors behind him.

"There would be no point, unfortunately. I didn't see his face clearly, and aside from bowling me over, his only crime was trespassing."

Lewis rattled the doors to make sure they were secure and frowned. "I feel uneasy about this."

Phoebe tried to smile at him, but the thought of that gun, pointed straight at Wittaker, the way he'd scooped her up and put himself between her and her assailant . . . .

Her legs felt a little weak and she sat down harder than she intended on the arm of a chair.

Lewis kept his gaze on her as he lifted his hand to ring the bell to the kitchen. Before he could tug it, the sound of someone on the front doorstep had them both turning their heads.

"My aunt back from the ball?" Phoebe suggested.

Lewis all but ran from the room to the front door in his haste to pass her into her aunt's care. A moment later she heard the low rumble of his voice, surprisingly deep in a man as slight at he was, and then the squawk of horror from Aunt Dorothy.

The sound of her aunt's distress helped her get a hold of herself. The little collapse of a moment ago was the only weakness she would allow.

"My dear! Lewis says . . ." Her aunt gave a cry at the

sight of her, and Phoebe belatedly remembered her dress. "You've been manhandled!"

"Only pushed out the way, and tripped over my own skirts," Phoebe told her. But she thought of the way the intruder had behaved when he'd seen her, the way he had lifted the gun.

Even in the weak light of the moon, there had been a focus on his face, a practised air about him as he'd taken aim at her down the sight.

It was the way he reacted. As if he'd come across her fortuitously. As if killing her was the reason for his being there at all.

She shivered.

If the Duke of Wittaker had not been with her, she would be dead.

"Look at you. How calm and brave." Aunt Dorothy put an arm around her and gave her an affectionate hug. "Lucinda would be having hysterics by now."

Phoebe was able to manage a real smile at the thought of her cousin Lucinda in this situation, and the tight squeeze of fear on her chest relaxed its hold. "I don't feel brave. Just lucky. And ready for bed."

She wondered what Wittaker had meant by seeing her later. She was not going back out into the garden to hang about for his return. He could see her tomorrow. In broad daylight.

That was, if he survived his chase with the intruder. Although she couldn't doubt he would.

She had seen the hunter in him, the almost eager way he'd taken after the man.

He didn't like to be bested. And from all accounts, especially at the gaming tables and the duelling field, he seldom was.

That part of his reputation, at least, was true.

When she finally sent her aunt to bed, and her maid had helped her undress, she stood beside the bath Lewis had organized and unpinned her hair, running her hand over the back of her skull where Wittaker had cupped her head, and then trailing her fingers down to the skin of her neck where the smooth warmth of his inner wrist had touched her.

As she sank into the hot water, she thought again of the way Wittaker had lifted her up and stood between her and a loaded gun.

She would tell him about the petition Sheldrake had sent her.

She owed him that much.

She owed him, in truth, her life.

***

James could hear the rasp of his quarry's breath as they came out of Upper Berkley Street, across Edgeware Row and onto a bowling green, which James belated realized was situated in the fields above Hyde Park.

It would be deserted this time of night.

The man realized it a moment later himself, stopped and turned, pistol waving in his hand. "Stop."

James didn't give him the time he needed to catch his breath and aim, though, he ran straight at him. He saw the intruder's face waver between disbelief that someone would be mad enough to come at him when he held a weapon, and fear.

Fear won and he spun and ran again, with James much closer than before.

"Let up, mate." The man reached the low stone wall at the far end of the bowling green and leapt it. His words came out hoarse and breathless. "I didn't mean *you* no 'arm."

James followed him, but Miss Hillier's intruder had decided to take a stand. As he reached the wall and looked over, he saw the pistol aimed straight at him and ducked down, crouching on the thick, smooth lawn of the bowling green.

The shot missed him by inches.

He leaned against the stone, trying to catch his breath, and he heard the intruder doing the same on the other side of the wall.

"You're like a dog with a bone, mister." The man choked and then cleared his throat. "I've got a second pistol loaded. I'm walking away backward 'cross the fields, with it aimed at the wall. Don't force me to pull the trigger again."

"Who paid you to kill Miss Hillier?"

The man gave a genuine bark of laughter at the question. "As if I'd blab. An' it's *Miss Hillier*, is it?" He gave a snort. "Sure you don't know her a bit better 'n' that, being as you were all alone wi' her in a little secret garden 'round ten at night?"

"Inconveniently for you." James turned back to face the wall, still crouched low.

"You might say that. You might say I'll have to get out o' town for a bit now, 'cause I don't think the lady will be caught by surprise again, and them what wants her out the way won't be well pleased by tonight's work."

"I think that would be best. I would certainly advise you against another attempt." James heaved himself up and onto the top of the wall again, but the intruder took a few stumbling steps back, fumbled with his second pistol and raised it.

"You stay right there. I'm warnin' you." He walked back slowly, disappearing into the dark of the open field, and when James judged he was too far away for an accurate shot, he leapt down, but after a few steps he heard the sound of a man running. The noise faded into the night and he knew he wouldn't catch him now.

He turned back and climbed the wall again.

He was getting very good at climbing walls.

Chapter Twelve

Phoebe had just slid between the cool, smooth sheets and was about to blow out the lamp beside her bed when there was a rattle at her window.

It sounded like a piece of gravel had been thrown at the glass.

She lay still, listening, and it came again, harder this time. Almost hard enough to smash through.

Wittaker.

It had to be.

She got out of bed and ran to the window, pulling up the lower half and leaning out.

The Duke of Wittaker stood below, arm flung back as he readied himself for another throw.

She'd been worried for him, running after the intruder with no weapon, and now, relief made her incautious. "You're all right!"

He dropped the stone in his hand. "Perfectly. And yourself?"

She gave a nod, and the thrill of exchanging pleasantries from her window at eleven at night wearing her night shift gripped her. Made her shiver.

"I need to speak with you."

She must have misheard him. "Now?"

"We have urgent matters to discuss."

She looked behind her, as if Lewis and her aunt were already rapping on her bedroom door, although thank goodness, they were not. "I'm afraid we'd wake the household and . . ."

She trailed off.

Impotent rage, her old friend, ran a familiar hand down her back and she stiffened under its hot, prickly fingers. Why shouldn't she speak with someone? With whomever she pleased? She was twenty-four years old, responsible, intelligent.

She had all but accepted the anger and the frustration as constant companions, but Sheldrake cutting her free, the incidents of the last day, opened her eyes to how big they had grown, hulking beasts that rubbed up against her. Crowding her and making her life smaller.

Tears stung her eyes as she fought for composure. For the stoic acceptance she'd forced on herself time and again.

Below her, Wittaker rubbed his face. "It *is* urgent, but I understand. I shouldn't have asked it of you. My apologies. I'll see you first thing in the morning."

He turned to go, and she thought again of the way he had run to her, had swung her behind him so that he stood between her and a loaded gun.

The fragile barrier inside her, the one that only just held her back each time she seriously contemplated stepping over the line, snapped.

"Wait." She leaned further out the window. "Can you

climb the wall using the trellis?"

He stopped. Turned back to her, and then walked up to the wall, patted it with his hand, and she heard him give a quiet chuckle.

It took him less than half a minute to reach her bedroom window, pulling himself up the wooden lattice covered in ivy, and she stepped back to allow him to climb through it.

He smelled spicy green, the scent of crushed ivy leaves and cool spring air clinging to him as he swung his legs over the window sill.

"What could be so urgent?" She stood with her arms crossed over her chest, feeling like a fish flopping about at the bottom of a boat. She had no point of reference for this, although she was prepared to trust him.

"The man who killed Perceval is to go on trial on Friday. Tuesday is almost over. We have hardly any time to solve this before Vinegar Gibbs orders him hanged, and all that Bellingham knows about who helped him in this dies with him." He looked from her to her rumpled bed and tugged a hand through his hair. "I'm sorry, Miss Hillier. I know this is extraordinary behavior on my part, but someone tried to kill you tonight, and I want to know if you have any idea why."

She didn't want what he said to be true, but she couldn't deny that the intruder's behavior had changed when he saw her. He'd raised his pistol the moment he worked out who she was.

"When Sheldrake said goodbye . . ." She couldn't help the way her fists clenched at the memory. "As he walked away he said something about how I should be safe enough." She tightened her arms around herself. "At the time I thought it a strange thing to say, but then, the whole conversation was strange. I think he was trying to convince himself he hadn't put me in danger, trying to rid himself of any responsibility to me."

"Not to excuse him, but I would have thought he was right." Wittaker seemed to realize how nervous he made her, taking up so much space in her bedroom, and he sat down on the window seat he'd just climbed over. "Unless someone saw you meeting him before he left?"

She shook her head. "He was very careful to make the meeting secret. I suppose it's the note he sent me. And my going to Newgate this afternoon. Someone must have been watching me, or saw me there."

Wittaker paused in the act of straightening out his legs. "I thought you said the note didn't say anything."

She gave a jerky nod. "He only wrote the address of the inn on it. But he enclosed something."

Wittaker stood again, and this time he made no effort to put her at her ease. "You never said this before."

She shrugged, completely unrepentant. "I didn't know which side you were on, before."

He narrowed his eyes at her. "And what did he enclose?"

She walked across to her small writing desk and drew out the letter and the petition folded within it. Handed it to him.

He stared at it a long time. "A petition to the Prince Regent." He looked as though he was trying to remember something. "I'll have to take it with me."

She nodded. "You can keep it."

He looked up at her, stared at her for a long moment. "Tell me, Miss Hillier, how on earth was it that you were Sheldrake's fiancée?"

There was rage, back in an instant, holding her close, almost smothering her, and she forced herself to breathe out. "The betrothal was a family matter, Your Grace."

He gave a slow nod. Then he folded the letter and slipped it into his jacket. His bow was formal, and he turned back to the window. "Please don't go anywhere tomorrow. Stay at home."

Phoebe frowned. "You think they'll try again?"

He crouched on the window sill. "I don't think they're going to stop trying because of one miss. However, I have the impression the intruder from tonight plans to leave town rather than inform his employers of his failure, so we have some time before they send someone new after you, I hope."

She narrowed her eyes. "You had a *conversation* with the man in the garden?"

He sent her a wicked grin. "Just a quick one. Between bouts of him shooting at me."

She couldn't help the soft laugh that escaped her. His sense of humour delighted her. "I admire your daring."

The look on his face changed, and as she watched him watch her, she suddenly remembered she had a man in her bedroom and that she was only wearing a night shift.

"Good night, Miss Hillier." He didn't flinch from looking directly at her, but his voice was rougher than it had been. Deeper. "Remember, keep inside."

She swallowed. "I can't stay indoors indefinitely. My aunt will wonder what's wrong."

Wittaker swung a leg over and tested the lattice. "I'll think of something. And I'll stop by tomorrow."

"Will you be calling at the front door?" she asked as he disappeared from sight, desperate to claw back the light-heartedness between them. What had replaced it a moment ago was intense. Hungry. Too out of control.

The soft rumble of his laugh drifted up to her, and she grabbed her drapes with relief at the sound.

"I don't know. I'm becoming quite fond of climbing walls."

Chapter Thirteen

Wednesday, 13 May, 1812

James couldn't remember when last he felt so well. He'd gone to bed at midnight, quite the earliest he'd had his head on a pillow in some time. He'd tried to find Dervish at their club after he'd left Miss Hillier's magnificent house, but he'd been nowhere to be found, and short of trawling London for him, James had been forced to send him a note and go home.

His good night meant he was up early, and as he came down the main stairs he could hear laughter from his kitchens, two deep male voices and a low, musical, feminine one.

Miss Barrington, Aldridge's fiancée, must be visiting his chef, although why she should do so at seven in the morning, he had no idea.

He hesitated near the bottom of the stairs, debating whether to interrupt them.

He wanted, in a way he couldn't explain, a piece of the unfettered joy he could hear.

He'd had a thin slice of it last night, laughing with

Miss Hillier in her bedroom, with its rumpled bed and scented bath standing full to one side. For a moment they had both forgotten she was in her night shift and they were alone.

And then they had remembered.

He gripped the bannister hard and heard the laughter from his kitchens again.

He took the last step and turned towards it, entering a part of his house he very rarely had cause to go.

"Your Grace!" Completely at his ease, and obviously delighted to see him, Georges Bisset, James's chef, waved him in, as if it were he who was the host, and not James.

Which, James decided, was quite true in this particular place. Georges ruled here, and no one, not even James, could deny it.

He walked towards the small group, noticing other kitchen staff scuttling about, far more nervous than their commander at his presence.

The scent of lemon and bread hung heavy and delicious in the air.

"Your Grace." Giselle Barrington gave him as warm a smile as Georges had. "Forgive our early morning visit, but Pierre and I met Georges at the market this morning, and he told us he had come up with a special brioche. We had to come back with him to see it and try it for ourselves."

"You know Pierre Durand?" Georges asked him, waving his hand at the older man standing next to Miss Barrington. "He was my mentor. I was his sous-chef when we worked together for Giselle's mother and father, many years ago."

Which meant the man before him, still in Giselle Barrington's employ, although more a second father to her than an employee, was likely one of the best chefs in the world.

James murmured a greeting, and wondered if the Prince Regent knew the man existed. He would try to hire him away from Giselle Barrington, if he did.

The Prince Regent had boastfully announced he intended to hire Georges Bisset over six months ago, and James had stepped in and stolen him out from under the prince's nose, making Georges a better offer, as part of a bet; one smoky, half-lit, drunken night over a gaming table when he'd been in character a little too well.

He had often been a little too well in character, towards the end.

Hiring Georges had been, he realized now, the turning point for him. When Georges had taken up his position, something about the force of the man's personality, his complete disregard for James's status when discussing matters to do with the kitchen, had been like a curtain pulled back to let the sunlight into a gloomy room.

There had been something in his demand that James be on time for meals, and present to actually eat them, that had held the warm comfort of coming home.

"*Énchanté*." Pierre Durand gave a formal little bow. The Frenchman's eyes were bright and sharp, and his dark hair was streaked with silver. "You are the one who Georges was able to go to for help when my Gigi needed it."

James thought back to the way Georges had tracked him down at The Scarlet Rose and pulled him out of a game of Twenty-one to help Miss Barrington a few months ago, and how close they had all come, Aldridge, Dervish and himself, to failure. His eyes lifted to Miss Barrington's neck, but the place where she had been cut was only a thin pink line now. "My part in it was very small."

"Bah, we are all heroes." Georges gave a dismissive wave of his hand. "Now we try my brioche." The scent of lemon intensified as Georges lifted a small basket and flicked back the cloth covers.

"Lemon rind in the dough?" Pierre asked him. "But surely that is not all?"

"Lemon rind in the dough, and *crème au citron* in the center," Georges said with a wide grin. "Truly, though I say it myself, *délicieuse*!"

The door to the kitchen opened, and Harding came in, a frown on his face at finding James in a place he had never been before. "Lord Dervish is here, Your Grace."

James wasn't sure what was more horrifying to his butler. The fact that James was in the kitchen, or that for the second time in a few days, Lord Dervish had arrived at an inconvenient time.

"I have to speak with him urgently, I'm afraid." James gave a regretful nod to the brioche. "Perhaps I can try your masterpiece at breakfast? I'll invite Dervish to join me."

Georges clapped his hands, loud enough to silence everyone in what had been a gently humming kitchen. "We 'ave a guest. Everyone, to work."

James grinned, and caught Miss Barrington doing the same, because clearly, everyone had been hard at work before. Although, as he said his goodbyes and left, he noticed the pitch had risen.

He realized with surprise as he pushed the kitchen door open and stepped into the hallway that he was still smiling. And had no inclination to stop.

Chapter Fourteen

"I wasn't cadging breakfast, arriving so early." Dervish sat down at the table and eyed the dishes that had started coming in from the kitchen.

"Georges is thrilled to have more than one person to make breakfast for. And you've arrived on the morning he's trying out his new brioche."

Dervish looked up. "I wouldn't have thought you that aware of what goes on in your kitchens, Wittaker."

James quirked a smile. "I'm not, usually." He took a sip of coffee. "Thank you for coming so quickly. I've made some headway."

Dervish shook his head. "I got your note. But I'm afraid I wouldn't have come at this hour except that I have some news for you."

James lifted his brows.

"Lord Sheldrake is dead. I saw the bulletin just before I went home last night from Whitehall. He was killed in a carriage accident."

James gripped the table. "I thought he'd fled the country." His thoughts flew immediately to Miss Hillier. To how she would take this news.

"Looks like he intended to. His accident was within ten miles of Dover."

"He's the reason I sent you that urgent message last night. He posted a letter to Miss Hillier from an inn he stayed at on the way. It proves he was involved somehow with Bellingham."

Dervish stopped cutting open his brioche and stared. "He admitted it in a letter?"

"No. He said nothing in the letter. And now I understand why. He was careful not to incriminate himself in any way. But he enclosed something. I couldn't understand why he would send it to Miss Hillier. It would have been better for him to destroy it, but it may have been he was using it as a way to keep the men he'd fallen in with from interfering with his escape."

"An insurance policy, you mean?"

James nodded. "Which means the document must incriminate someone other than himself. It would have no value, otherwise."

"He may have realized he was being followed, or hunted down, and sent the only thing he thought could save him somewhere safe."

James tapped a little rhythm on the table. "It would also explain why someone tried to murder Miss Hillier last night."

"What?" Dervish dropped his silver cutlery with a clatter. "You think they knew she had the document?"

"If we think Sheldrake's accident wasn't an accident at all, he may have been forced to say where the document was before they killed him. And given his personality, if he thought they would spare his life if he told them, he would have endangered Miss Hillier to save his own skin, I have no doubt.

"In fact, that would fit her assassin's actions last night better." He thought of how the man had aimed at Miss Hillier, but had not taken the shot, giving James time to get between them. "If they know she has the document, then the intruder would have wanted to find out where it was before he killed her. He hesitated. That's how I was able to stop him."

"We'd better get that document—" Dervish stopped short as James pulled it from his inner jacket pocket and handed it over.

"A petition?" Dervish scanned it, his eyes widening when he saw whose name was on the document. "But that's strange . . ."

"Yes, something is niggling me about it, too."

"It's having the thing at all." Dervish studied it thoughtfully. "Somewhere in the committal proceedings that were conducted after they arrested Bellingham, he spoke of sending a petition to the Prince Regent."

"When did you see the transcript of the proceedings?" No wonder Dervish looked pale and dark-eyed. He could hardly have slept.

Dervish rubbed his forehead. "I skimmed it at Gibbs's office into the early hours of this morning. There is only one copy and he won't let anyone take it away, which I agree with. But I can't remember what Bellingham said about the petition. We'll need to check it again to find out when he said it was submitted, but he spoke clearly as if it had been received—that was part of his grievance, that even the Prince Regent had denied him justice."

"So that begs the question," James held out his hand and took the petition back to look at it again himself, "if this was submitted to the Prince Regent, how are we holding it in our hands?"

Dervish rubbed his forehead again. "We shouldn't be."

James drained his coffee. "I'll take a look at the transcript. I was going to, anyway. I heard something about that hearing that I'd like to check for myself."

"You were able to get information from Bellingham?" Dervish leaned forward.

James shook his head. "All I got from Bellingham was an impression, nothing definite. I think he was helped. How much, I don't know, but he had advice from someone. Someone convinced him the law would be on his side if he killed the prime minister. He's spouting legal terms, but he doesn't understand them properly." James thought back to the calm, the focus of the man, and he felt pity. There would be no saving Bellingham on Friday. He had killed Perceval in cold blood, no matter what he kept telling himself and everyone around him.

"The information I have about the proceedings is that Gascoyne outright lied during them. I'd like to read what he said for myself."

Dervish paused with a coffee cup halfway to his lips. "Gascoyne lied?"

"Jerdan, the *British Press* correspondent who was right behind Perceval when he was shot, said his testimony was false. He couldn't work out why, though. Could just be self-importance. Or something more sinister."

"Good God. Won't that go down well in all quarters? Especially as Gascoyne's the assassin's member of parliament." Dervish leaned back in his chair and closed his eyes. "Do you have any good news?"

"Depends what you think is good." James tucked into his omelette. Georges might resign if he didn't eat it while it was hot. "One of your Home Office spies was there when Bellingham shot Perceval, as well."

Dervish opened his eyes and stared at him, his bright blue gaze patient and flat.

James grinned at his air of exasperation. Dervish needed a little teasing in his life. "Vincent Dowling. I've read some reports by him when I've sat on that radicals committee you chair."

"You're sure it's the same person?"

"I checked. It is. Jerdan mentions him as arriving on the scene at the same time as Gasgoyne. His real employment, when he isn't spying for the government, is as the political correspondent for the *Day*."

"Someone needs to speak to him."

"I plan to." James leaned back. "I'll be very interested to hear what he has to say."

But there was something he had to do first. "Who will the authorities approach with news of Sheldrake's death?"

Dervish's eyes narrowed. "His heir, most likely. If he has one. I know his parents are both dead."

"And Miss Hillier?"

"Eventually someone will speak to her. Most likely

she'll hear it in the press before anyone official gets to her."

"I'll tell her."

Dervish looked at him over the rim of his coffee cup. "She'll most likely not thank you for it."

James shrugged. "I don't want someone else telling her, in case they upset her."

"She'll be upset, no matter how she's told."

James shrugged. He would do it. He couldn't explain why he felt so strongly, but it was almost a compulsion. "I'm also worried she might come under another attack."

Dervish tapped his lips with his forefinger, watching him with a strange, knowing expression. "You're sure she can be trusted? You mentioned before you thought she was hiding something?"

James stared back at him coolly.

Dervish gave a grunt, and scraped back his chair. "As you like. Do whatever you need to do."

Chapter Fifteen

"The Duke of Wittaker is here to see Miss Hillier." Lewis sent her a quick look, and she wondered if he was debating whether to tell her aunt this was the duke's second visit in two days.

She smiled to herself. Make that the fifth.

"The Duke of Wittaker?" Phoebe could see her aunt trying to recall what she knew about the duke. "Didn't I hear . . .?"

"Please show him in, Lewis." Phoebe took control.

Lewis bowed, slid another look at her and left the room.

"I'm sure I've heard something . . . "

Phoebe ignored her aunt and stood. She caught Wittaker's gaze as he appeared in the doorway.

He looked grim. All traces of the playfulness she'd seen in him last night were gone. He didn't look capable of laughter.

"Miss Hillier." He bowed to her.

"Your Grace, allow me to introduce my aunt, Mrs Patterson."

"My lady." Wittaker bowed to her as well.

"I had no idea you knew His Grace, my dear." Her aunt slanted her a look but Phoebe merely nodded. Her aunt had only been a regular visitor to London since Phoebe's father had died and she'd been in need of a chaperone. She wouldn't know who Phoebe had and had not met.

"I'm afraid I've come to give you bad news."

Phoebe's eyes jerked back to his face, and she frowned. "Bad news?"

Was this his solution to arrange for her safety? Some ruse to give her a good reason to remain indoors or go into hiding?

"Please, I think you should sit."

He seemed too serious for this to be some plan he'd concocted. She shivered, suddenly cold. Her aunt sank slowly into a chair, and Phoebe followed suit. Wittaker did not join them.

"I heard this morning from a government official that Lord Sheldrake is dead." He was looking only at her as he spoke, and she could not read him. Could barely understand what he was saying.

Her aunt gasped. "How?"

"It appears to be a carriage accident."

Phoebe could not look away. She heard the word 'appears', heard his inflection.

They had killed Sheldrake. She reached out blindly to hold onto something, and ended up clutching the armrests of her chair. "I thought he was leaving the country." She tried to make sense of it. "Did he die in England, or abroad?"

Her aunt turned to stare at her. Too late she remembered she still had not told her of Sheldrake's betrayal.

"He died ten miles from Dover."

"What is this, Phoebe? Why was Sheldrake leaving the country?" Her aunt's voice was sharp and high.

"He called off our betrothal on Sunday evening." At last Phoebe tore her gaze from Wittaker's face to look at her aunt. "I'm sorry, I didn't tell you because his rejection was difficult for me to explain. He told me he was leaving the country, that he was in trouble and owed money . . ." She trailed off in the face of her aunt's horror.

"The . . . the . . ." Too well-bred to say what she surely wanted to say, her aunt looked down at her lap, her hands so tightly entwined Phoebe could see the whites of her knuckles. "After the promises he made. After everything your father went through . . ." She stopped short, and glanced across at Wittaker. "Thank you for giving us the news, Your Grace. I am not sure why someone as high-placed as yourself was so kind as to come and inform us personally . . ." There was stiff formality in her aunt's voice now, as she rallied herself like a general facing poor odds.

"I came because I consider myself a friend of Miss Hillier's and I didn't want her to hear the news from anyone else."

Her aunt's mouth opened and then closed with a snap. "I . . . see." She looked at Phoebe, and Phoebe could see she did not see at all.

"May I have a word with Miss Hillier in private?" He was already walking forward to take her hand, as if the question had merely been for form's sake. He didn't care whether her aunt gave her permission or not.

And the permission was Phoebe's to give, and no one else's. She was mistress here. She had to keep remembering that. Society conspired to make her feel in need of following rules or obeying instructions from others, but she *was* mistress here.

"Certainly, Your Grace." She raised her hand and allowed him to help her to her feet. "We can take a moment in the garden."

She led him out the room to the library, avoiding her aunt's gaze, her back straight and stiff.

The doors were still locked from last night, and she turned the key and stepped out, with Wittaker close behind her.

She waited until they were down the steps from the house and in the garden itself before she turned to him. "Is it true? Sheldrake is really dead?"

He looked genuinely shocked at the question. "I would never lie about something like that."

She looked at him for a long moment, and eventually turned away.

"I'm sorry. For your loss." There was an edge to his tone, and she turned to face him, but he was looking away, across the garden toward the wall.

"Thank you." She crossed her arms and hugged herself, her head down. "You might be the only one who understands this, but while I'm sorry that Sheldrake is dead, I'm finding it hard to feel the level of grief expected of me."

She sensed his quick look, but he said nothing.

She kept her head bowed. "I've been so angry with him. And before . . . " She sighed. Steeled herself to speak the words, because she didn't think she could say them to another person and they were bubbling up inside her, demanding to be voiced. "I held him in a sort of contempt." She rocked back on her heels. "He treated me like a brainless ninny, like some dim-witted little twit. He never saw me. Never saw me as I was. I think he genuinely thought he was my intellectual superior. It galled me. The only way I could bear it without screaming was to make snide comments about him in my head. It's lowering now to think that I had to do that. That I couldn't rise above it. But I had to make myself hold still as he patted my arm in that patronizing way he had, count numbers in my head instead of thinking how I was to be married to him. That this would be my life forever . . ." She drew in a deep breath. Finally looked up to find him much closer to her than he had been.

"I don't understand why your family bound you to him."

She gave a dry laugh. "Don't you? Surely you must have seen a hundred such matches, poorly conceived and for practical matters that have nothing to do with the personalities of the bride and groom?"

He conceded her point with a nod. "What reason did your family have?"

Long years of keeping her secrets made her hesitate, but she had already said the worst. What harm could it do to explain the whole thing?

"My father was a third son. Both his older brothers died before he did, though, and without heirs; the last one only a year before my father himself passed away. I'm my father's only child. My father's title and the part of the estate that is entailed were to go to the next male heir, and that happened to be Sheldrake, who's my father's second cousin. My father's title is lower than Sheldrake's family's, so Sheldrake had no use for it, but the estate, that he wanted. That, and the fortune my mother brought to her marriage with my father."

She sighed. "I'd been difficult about accepting a husband since I came out, something that had once caused my parents considerable distress, but when my father inherited his brother's title and lands, it was suddenly treated as if it had been my father's idea all along. That he was keeping me free for Sheldrake, who would inherit the estate and title on his death, and through marriage to me, my father's, or rather my mother's, fortune."

Wittaker angled his head. "I can see why that would be beneficial to Sheldrake, but how was it beneficial to you?"

"Keeping it all in the family? Continuing my father's line through my children? My son to inherit the title from Sheldrake?" She spoke without bitterness. She had let that go. Or thought she had. "My father only died six months ago, and he had the contract drawn up on his deathbed. It was all that kept him alive in the last few weeks, finalizing that document."

"I see." His eyes narrowed. "And what did your father think of your son inheriting nothing but debt in Sheldrake's wake?"

"My father knew what Sheldrake was like. He talked up his virtues to me, to the point where I started avoiding him altogether it was so painful to hear, but the contract he made Sheldrake sign shows he had no illusions about

Sheldrake himself, no matter what he wanted *me* to think."

That betrayal still had the power to hurt. He had known, *known* what he was shackling her to. But keeping things in the family, the idea of dynasty, was more important to him. More important than her. "Sheldrake would have done anything to get even part of my dowry. I don't think he even read the contract properly, but he discovered the terms were . . . strict . . . when he decided to leave the country. It seems my father has all my money tied up in a trust that Sheldrake was unable to touch." That she was unable to touch, as well. Or only as her trustees saw fit. "He was most surprised to find he had no access to my funds when he was preparing to leave the country."

She was sensible, intelligent and old enough to decide her own future, but since her mother's death her father had taken as much power away from her as he could.

He'd regretted her education, her mother's insistence on the best tutors and the widest possible range of subjects for her daughter. Her mother had come from a practical, hard-working merchant family who had risen to wealth through brains and effort, and she had wanted Phoebe to understand as much about the world as she could. Her father, though, would have preferred her to be ill-informed and more pliable.

She clenched her fists and tried to breathe through the tightening of her chest. She needed to stop thinking of this. To calm the rage that kept gripping her.

Her father was dead and the deed was done.

She knew she was privileged. That she lived in surely one of the most beautiful houses in London, and had everything she could ask for. But she would give up much of what she had for some acknowledgement of herself. Of her worth. Of her capabilities.

"Sheldrake told you this? That he had tried to get hold of your inheritance?" Wittaker's incredulous question drew her back to the present.

She forced herself to let the anger go. "On Sunday night. He said he'd approached the trustees, trying to get his hands on some of the money. To make his life in exile a little easier."

"My God." Wittaker took two steps away, and she could hear he was breathing heavily. "The man was a fool."

"Yes," she said, and even she could hear the regret, the sadness in her voice. "He was."

He smiled at her suddenly, and it was so unexpected she blinked.

"His loss."

She looked away again and let her arms fall to her sides. She felt the same edge of panic she had last night, as Wittaker crouched on her windowsill, looking at her with hungry eyes. She grasped desperately at a new topic. "However wrong it was of them to kill him, it will have one consequence perhaps they didn't expect."

His gaze was steady, but the heat in them was still there. "What's that?"

Phoebe avoided his eyes. "I have the perfect excuse to stay close to home for a few weeks."

He raised a questioning eyebrow.

"No one knows Sheldrake broke our betrothal. I'll be expected to be in mourning."

Chapter Sixteen

Wittaker almost enjoyed sparring with Gibbs's clerk when he arrived at the Attorney General's chambers, and only produced his card, thereby winning the war of wills, some time after he could have done.

He longed for a little violence.

It was easy to work out why, but it didn't lessen the need.

He could go to The Scarlet Rose and stir up enough trouble to satisfy the pounding in his veins, the hot-blooded energy that was coursing through him. Initiate a fencing duel or fisticuffs.

The thought enticed him. And it would have the added benefit of keeping himself in character for the meanwhile.

He smiled, and Gibbs's clerk lost the supercilious look on his face and almost fled the room in his haste to show James where the transcripts were kept.

He left James in the small, airless room almost as fast, and James forced himself to sit. To concentrate, while trying to ignore the redolent smell of mold and damp.

Looking at the hastily scrawled date and time at the

top of the document, he wondered what they had been thinking, hearing the case less than a few hours after the crime had been committed? Tempers and emotions had been high, on all sides.

He read through the opening rhetoric some of the members of parliament had spouted about the evil nature of the assassin and winced. Bellingham may have shot Perceval and admitted to it, but James had never seen a more open and blatant misuse of the justice system.

He began to skim, looking for mention of the petition, and eventually found it. Bellingham stated he had sent a petition to the Price Regent in January, but that it had been unaccountably lost in the system, and when the error was discovered, he had to submit a second one.

According to him, the loss of the first petition, which had taken all his funds to hire a lawyer for, had spelled almost total financial ruin and the end of his chances at justice.

And yet . . . it hadn't.

James leaned back in his chair. Far from being ruined, Bellingham had stayed on in London for a further two months and submitted another petition.

Not only that, Bellingham mentioned pamphlets he'd had printed and distributed after the second petition was lodged. He'd asked at the committal proceedings that the pamphlets he'd had on him be returned to him, as well as his other papers.

James recalled Bellingham saying something about having documents returned to him yesterday when he'd interviewed him in his cell, and now he understood what he was talking about.

Printing pamphlets cost money.

How had he afforded it all?

Bellingham had rented rooms at a reasonable address, and James saw that the Bow Street officer assigned to the case, John Vickery, had given evidence at the hearing as to Bellingham's lodgings. He said he'd interviewed a woman who had something of Bellingham's in her keeping, and . . . James leaned forward. At that point, for the first time, Bellingham had become agitated. He only calmed down when Vickery explained the possession in question was a memorandum for twenty pounds owed to Bellingham by a Mr. Wilson, which his landlady was holding for him.

So what had Bellingham thought Vickery meant that had him so concerned? What woman and what possession could have caused him that much distress? Obviously not his landlady and the twenty pounds.

And, now that James thought of it, how did he have twenty pounds owed to him at all? By his own admission he had not worked while in London and had no money left as of January, when the first petition had been submitted. A petition that had somehow found its way into Sheldrake's hands. A petition that was supposedly lost.

The Bow Street officer, Vickery, was someone he obviously needed to speak with.

"Who the devil are you?"

James lifted his head from the transcript and tipped his chair back a little to take in Vinegar Gibbs standing in the doorway. Sir Vicary had his head angled back a little, all the better to look down his long blade of a nose at James.

"Wittaker." Gibbs's eyebrows rose when he recognized James. "What are you doing here?" Gibbs's voice had always grated on James's nerves, and he fought to keep his face neutral.

He waved his hands over the transcript. "Familiarizing myself with the Perceval case."

"What for?" Gibbs drew himself upright. He was a tall man, lean and angular, his eyebrows a dark slash over his eyes. He thrust his jaw out bullishly. "What could possibly be your interest in this?" Was it James's imagination, or was that a flicker of fear that skittered across Gibbs's face before he replaced it with puffed-up affront.

James worked up a supercilious smile. "Do I need a reason? I'm a member of the House of Lords, after all. Of course I want to know the facts of what happened."

"Well, you can wait for the trial like everyone else. I can't have you monopolizing the transcript."

James raised his brows and looked beyond Gibbs's shoulder. "I don't seem to be holding anyone up. But I'll be sure to withdraw if someone involved in the case requires the use of it." He tapped the papers in front of him. "And, to be honest, I wouldn't call what's happening on Friday a trial. More a sweeping under the carpet."

A vein began to throb at Gibbs's temple, and his eyes bulged. "What did you say?"

This time, James didn't bother to hide his wince at the way Gibbs's voice set his teeth on edge. "You heard me. The word is you're calling the trial for Friday, a mere four days after Perceval's death. You know Bellingham is from Liverpool. It will be almost impossible for witnesses to come down to London in time, let alone for the investigators to question them. That's aside from letting the Bow Street officers do a thorough job with the evidence in London."

Gibbs said nothing, his breathing heavy, his face almost purple.

"It also hasn't escaped anyone's notice that you're charging Bellingham with murder, not treason. If you'd done that, by law you'd have to wait fifteen days before the trial could commence. So what are you trying to hide?"

James had hoped to see Gibbs during this visit and do a little stirring, but Gibbs's reactions went beyond his expectations.

The Attorney General was rarely at a loss for words, but now he gaped like a fish out of water.

"I'd like the answer to that, myself." The man who appeared suddenly behind Gibbs was James Stephen, one of Spencer Perceval's best friends. His voice was a little hoarse, his face white and grim.

While Gibbs turned to face him, James rose from his chair. He'd prefer to be standing for this confrontation. It should prove interesting.

"I've already spoken to Ward about the trial date—" Gibbs was forced to step into the room with James as Stephen crowded him.

"I've seen Ward. He told me what you said." Stephen flicked a curious glance at James, and then focused on Gibbs again. "Neither of us found your excuses reasonable. While the crowds were out of control on Monday evening, things are much calmer now. You risk fouling the case by forcing the trial date so soon after the crime. We need to know the truth of why Perceval was killed, damn it. He was our friend. It doesn't make sense . . ."

Stephen trailed off in genuine distress, and James noticed Gibbs had edged even further from him. A nerve ticked under the Attorney General's eye.

"I would like to know how you all know the trial date, anyway. It hasn't been announced yet." It was bluster, an attempt by Gibbs to divert the conversation.

Stephen gave him a contemptuous look. "Perceval deserves justice. That means giving the investigators the time they need to investigate. You're perverting the course of justice with this jumped-up excuse for a trial."

"That is enough!" Gibbs's face contorted. The vein was throbbing on the side of his temple again, and James wondered if he was going to suffer an apoplexy. "Out. Get out of my office."

James exchanged a look with Stephen, and gave a slight nod. He moved past Gibbs, still standing just in the room, panting as if he'd run up stairs. Stephen followed him out, past the wide-eyed clerk, and into the street.

"Surprised to see you in there. What's your interest in this, Wittaker?" Stephen stopped and turned to face him. This close, James could see the dark rings under his eyes, and the deep grooves on either side of his mouth.

"It's legitimate, that's all I can say." James paused, then held out his hand. "I am very sorry for your loss. I know you were close to the prime minister." Stephen was one person he knew would have had nothing to do with Perceval's death. He and Perceval had been an almost indestructible team.

Stephen shook his hand, his gaze thoughtful. "When we challenged him, Gibbs looked like he might fall down in a blue fit."

"Yes." James looked back toward the building, but the clerk hadn't come running out screaming for a doctor, as James half-expected him to.

"He's the Prince Regent's man, you know?"

James shook his head.

"He was the Prince Regent's legal council for many years. And as an ally of the Prince Regent, you can bet he is . . . was . . . a bitter enemy of Perceval's." Stephen rubbed his face. "I can't believe he would do this out of a sense of spite—but what else is there? Gibbs could lose his reputation with this miscarriage of justice, and what does he have to gain?"

Before James could answer, Stephen turned abruptly and walked away, not at any great speed, but more like a man completely at a loss as to where to go at all.

James watched him until he disappeared into the crowds.

He'd brought up an interesting point. Was this rushed trial Gibbs being ultra-cautious about the state of social unrest, or was there something more to it?

James turned in the direction of Bow Street. Time to find out what John Vickery of Bow Street knew.

Chapter Seventeen

Aunt Dorothy added two extra spoons of sugar to her tea and stirred it vigorously. "I still can't believe—"

"Please." Phoebe rose from her chair and lifted her hands up to her ears, realized how ridiculous that was, and dropped them. "I would prefer not to talk about it."

Her aunt's sharp intake of breath made her wince.

"But that he would renege. I thought he was desperate for your money—"

She turned to give her aunt a cool stare. "He was. He tried to help himself to it before he left. Perhaps he thought to flee and leave me in a perpetual state of betrothal." Phoebe walked to the window and looked out into her garden. She wanted to go out into it, but she knew all too well now how easily her walls could be breached.

"But flee from what, and how do you know about the money?"

"I don't know exactly what he was running from, but he told me about the money. He approached the trustees. Tried to negotiate some of the funds early. But Father had anticipated that and Sheldrake found himself outmaneuvered."

"He told you?" Aunt Dorothy's voice was without any animation now. As if every drop had been wrung from her. "I can't believe he would be so crass."

Phoebe thought of how Wittaker had looked just after she'd told him this same thing. The shock, and then that smile. Hungry and wild.

His loss.

She shivered, her eyes on the back wall of the garden.

"Phoebe."

She blinked and turned to her aunt.

"What are we to do?" Her aunt looked lost.

"What is there to do? I didn't tell anyone Sheldrake broke off the betrothal. I didn't even tell you." Phoebe shrugged. "I will mourn him, and then I will be free."

"But what if *he* told anyone?" Aunt Dorothy stopped, then took a breath. "That is what I worry about. Sheldrake was not discreet. If he told anyone at all, you are ruined. You were together too often unchaperoned during your betrothal for it to be otherwise."

They remained in silence for a long moment, Aunt Dorothy with her eyes closed, as if to escape reality entirely.

The sound of someone knocking on the front door broke the quiet. Phoebe heard Lewis's steady steps to the front hall, the low murmur of his conversation.

A woman's voice rose over Lewis's deep bass, her tone strident, and Phoebe pushed away from the window and stood facing the door.

Aunty Dorothy didn't even turn around when Lewis stepped into the room.

"Lady Halliford asks if you are at home." Lewis's

words were clipped and a flush of color burned his cheeks.

It had been Lady Halliford's ball on Sunday where Sheldrake had ended things between them. She had never visited Phoebe before, and a feeling of unease settled on Phoebe's shoulders, heavy and prickly as a winter shawl.

The timing was suspicious.

Before she could speak, her aunt seemed to snap out of her listlessness. "Of course we are at home for her ladyship. Send her through, Lewis, and then bring in some fresh tea and some cakes."

Phoebe regretted not having the courage to decline, but of course, as her aunt said, they would be at home for someone of her ladyship's calibre.

Lewis ushered her in, and Phoebe felt a fleeting sense of satisfaction at the look on Lady Halliford's face. People often had that look when they entered the house for the first time and saw her staircase.

It was a look of wonder, and sometimes, as was the case with her current guest, of envy.

"I had no idea you lived in such an elegant house, Miss Hillier. You should host a party here. I could help you with the arrangements."

Phoebe dipped into a curtsey. "Good afternoon, Lady Halliford. How lovely to see you."

Lady Halliford stopped short, and her small mouth pursed into a perfect O. She inclined her head. "And likewise, I'm sure."

Behind her, Lewis's lips twitched, and he closed the door with a flourish.

Aunt Dorothy shot Phoebe a look of horror. One did

not point out a social superior's lack of manners. "Won't you take a seat, my lady. How gracious of you to visit."

Lady Halliford gave her a nod and sank elegantly into a velvet armchair, looking at the low table around which the chairs were set in surprise. "You do not take cake with your afternoon tea?"

"We do, but I'm afraid you find us a little in disarray today. A new tea tray is coming."

Phoebe caught her aunt's eye and made sure she knew Phoebe would not countenance a single word about Sheldrake as she sat down, herself.

"I'm sure disarray is an understatement, Mrs. Patterson, although why just today? Surely since Sunday evening?" Lady Halliford smiled, eyes gleaming.

Phoebe stared at her, and Lady Halliford held the look for a moment before looking down, modestly, at her clasped hands in her lap. Her smile remained fixed in place.

"I beg your pardon?" Phoebe saw her aunt wince at the aggressive edge to her question.

Eyes shining even brighter, Lady Halliford lifted her head. "You and Sheldrake, of course." She gave a little frown, as if confused.

"What about Sheldrake and I?"

"Oh, my dear girl." Lady Halliford gave a little cluck, like a contented hen. "When I heard about how he threw you over and left the country, I was horrified. I felt it my duty to come and speak to you, and extend my commiserations. I would have come sooner, but this dreadful business with the prime minister delayed me until today."

Phoebe could do nothing but sit mute.

Lady Halliford presided, plump and elegantly dressed in pink silk, artful ringlets framing her face; a perfectly sweet bonbon with a poison centre. "And from what a little bird told me this morning, you haven't let the grass grow under your feet." She lifted her eyebrows at Phoebe's blank stare. "You and the Duke of Wittaker? I scarce think he's been to a single respectable gathering this season, so I can't imagine how you are acquainted enough for an early morning visit. But word is you are." She gave a sugary smile.

Aunt Dorothy made a noise beside her. A little animal groan that she swallowed as soon as the sound emerged.

"I'd very much like to know how you came by your information." At last her jaw loosened enough for speech, although her words were stilted. Phoebe had the small satisfaction of seeing Lady Halliford lose a little of the pink of excitement in her cheeks when she caught sight of Phoebe's face.

"Why, it is all over town."

"No, it isn't." Phoebe was quite sure of that.

"But . . ." Lady Halliford frowned again, although this time in genuine confusion. "I heard . . ."

"You find us unsettled because Lord Sheldrake is dead. He died yesterday. The Duke of Wittaker kindly took the time to inform me of the news this morning."

For the first time, Lady Halliford looked out of her depth. "Dead . . ." She fiddled nervously with the rings on her fingers. "I wasn't aware—"

"Weren't you?" Phoebe kept her gaze fixed on Lady

Halliford, but she would not look at her, now.

"No. How perfectly rude of you to suggest I would —"

"Who told you Sheldrake broke off our betrothal?" Phoebe's question was sharp, cutting through the bluster.

"Why, it was . . ." She paused, then rose to her feet, her cheeks flushed with anger, now, not excitement. "Your attitude is hardly appropriate, Miss Hillier. I will excuse it in light of the shock you must be in, but I'm sure my source was accurate, he hasn't ever been wrong in these matters before. Which puts you in an awkward position. You are neither the grieving financée, nor the disinterested acquaintance." At last, all pretense was gone, all artifice. She looked down on them both with a supercilious expression.

"Why did you come here?" Phoebe rose to her own feet.

"I . . ." Lady Halliford hesitated, and Phoebe guessed her purpose had been derailed by news of Sheldrake's death.

"I don't think it's appropriate of me to impose myself on you further, given the tragedy of the moment." Lady Halliford took up her reticule and straightened her gloves.

Aunt Dorothy rose, almost swaying on her feet at the prospect of the scandal about to hit them.

Sheldrake. Wittaker.

One or the other would be bad enough. It looked like they would have to contend with both.

Phoebe's temper spiked even higher.

She looked directly into Lady Halliford's eyes. Let her see she had made an enemy for life. She pulled the cord for Lewis and he appeared almost instantly.

"Lady Halliford is going, Lewis. Please see her out."

They exchanged stiff, polite nods, and then her ladyship swept out of the room.

In the quiet that followed in her wake, Aunt Dorothy began to weep.

Chapter Eighteen

Bowstreet Runner John Vickery was a large man, but with a surprisingly gentle face. His blue eyes fixed on James with interest as he stood from his desk and made a formal bow.

"Good afternoon, Your Grace." His gaze flicked to the clock on the wall behind James's shoulder. "The magistrate says you've come here straight from the Attorney General's office." There was a suspicious lack of inflection in Vickery's voice.

"Yes, the Attorney General kindly allowed me to read through the transcripts of the proceedings, and I have a few questions for you, if you don't mind." James kept his voice neutral, as well.

Their thoughts on Vinegar Gibbs went unspoken, although James sensed their views would probably align quite nicely.

"The Attorney General is most insistent that I have something for him by tonight, Your Grace, and if I don't get going very soon, I'll miss an important appointment." Vickery glanced at the clock again.

"I'm more than happy to walk with you and talk, if it

will make things easier." James stepped to the side and indicated the door, and with a reluctant nod, Vickery walked out of the station, with James following behind.

Vickery wanted to ask him what his interest was, James could see it in the way he hesitated on the pavement, but he couldn't bring himself to question a duke.

"If Sir Vicary has sent you because he's getting anxious, you can tell him I will be round with Sir Harry Combe, the magistrate, tonight." Vickery stood, stoic and unmoving.

James shook his head. "This has nothing to do with the Attorney General. I'm interested for my own reasons, and as I say, I'm happy to walk with you, so as not to impede your progress."

Vickery hesitated another moment more, then accepted he would have the company of a duke for some of his afternoon and began to walk.

"I saw from the transcript you found a great deal of evidence against Bellingham in the room where he was lodging?" James kept up easily with Vickery's long stride.

"A cast to make bullets. Gun powder. Papers and pamphlets." Vickery kept his eyes ahead.

"That all cost money."

Vickery slowed, and gave him a sideways look. "It did."

"And I also read his landlady is holding a promissory note for twenty pounds for him."

Vickery grunted in assent.

"The pistols would have cost money, too, unless he already had them—"

Vickery made a sound at the back of his throat, then stopped.

"What? You don't think he did?"

Vickery hesitated, then shook his head. "The guns were special. Designed to be concealed and broken down into smaller pieces. They looked custom-made and I wouldn't have thought someone like Bellingham would have had pistols like that lying about."

"Something like that would be expensive." James was forced to walk behind Vickery as they edged past a fruit seller taking up most of the pavement. "I wonder where he got them?"

Vickery looked over at him suspiciously. "You seem caught up in the cost o' things. You know something I don't?"

James shook his head. "As I said, I've just come from reading the transcript, and in Bellingham's own words, he was destitute by the end of February. How did he support himself?"

Vickery shrugged. "Something worth looking into, I'll grant you, but I've got no time for that. Might have had some money sent down to him from Liverpool, maybe? It's all we can do to get the facts straight in the time we have. Sir Vicary wants an open-and-shut case, he says. No room for doubt."

"Will you be able to give it to him?" James's sense of Vickery was that he was straight. And thorough.

The big man gave a nod. "No doubt he did it. Made the bullets, even if he didn't buy the gun. He's well-known to everyone, even some clerks at Bow Street have spoken to him. He's been all over with those pamphlets, demanding justice. Took justice into his own hands, looks like."

His voice was calm, but something in the tone told James he was angry at the thought of Bellingham taking the law into his own hands. If that was what he had done.

He hadn't known what to expect of the Bow Street officer, but so far this big, steady man impressed him. He didn't want James with him, but he'd taken his presence with good grace.

"Where are we walking to?" James noticed they were in the commercial district now, coming up to High Holborn.

"A Mr. Taylor sent a note round. Has some information." Vickery didn't say anything else, but James guessed the note said more than that, to have gotten the head investigator's attention with so little time at his disposal.

"Do you mind if I accompany you to the interview?"

Vickery's face tightened.

"I won't introduce myself, or talk."

Vickery waited for a carriage to pass, and then crossed the road before he finally gave a nod.

James liked him all the more for his obvious reluctance.

Vickery slowed his pace as they approached a tailor's shop. He gave James a last look, as if willing him to change his mind, and when James looked back at him with a smile, he sighed and pushed the door open.

A small bell rang to announce them, and a thin man with receding blond hair in shirt sleeves and a waistcoat stepped out from the back room. He was using his sleeves as pin cushions, with silver pins woven into the fabric all along the cuff.

"Mr. Taylor?" Vickery stepped forward and shook the tailor's hand. "I'm Vickery, from the Bow Street Magistrate's Office."

He didn't introduce James and James took his cue, standing quietly to one side, as if only an observer.

Taylor peered at him in the gloomy light, and then faced Vickery, fiddling nervously with the pins at his wrists. "Saw what they said in the paper. About who killed the prime minister. My Mary, she tells me to send round a note to you. We knew him. Or, I did. From the tavern down the road a little ways, near Red Lion Square. And I did some work for him, though now I know what it was used in, maybe I shouldn't admit to that." His words tumbled over each other, like water down a steep mountain stream.

"No harm will come to you." Vickery looked like every word he said could be trusted.

James wondered if it could.

"Well." Taylor looked cautiously at James again, nervous not knowing who he was. "Bellingham caught me a few weeks ago, by chance, I think. We bumped into one another up on Guilford Rd, and he asked me if I could do a sewing job for him, seeing as I'd made a few other things for him. Right away, he wanted it. A small pocket sewn into the inside of his jacket. He ran to his lodgings to draw the size and shape of it for me, and brought the pattern down to the shop."

"What jacket was this?" Vickery made it sound like it didn't really matter, but James noticed he looked sharper than he had. More aware.

"Dark brown jacket. Very good fabric and the most up-to-date style."

"And what was the pocket for?"

Taylor flicked a look at him, then away. "He didn't say, but given the shape and size, I'd say to conceal a pistol. 'Twas a pistol, wasn't it? That he used on the prime minister?"

Vickery rocked back on his heels and ignored the question. "Do you have a record of the transaction? A receipt for payment?"

Taylor nodded. He reached behind him, to the counter, and took up a ledger. He lifted it up for Vickery to see, running his finger along an entry.

Vickery leaned in to look. Gave a sharp nod. "Appreciate your help, Taylor. Most likely, I'll have to call you as a witness. I'll let you know when the trial is scheduled."

Taylor did not look happy about it, but he murmured his assent.

James stepped in a little closer. "Can you tell me the name of the tavern where you became acquainted with Mr. Bellingham?"

Taylor's gaze jerked up to him, and then to Vickery, who was staring at James with no little annoyance on his face.

"Legge's." Taylor's gaze shifted between the two of them.

"Thank you." Vickery spoke as if it were he who had asked the question, gave Taylor a small bow in farewell and led them outside.

He kept his silence, but when they were a few doors away from the shop, heading back to Bow Street, he looked across at James.

"I know I said I wouldn't speak." James kept his tone mild and apologetic. "I'm sorry, but I wanted to know the name of the tavern, and couldn't think of a way to get you to ask it for me."

Vickery sighed. "No harm done. I suppose." He focused on the pavement ahead of them. "This is the final nail for Bellingham, you know. He's going to swing."

James frowned. "Why do you say that?"

"We have his confession. And the pamphlets. And the weeks of badgering officials for his blessed compensation. And asking reporters in the gallery at the Houses of Parliament over the last month to point Mr. Perceval out to him. But more than that, now, we have Mr. Taylor telling us Bellingham arranged in advance to have a hidden pocket sewn into his coat, so he didn't have to put the gun together at the scene. He screwed it together beforehand and hid it inside his jacket."

"Completely premeditated, you're saying."

Vickery laughed. "Well, it's not the actions of a madman. This wasn't done in the heat of the moment, or in a fugue. He planned it weeks in advance."

"Perhaps." James wasn't convinced there wasn't some madness there, though. Could a man be so in the grip of a certain idea, so obsessed with something, that he became mad in that thing alone, but could otherwise behave in a way that looked normal?

Whatever it was, he was convinced someone helped Bellingham. Pushed him along and encouraged him. Funded him.

"How did he pay for it all?"

"Back to this, are we?" Vickery shrugged. "He didn't stint himself at his lodgings, I'll give you that. He paid extra for a fire in his room, and sent his clothes to be laundered down the road." Vickery spoke slowly. "He must come from money, or have saved some."

"According to him, that's not the case. And if he's telling the truth, where did he get it? He's been in London since December with no means of support, let alone enough to pay for new clothes, and rent, and the guns, if he bought them and wasn't given them by someone. He also commissioned those pamphlets, not to mention the second application to the Prince Regent for compensation." James was talking to himself, but he saw Vickery stiffen a little.

"I don't have time to find out about that. Gibbs wants answers by tonight."

James said nothing.

"What are you implying?" Vickery's voice was a little strident, now, either forgetting James was a duke, or not caring. "That he was paid to do what he did? That someone was funding him?" The Bow Street officer's eyes were narrowed.

"No." James walked more slowly, and Vickery cut his own pace to match. "He says he acted alone, and I think he believes that. But someone made sure he could keep going. Fed his obsession."

Vickery shook his head. "Even if they did, what can I

get them on? Giving money to a murderer? He's the one who planned it. He's the one who pulled the trigger. Can't get him to say different."

"You're quite right." James saw Vickery flinch at his soothing tone. The big detective gave him another narrow-eyed look.

He stopped, and James realized they'd reached Bow Street.

Vickery squared his wide shoulders, and looked up at the building where he worked, then back at James. There was something in his eyes. Frustration, but acceptance as well. "It doesn't matter. It should, probably, but in this case, it doesn't. With what I'm going to take to the Attorney General tonight, Bellingham is going to hang."

Chapter Nineteen

Phoebe couldn't stand being inside any longer. Her aunt's dread pressed in on her and the stench of malice left by Lady Halliford lingered in the rooms. She needed air.

She stepped out into the landscaped area in front of the library, and watched Jake, the gardener, deadhead the roses to her left.

He would come to her rescue if someone scaled the wall again. And besides, it was daytime.

She had the feeling whoever meant her harm preferred to work under cover of darkness.

"My lady."

She turned at the sound of Lewis's voice. He was frowning at her from the top step. He couldn't know everything that was happening, but he was intelligent enough to work out something was wrong, and he didn't like it.

He looked down at the tray he was holding in his hands and his face changed, shedding the disapproval as he walked down the stairs toward her. The way he carried himself, the excitement in his eyes, made her focus on him more sharply.

Something had happened.

"A note for you." The way he said it, the word 'note' had a capital N. He held it out on the good silver tray, and that in itself was so unusual that she stopped short.

She said nothing, but she thought Lewis's cheeks reddened a little.

"A note from the Prince Regent." He proffered the tray to her, and it trembled a little.

The Prince Regent? Phoebe stared down at embossed gold on linen paper.

"It was delivered less than five minutes ago." Lewis lifted the tray to her again.

She picked the note up, reluctant, though she couldn't say why. Perhaps because recently none of the surprises in her life had been particularly pleasant.

Lewis presented a letter knife with a flourish, and she slit the seal.

A card lay within, an invitation to a private dinner that evening. Written on the paper beneath it was a short note in a scrawled hand:

My condolences on the death of your betrothed. He was a friend. To commemorate his passing, I'm holding a small dinner in his honor. I could not think of having it without you.

The Prince Regent's scrawled signature adorned the bottom.

She lifted her head. "I'm to attend a private dinner tonight with His Royal Highness."

She held up the invitation that had been enclosed with the note, and saw the dinner was for eight o'clock at Carlton House.

"I will have to go." She spoke to herself, thinking of the Duke of Wittaker's warning to stay at home, but this was a direct summons, however politely couched, and one she couldn't ignore.

Lewis looked at her strangely. "I'll instruct your maid to get out your best gown."

"Is the messenger waiting for a reply?" There was no mention of her aunt in the invitation, but it was unthinkable that she go without a chaperone.

Lewis gave a nod.

"Let him know my aunt and I would be honored to attend." She put the invitation and the note back on the silver tray and Lewis disappeared inside.

She did not want to follow him in.

The gardener was still working on the rose bed on the other side of the garden, but well within earshot should she need him.

She turned and walked into her enclosed sanctuary, the thought of attending the dinner making it harder and harder to breathe.

Lady Halliford would have been at work since her visit earlier. Spite had shone out of her like the glitter of cold, sharp crystal. The news that Sheldrake had ended their betrothal, that she was ruined, may well reach the Prince before tonight, but even if it didn't, given Lady Halliford's reach, at least some people at Carlton House tonight would know. And they would be only too happy to spread the word.

Tonight would be awkward. Possibly a social disaster.

She started walking the paths, blindly picking herbs as she went and she had a fragrant bouquet by the time she reached the far end of the row.

"Do you not understand the meaning of 'don't go out'?"

The words were murmured just above her head.

She froze in surprise, and jerked her gaze upward. The sight of Wittaker, crouched above her like a vengeful angel, helped to steady her, but too late. Hot tears stung her eyes and she turned away immediately, breathing hard.

He jumped down instead of climbing, and before she was ready to look at him again hands gripped her shoulders and turned her around.

"What is it?" He studied her face with such intensity she looked down at his highly polished boots to hide from him.

A single tear escaped, sliding down her cheek, and a warm finger brushed it away. His arms enfolded her, so she was pressed against his chest, the herbs in her hands crushed between them, the scent of rosemary and sage mingling with the smell of wool and sandalwood. For a moment she let her head rest against the beat of his heart.

It was hard to pull away.

Harder still because he resisted, only releasing her when she jerked back. He seemed to have no sense of propriety.

"Why are you hiding in your garden, when you know it's not safe?" He looked bigger, somehow. More dangerous than before.

"It should be safe. This was the one place I could

count on." Sheldrake, with his schemes and deceptions, had taken that from her, and the rush of anger at the thought gave her what she needed to find her equilibrium. She was fast friends with anger, and happy to use its steadying hand.

He said nothing, watching her intently.

He kept doing this to her, making her so uncomfortable she had to look away. The herbs were a mangled green mess in her hands and she concentrated on them. "I'm in trouble."

"Someone is trying to kill you. Of course you're in trouble." He spoke softly, the way some men she'd seen at balls or dinners spoke to their wives, head bent close to her ear, warm breath soft against her skin.

"Not that." She shook her head to hide the shiver that shimmered through her.

His hand reached out and cupped her shoulder, drawing her even closer to him. He held her gaze and she drew in a breath at the banked fury there. "You have more pressing troubles than someone trying to kill you?"

"Someone knows Sheldrake broke off the betrothal." She tried to keep her voice steady. "And now the Prince Regent has sent me a command to attend a dinner at Carlton House tonight in Sheldrake's honor, and I don't want to go."

He stared at her, and she realized she had rendered him mute.

"The invitation arrived a few minutes ago."

"Was Sheldrake a particular friend of the Prince Regent?" Wittaker's hand gripped her shoulder a little tighter.

"He said he was. That he was regularly in the

Regent's company. I thought he was exaggerating the connection, but . . . perhaps not." She let the crushed herbs fall onto the path and looked down at her green-stained hands.

"Why don't you want to go? Aside from the fact that leaving the safety of your house is dangerous?"

"Because the invitation makes it clear he thinks Sheldrake and I were still betrothed when Sheldrake died."

Wittaker frowned at her. "You said someone had found out you weren't. Who?"

She rubbed her hands together, smelled the scent of thyme again. "Lady Halliford came around well before the visiting hour today, and let me know she knew."

"She didn't say who told her?"

"She let slip it was a man, but that was all. She . . ." Phoebe thought back to the open glee on her ladyship's face. "She was thrilled to have such a scandal. She began the visit by pretending to offer her support, but she was after gossip. Only, finding out from me that Sheldrake was dead derailed her plans. She didn't know how to respond."

"She may be at the Prince Regent's tonight. Her husband is a close confidant of his."

Phoebe closed her eyes. "Then the Prince will definitely find out I wasn't Sheldrake's betrothed when he died." She shrugged. "I assumed she would spread the word, anyway, though."

His free hand came up, and grasped her other shoulder. "It would seem someone has set Lady Halliford on you. I've heard she's a gossip, but this seems a level above how she usually operates."

"Who, though?"

He raised his brows.

"Not the men trying to kill me, surely?" But why not? Sheldrake was too vain and too conceited to get involved with anyone less than his social equals or betters. Which meant whoever he had plotted with had been his contemporaries. They would be exactly the people she would be dining with tonight.

"I will see if I can get an invitation to Carlton House as well." Wittaker's voice was tense.

She looked up, surprised. "I don't expect . . ." She frowned, and realized his hands were still on her, still holding her. "You are surely busy with this investigation, Your Grace, you don't have time to watch over me. I'll be safe enough with the Prince Regent. He must be well-guarded, especially after the prime minister's death."

He gave a slow nod. "He will be. But you have to get to Carlton House and get back. I will escort you and your aunt."

She thought of Lady Halliford, and how Wittaker's name was already linked to hers, and shook her head. "I don't know if that would be a good idea."

He finally dropped his hands. "Why not?"

"Lady Halliford had another little surprise up her sleeve. She knew about your visit to me this morning." Phoebe blushed. "She was already speculating about it."

Wittaker went still. "Your house is being watched. And whoever has arranged the watching is at a high enough level to feed gossip to the likes of Lady Halliford."

It came back to whoever told Lady Halliford about

the end of the betrothal. It had to be the same person, or she suddenly had more enemies than she knew.

"But surely, by giving her that information, they're revealing that they are watching me. Do they not mind that I know?"

"Perhaps they want to intimidate you. They don't know the true nature of our relationship, and they may think you are alone, with no one to help you." Wittaker looked thoughtfully up at the house, then back to her. "Or perhaps she was told the information in confidence but couldn't resist using it to stir up trouble." He gave a sudden grin. "I doubt they know I'm here now."

Phoebe felt a little sick at the thought that he might be wrong. "What about last night?"

Their gazes met, and Wittaker lifted his hand again, sliding it along the back of her neck to cup her head like he had done in the dark of the garden yesterday evening. "They only know about last night if they've spoken to their assassin, although I doubt it. He's hiding somewhere out of their reach, is my guess."

Phoebe let herself enjoy the warmth of his hand, the shocking frisson of excitement at their closeness. She wanted to step even closer, press herself against him, and so she did.

He drew in a sharp breath.

"Phoebe?"

The horror in her aunt's voice, calling from the entrance to the garden, froze her, and she closed her eyes. Wittaker brought her head forward, to rest on his chest, his fingers smoothing her hair in a gentle stroke. It was a small movement, incredibly intimate. The significance of it astonished her.

It was the action of an ally, and she gained strength from it. Enough strength to reluctantly turn in his arms and face her aunt without a hint of shame tinting her cheeks.

Wittaker did not release her, as she thought he would, he stood behind her with his hands resting lightly on her shoulders, and whatever was on his face, her aunt closed her mouth and flushed a bright red.

When she spoke again, her tone was less strident. "Phoebe, what is going on? Lewis says we are to dine with the Prince Regent tonight." She flicked a glance at Wittaker. "And when did His Grace arrive? I didn't hear him announced."

"He only just arrived a few minutes ago." Phoebe looked up at him.

"And I'm afraid I must be going already. I have an invitation to procure." In an outrageous flaunting of the rules, he touched her cheek with his fingertip. "Will you go inside? Please?"

She nodded, and at last he dropped his hands.

"I will spend another moment admiring your garden, and then see myself out." There was a hint of laughter in his eyes, as he reminded her that he had to climb back over the wall, and didn't necessarily want her aunt to know.

"Your Grace." Her aunt's voice was sharp, her courage back at the sight of his flaunting of the proprieties. "Am I to understand—"

"I will explain." Phoebe walked to her aunt and took her arm. "Let's go inside and choose our gowns for tonight's engagement."

She looked over her shoulder. "Good afternoon, Your Grace."

He bowed. "Until this evening, ladies."

Her aunt looked between them, and the eyes she raised to Phoebe's were unhappy.

"Come." Phoebe led her out into the main garden, and knew Wittaker was most likely already gone.

She had told him she didn't expect his protection, but she acknowledged now that she was glad to have it.

"He is a duke, and you are only the daughter of a baronet. Your mother was a commoner, and there is no social advantage to a match with you for him." As they approached the open doors of the library, Aunt Dorothy slowed her steps, to give them privacy before they were back amongst the servants. "Are you trying to ruin yourself?"

"No, Sheldrake did that for me. This mess is his doing, and Wittaker is merely trying to extract me from it, with my reputation intact."

"That's not what it looks like to me." Her aunt's words were short.

"What does it look like?" Phoebe looked across at her.

Aunt Dorothy shook her head. "Seduction."

Chapter Twenty

James had never been so glad of his reputation as a rake and a scoundrel. The Prince Regent liked to think of himself in those terms, and enjoyed the company of others of the same ilk.

He was invited in immediately at Carlton House, and ushered upstairs to the Prince's dressing room. The Prince Regent sat surrounded by waistcoats and jackets, his color high and a glass of red wine at his elbow.

"Wittaker. You will have to choose a waistcoat for me." The Prince Regent leaned back in his chair and motioned James in.

There were two other men in the room. Wittaker knew one of them, Lord Bartlett, but the other was young and foppish, and James had never seen him before. Bartlett stood by the window, a glass of wine in his hand. He raised it in James's direction.

"Wittaker."

They exchanged a nod.

"Do you know Mr. Fortescue?" The Prince Regent waved a hand at his young companion.

"No." James gave a shallow bow in the man's

direction, and Fortescue pouted mullishly at him, without responding.

James raised an eyebrow in utter disdain and boredom, a man of the world in the grip of ennui, and as he turned back to the Prince, saw Fortescue flush at the set down.

The Prince Regent noticed as well, and smiled rather more warmly at James.

Let the one-upmanship begin.

James had avoided it for more than a month, and being back in it for even a few minutes sapped his strength.

"What's the occasion, Your Highness?" James eyed the waistcoats. They were certainly ornate for a private dinner held in memory of a departed friend.

"You should know, Wittaker. You're coming. Aren't you?"

James lifted his head sharply. "I have no idea what you're talking about, Your Highness, although, of course, I am at your disposal."

"What?" The Prince Regent looked carefully at James, and frowned. "You're not bamming, are you? You really don't know?"

James shook his head. "Something you've organized?"

"Spur of the moment. If you've been out this afternoon, then the invitation is probably waiting for you at home." The Prince Regent took a gulp of wine, peering at James over the top of the glass with heavy-lidded eyes. "An acquaintance has passed away suddenly. I'm holding a small dinner in his honor and Lord Halliford told me you were a friend of his. Lord Sheldrake."

James hid his surprise, staring back with mild interest. To call Sheldrake a friend of his was so tight a stretch of the truth, he wondered it didn't snap and lash them all.

And hadn't the Hallifords been busy bees? He wondered if Lady Halliford had told the Prince of Sheldrake's death after learning about it from Miss Hillier, or whether he had already known.

He should have gone home first to see if he had an invitation rather than subject himself to this farce of a visit. "Yes, Sheldrake's death is terrible news."

He wondered if the Prince Regent would comment on his visit to Miss Hillier this morning, as Lady Halliford had done. It would be interesting to see just how much the Hallifords had shared with him.

"I've invited his betrothed. Or rather, I've been made aware she is his former betrothed. Miss Hillier. You know her?" The Prince Regent lifted a kerchief in a plump fist and dabbed the side of his mouth. It came away red with wine.

James almost laughed at the gleam in the Prince Regent's eyes. He was the biggest scandal-monger James knew. "I'm a recent acquaintance. I was asked to convey the news of Sheldrake's death to her this morning."

Lady Halliford had obviously told him, because there was no surprise on his face. "How'd she take it? Given he'd thrown her over." The question was sly.

James shrugged, as if the matter was of no particular interest and he didn't know or care, either way. He leaned back against the wall and crossed his arms over his chest and tried to forget the warmth of her body, pressed against his in the garden, the smooth silk of her hair under his fingers.

These people wanted to take bites out her, draw blood, just to amuse themselves, and anger and a taste for vengeance rose up in him. "Are you having a dinner in memory of the prime minister as well?"

The Prince Regent set his glass down hard on the side-table. "Lord and Lady Edgeware turned their ball on Tuesday into a memorial to him. I couldn't go, because it was decided it was too dangerous for me to be out on the roads so soon after the riots on Monday, but I hear almost everyone was there. No sense in my having another one for him. And I actually liked Sheldrake, whereas Perceval—" He paused, and narrowed his eyes at James.

James grinned in response, trying to hide the satisfaction of having drawn a little blood of his own.

"You . . ." The Prince Regent was momentarily at a loss for words, and James wondered if he'd overreached. This was not a topic the prince could always respond to light-heartedly. "You asked that just to work me up, didn't you?"

James let the grin develop into a full smile. "Perhaps."

In what could only be interpreted as a fit of pique at being ignored, Fortescue gave a huff of impatience and stood, flouncing to where the waistcoats were laid out on a table and lifting up one with a brown and cream floral pattern. "I think this is the one." He sent James a vicious look before facing the Prince Regent with a smile, and James didn't try to hide his amusement.

Bartlett let out a laugh, derisive and cruel, and Fortescue flushed. "You are fighting well above your weight, Fortescue." He drained his glass, and walked on unsteady feet to the sideboard to pour himself another.

"I hated him, you know. Perceval." The Prince Regent ignored the byplay, and focused his attention on James. "Hated him. In his time in government he blackmailed me, ridiculed me, made me a laughing stock—" The Prince Regent held out his glass, and Fortescue hurried to fill it. "The only drawback in his death, as far as I'm concerned, is that it's fed the radicals' desire to see me go, as well as that jackanapes." He drained his full glass in one gulp.

There was silence in the room. None of them, not even Fortescue, was stupid enough to make a comment.

The Prince Regent looked down into his empty glass, and then up at them each in turn. "What, my wit struck you all dumb?"

James gave him a mock salute. "What about speaking no ill of the dead?"

The Prince jerked his head back as if he'd been slapped. "Everyone knew I couldn't stand the fellow before he was dead. Why would they think I can stand him now?" He played with the empty glass in his hand, tipping it this way and that. "You know he forced me to sign a document saying I was well-pleased with the job he was doing at the beginning of February? Forced me!" He set the glass down, and James was relieved he hadn't thrown it at the wall.

James made a sympathetic sound of agreement. The Prince Regent had wanted Perceval out of office so that he couldn't renew the Regency Bill, and all the restrictions it placed on the Regent's power.

He had lost the battle.

His plans to remove Perceval had backfired and he'd been humiliated. Perceval had rubbed his nose in it by forcing him to publicly praise him.

Looking at the cold hatred in the Prince Regent's eyes, James decided Perceval had been playing with fire.

"Who will rid me of this troublesome priest?" Bartlett spoke from the window, his words jumbled and slurred, almost unintelligible.

"Get out, Bartlett, you're drunk." The Prince Regent heaved his bulky frame to his feet. "Choose a waistcoat for me, Wittaker, and get out, as well. I need a rest before tonight."

James walked to where Fortescue was pouting beside the table. He chose one at random, keeping a look of bored amusement on his face. He lifted up one of cream satin with a raised fleur-de-lis pattern in the same color and turned to present it with a bow.

The Prince Regent took the item as carelessly as James had chosen it. "What was your view on Perceval, Wittaker?"

James lifted an eyebrow. "You know me, Your Highness. What do you think?"

The Prince seemed to search his face for a beat too long, then gave a laugh. "Quite so."

James bowed and walked out. The silence behind him had the feel of men waiting until he was gone before they spoke freely again.

Chapter Twenty-one

Carlton House was sumptuous.

A butler led them through the massive white and black tiled entrance hall to a reception room heavy with gold gilt and sparkling chandeliers.

Between her aunt and herself, they had chosen a deep shade of purple for her gown. If Sheldrake had been her betrothed, she would have been in black, but with some knowing she had been thrown over before he died, they decided on dark colors without the commitment of full mourning.

Phoebe was aware of every stare, every head turned in their direction as they entered.

She must have slowed her step, because she sensed Wittaker drawing up sharply behind her, doing a complicated quickstep to not run into her.

His hand brushed her lower back. It was nothing but a light touch, invisible to everyone in the room, but her breath caught in her throat, and she had to look down at her mauve slippers so no one would see her reaction. If the Prince Regent himself had addressed her at that moment, she would not have been able to speak.

Wittaker overtook her, tall and striking in his dark evening clothes. She realized he was shielding them, drawing attention away from them as he placed himself as a buffer in front of the open stares and the sidelong glances of the small gathering.

Could someone have influenced the Prince Regent to hold this dinner tonight? It seemed a complicated and uncertain way of getting her out of the safety of her house, but whatever part Sheldrake had played in the prime minister's death, at least some of his friends must be involved too, might have persuaded the Prince a memorial dinner would be a good idea.

That was more plausible. Although the reason for it eluded her.

If it was to ensure her house was empty, so they could search for the letter Sheldrake had sent her, they would find nothing—not even her servants. She had made sure Lewis had given everyone, including himself, the night off. No one would be hurt by accidentally running across a housebreaker if she could help it.

"My dear, you have heard the terrible, terrible news." A thin, wrinkled hand reached out to grip Phoebe's arm, too tight, too hard, and she looked up to find Mrs. Wentworth at her side. Sheldrake's second cousin was dressed head to toe in lavender and her watery blue eyes were cold as a pool in midwinter.

Phoebe tried to tug free, but Mrs. Wentworth hung on, drawing even closer and patting Phoebe's hand. "Such a shock. To be taken so suddenly."

"Good evening, Mrs. Wentworth." Aunt Dorothy

held out her hands in greeting but Mrs. Wentworth ignored them, her grip relentless.

"And aren't you the bold one, my dear? Showing your face at a memorial for the man who broke off with you?" Her words were sing-song, spoken under her breath and said with a knife-sharp smile. "What did you do, you stupid girl?" She turned protectively to block Phoebe from view as three other women drifted closer, scenting blood—as if Phoebe was her kill to take.

Phoebe felt a laugh bubble up inside her at the thought. Mrs. Wentworth's scrawny neck did remind her of a vulture.

She lifted her gaze to Wittaker, and found him watching her.

He was still close by, hemmed in by two gentlemen, but only a few strides away. She had the sense that he saw it as his responsibility to save her.

The thought of it was as seductive as the touches he had given her in the garden, but she had relied on no one since her mother died, four years ago, and it would be more than dangerous to change that now.

She glanced back at Mrs. Wentworth. Vicious anger, condescension and disapproval warred on her lined, pinched face.

It was a look she had come to know well over the last year since her father became a baronet.

"I can't think what you mean by asking what *I* did, Mrs. Wentworth." She kept her tone even, and wanted to laugh at the surprise on Mrs. Wentworth's face. "Sheldrake betrayed *me*. He broke his word. But despite that, he was a childhood friend. I surely knew him as well as you did, as anyone here did. I have no need to be ashamed to show my face."

Her aunt gave her a warning look, but Phoebe had broken free of the reins. The thought of shedding this restricting life was exhilarating.

Suddenly the fear and dread that had gripped her all afternoon slid off her, and she appreciated the waste of it all.

Mrs. Wentworth sucked in a breath. "Indeed? If you hadn't dragged your feet, if you'd married him sooner, he wouldn't have been in the trouble he was."

A woman nearby tittered nervously, and Mrs. Wentworth turned a dark shade of pink.

"Oh." Phoebe could feel herself gathering speed for a wild, spectacular run for freedom. "Are you mourning the loss of Sheldrake's life tonight, or the money your son might have inherited if I had already been married to Sheldrake?"

Mrs. Wentworth opened her mouth, but before she could say anything else, a high-pitched bell rang from the doorway, and the Prince Regent stepped into the room.

Everyone turned to him, and there was a flutter of curtseys and bows through the crowd.

At last Mrs. Wentworth released her grip and edged away, to get closer to the Prince Regent.

Phoebe had never met him in person, and she shifted uncomfortably as he walked forward, rubbing the place where Mrs. Wentworth had bruised her arm. He looked closer to the newspaper cartoon parodies of him than his official portraits. And he was drunk.

Not fall-down drunk, but his eyes skittered over the

gathering and he stepped too carefully when he walked. "Welcome. And dinner is served. Absolutely no standing on ceremony."

Most people applauded, and there was a general movement to the room beyond, the crowd having been relieved of filing in in order of status.

Phoebe guessed if proprieties had been observed, it would have been the Prince Regent first, and Wittaker second, as the only duke present. Instead, Wittaker made his way against the stream of diners to her and her aunt's side, and held out an arm for each of them.

She should object, ask him not to draw such attention to them, or keep his distance to stop tongues wagging, but after her encounter with Mrs. Wentworth, she knew they would be wagging anyway.

Her aunt was greeted by a friend, who drew her to one side, bright eyes on Phoebe before she bent her head close to Aunt Dorothy's to talk. Phoebe didn't miss the quick glance at Wittaker, either.

"You're risking your reputation by being so gallant. Why?" She slipped her arm through his.

He leaned in. "I don't have much reputation to risk."

She couldn't see his face, it was too close to hers, and she pulled back. "You were trying to reclaim it, though, before this. It will be harder for you to do that when this is over, because whatever ruin I've found myself in because of Sheldrake, I'm still considered an innocent. I'm more vulnerable than your usual victims, in their minds."

"My usual victims?" He tilted his head, so she was looking straight into his eyes, and she could see humor there.

She smiled. "Well, I know you haven't had any, but they don't."

Something changed. He lowered his lids, but she glimpsed a darkness in him before he hid from her.

"What is it?"

He stiffened beneath her fingers. "Nothing, except, I'm no saint, and sometimes I was in character too well. I couldn't build my reputation on nothing. Just remember that."

Still deep in conversation, her aunt and her friend began to drift toward the dining room and Wittaker steered her after them.

Lady Halliford stood at the dining room door with her gaze focused on them. When she saw Phoebe had noticed her she looked straight through her and turned her back.

The cut direct.

"Won't this be jolly?" Phoebe whispered in Wittaker's ear, and when he looked at her with a straight face but laughter in his eyes, she had the satisfaction of seeing the darkness was gone.

***

To James, the dinner seemed interminable, although he had taken careful note of the dishes—Georges would demand an account of what the Prince Regent's chef had produced.

He had passed much of it sunk deep into his own thoughts. Neither Miss Hillier nor her aunt had so much as looked his way, and he knew it was a protection for themselves as well as him. They had already stirred up too much interest.

As Miss Hillier had said before, they weren't his usual victims.

He winced at the image that comment had dredged up. The early hours of the morning, two years before, when he'd found himself drunk, in a room at The Scarlet Rose, with a twelve-year old cowering on the bed.

He'd downed a jug of water and walked around the room for ten minutes to get himself as sober as possible before he'd asked her what the hell was going on.

Betty. He smiled at the memory of how she'd started out crying, then slowly, as she realized he wasn't planning to do anything to her, sat up and began to watch him warily, and then, at last, with a little hope.

When he'd finally felt capable of a lucid conversation, they had spoken for more than thirty minutes. Then he'd taken her downstairs, threatened to shut Madame Rouge down, and negotiated his deal with her.

He had never slept with another prostitute again.

It should have made anyone looking at him too closely suspicious of his credentials as a rake, but in fact it had only increased his prestige amongst the crowd he spent his time with. They all thought he had some secret stash of girls somewhere, and vied with each other to get an invitation.

A scrape of chairs jolted him from his thoughts as the women rose to leave the men to their port and cigars. As they made their way to the withdrawing room, Miss Hillier's aunt went immediately to her niece's side, presenting a united front. He was pleased to see she seemed to support her niece no matter what she thought of his and Miss Hillier's unusual relationship.

She was right to be concerned. He needed to remember that there were rules. He had spent so long ignoring them, or deliberately flaunting them, he sometimes forgot there were consequences to those who did not obey.

People like Miss Hillier, who society would take enjoyment in vilifying, while those same people looked on him with almost amused indulgence for the same indiscretions.

"A striking pair, aren't they?" Lord Fairbanks leaned in from his left, his round face flushed. He turned, like James, to watch the ladies depart. "Those fair curls with the dark blue eyes. I remember Mrs. Patterson from her coming out, back when *she* was Miss Hillier. She's kept her looks." He paused, as if to consider his next words carefully. "I saw you were paying the young Miss Hillier some attention, earlier. Bit quick off the mark, aren't you? Sheldrake's not cold in his grave."

James frowned at the insult. "I was merely being solicitous."

"That what they're calling it nowadays?" Fairbanks smiled, but it had a nasty edge to it.

James narrowed his eyes. "I was hardly propositioning her. I merely escorted her in to dinner."

"And escorted her to Carlton House. I was in the carriage behind you, saw you followed her and her aunt's carriage with your own." Fairbanks leaned closer. "Not like you to do anything you don't want to, Wittaker. So what's in it for you?"

Fairbanks's stare was not friendly, and James realized the man thought he was helping Miss Hillier. Protecting her now she was in a vulnerable position.

He gave a slow, understanding nod. "I have no plans to hurt Miss Hillier. In any way."

Fairbanks shook his head. "Think I was born yesterday, Wittaker? I can read a man's interest as well as the next person. You want her. Preferably up against a wall with her legs around your waist, and there's no hiding it." He looked away suddenly, his drink-flushed face turning an even deeper shade of red at the crudity of his words.

Well.

James leant back in his seat. "Perhaps I do, at that." He spoke slowly. "But we don't always get what we want."

"You seem to." Fairbanks swirled the port in his glass. "Never could understand the way of things between your father and you. He was such a principled, decent man. Never said a word against you, though. No matter what you go up to, he always said you were his son and had his regard."

Bitterness welled up in James, strong as acid. His father had made him, and then looked like a saint for putting up with his creation. It had always annoyed James, but now, he felt the anger rushing through him, hotter and more corrosive than ever before.

Fairbanks looked away, as if he could see the tight grip James had to exert on himself. "Just see that you take care. I knew Sheldrake, and he never could look after what was given to him. Damn fool. Miss Hillier has enough trouble without you stirring up more for her."

James stared at him, the anger barely manageable. "Miss Hillier is in no danger from me."

Fairbanks gave a reluctant nod and rose, moving toward the sideboard to choose a cigar from the selection the footmen had set out. James stood himself, too agitated to stay seated.

Most of the men had moved to the gaming tables that had been set up in the reception room they had gathered in before dinner but the Prince Regent stood to one side, watching the play, a whisky glass in his hand.

James wondered if he'd been sober at all today.

He caught James's eye and inclined his head. James had sensed a palpable tension about him since they'd sat down for dinner. A nervousness that manifested in the way his hand shook as he lifted his glass, and the quick, compulsive gulps he took of his drink.

James let himself stumble a little on the way over to join him, taking a glass of whisky from a passing footman, and forcing a vacuous smile on his face.

He wanted to find out if anyone had suggested tonight to the Prince, or if he'd come up with the idea on his own. For all that it was a memorial dinner for Sheldrake, the dead man had hardly been mentioned. But that might be because the Prince Regent was three sheets to the wind, as much as anything.

He'd long ago found that information was easier to come by if everyone thought he was drunk. And if he were any judge, he would need every trick he'd ever learned to get something useful tonight.

Chapter Twenty-two

Phoebe looked into the sly, nosey face of Miss Hepridge, who stood beside her with a cup of tea in hand, and realized she could take no more.

Mrs. Wentworth stood nearby, talking loudly enough to ensure Phoebe could hear her mention how her son was not able to attend the dinner this evening because he was over at Sheldrake's town house, making arrangements for their imminent occupation.

She had thought to offer some financial aid to Sheldrake's employees when she realized Sheldrake had run off without telling them he wasn't coming back, and their circumstances hadn't changed with his death; they'd gotten worse. She would need to help them anyway.

The Wentworths had no money of their own, and other than the entailed properties he could not use as collateral, Sheldrake had surely left them nothing but debt.

Phoebe could imagine Wentworth would have to let most of Sheldrake's staff go.

She sighed and offered her excuses to Miss Hepridge, moving away from Mrs. Wentworth and seeking out her aunt.

No one had approached her with a warning or a threat. So either tonight had been a genuine gesture on the Prince Regent's part, or someone had been searching her home for Sheldrake's letter.

However, if tonight had been engineered to let Phoebe know that a woman whose engagement had been broken was deemed ruined, then they had succeeded.

She'd known it, but the reality was an ugly, spiteful monster that leered at her from the faces of the women standing around her, sipping coffee and eating petit fours.

Relief that it was not them, or one of their daughters, and a compulsion to make it her fault—to hide the truth that they had no control over whether a man kept his word or not—shone from them in ugly greens and dirty reds.

She took all her hopes for acceptance in the world her father so desperately wanted her to live, all the personal wishes for friendship and connection, and crushed them like autumn leaves, grinding them to dust and then letting them float away.

There didn't seem to be a friendly face in the room besides her aunt, whom she finally spotted in a corner, looking as uncomfortable as she felt. Their eyes met, and Phoebe gave a tiny nod of her head, which Aunt Dorothy returned.

They made their way toward each other and Aunt Dorothy bent her head close to Phoebe's ear. "Leave?"

"Yes."

There was no mistaking the relief on her aunt's face, and Phoebe felt a renewed rush of anger. Sheldrake hadn't just ruined her, he had tainted her aunt's social standing, as well.

They stepped out into the corridor, and Phoebe motioned a footman closer. "We need to take our leave. Could you convey our thanks to His Royal Highness?" As he bowed, Phoebe worried her bottom lip, wondering how to let Wittaker know they were leaving, as well.

He had planned to follow them home, to make sure they got there safely, and she wanted his protection. For her aunt's safety, if nothing else. "One moment."

The footman had already turned to go and he looked back at her.

"I would like to give you a note for the Duke of Wittaker, if you would wait a moment." Phoebe couldn't help the heat that burned in her cheeks as she spoke. She knew the implications that could be—would be—drawn from a private note, but she couldn't risk her aunt's welfare.

Besides, the guests here tonight had made it clear she was ruined. She may as well do as she pleased.

The footman directed her to an exquisite table in the massive entrance hall that contained paper and pen in its little drawer, and she wrote quickly and handed it to him.

They settled in to wait for a response besides one of the massive pillars in the great room and were approached by the doorman, wanting to know which carriage to call.

Phoebe clasped and unclasped her hands, in a quandary as to whether she should presume to call the Duke of Wittaker's carriage around as well as their own.

She didn't have the nerve, she decided as she gave only her name to the doorman. To do so would be to presume too much, no matter what he had said.

The footman reappeared, his eyes refusing to meet theirs. "His Royal Highness sends his best wishes, and was pleased you could join him." He bowed, and when he straightened, his gaze was firmly fixed on his own feet.

"I . . ." Phoebe exchanged a look with her aunt. "Thank you."

He gave a nod and turned back, and Phoebe raised a tentative hand, which her aunt gripped, hard, and pulled down.

"Do not ask about that note." Her whisper was fierce. "You are *not* desperate. You are a Hillier."

Phoebe watched the footman disappear, and felt an odd mix of fear and disappointment. "I wish you hadn't done that." She flicked a glance at the doorman, but the carriage must still be coming round, because he did not look their way to call them.

"Sheldrake was in trouble." The words leapt from her mouth, and her aunt's eyes widened.

"Debts, you said?" Her expression was one of disgust.

"Not debts." Phoebe paused, then shrugged. "Or, not only debts. He had done something criminal. And the people he was in league with have decided he might have told me something dangerous to them. They tried to kill me last night. That man in the garden, he held a gun at me."

Her aunt's mouth fell open.

"I am only telling you this so that if they try again, you are aware and can take precautions. And so you understand why I'm going to ask you to leave tomorrow. Go back home, where it's safe."

"Phoebe?" Her aunt grabbed her arm again, her grip

as tight as before, her eyes confused.

"Your carriage, my ladies." The doorman held one of the massive double-doors open for them.

Phoebe glanced back one last time to see if Wittaker was coming, and then stepped into the night.

***

James noticed a footman approach the Prince Regent. He wished him luck getting any sense out of His Highness. The Prince had been slurring his words since James had joined him after dinner.

James had since insinuated himself into a group playing Hazard, hoping to hear something that would help Dervish's enquiry, but he began to ease himself out of the crush.

The restlessness that had gripped him since dinner made it difficult to concentrate on the talk around him, and his thoughts kept turning to Miss Hillier. The rigid line of her back as she'd left the room spoke of a fighter going into the ring already outmatched.

The footman had left by the time he broke from the rowdy crowd. He thought he might go check on Miss Hillier. At least a half hour had passed since dinner was over, and the men would be expected in the withdrawing room soon, anyway.

"Wittaker?" An hand came down hard on his shoulder, and James turned to find Lord Halliford standing behind him.

"Halliford. I hear you're responsible for my invitation here tonight." James made no attempt to hide the dislike that flared up inside him.

Halliford took a step back. "Did you, now?"

James gave him a long, cool look. "Yes."

Halliford looked across to the Prince Regent and then let his gaze jump back to James. "Well, I might have mentioned you knew Sheldrake."

"You and your wife seem particularly interested in me today." He kept his gaze on Halliford steady, and Halliford shifted uncomfortably.

"My wife?"

James flexed his fingers. "Miss Hillier told me about her visit this morning. The timing is quite interesting to me."

Halliford turned his head away for a moment, his cheeks and throat going a dark, mottled red. "Interesting in what way?" His voice was thick.

James hesitated. In the past, this conversation would not have happened. He would have played drunk and bumbled his way through a meaningless five minutes before wandering off. But the Hallifords' interference had caused harm to Miss Hillier and it had made him forget his usual role. "In something I'm looking into for Lord Dervish." He smiled.

Halliford frowned and took an uncertain step back.

James laughed loudly, slapped Halliford on the upper arm and turned away. As he did, he caught a glimpse of Halliford's confusion.

His act should keep Halliford off balance, and not quite sure if James was telling the truth or not. It might even force some results, stir up the hornet's nest. His usual methods certainly weren't working.

He started for the door, and knowing Halliford's eyes

were still on him, allowed himself to list a little to the left and stumble. When he stepped out of the room and out of sight, he straightened and started toward the withdrawing room.

"Your Grace?" The footman he'd noticed talking to the Prince Regent hovered a few steps from the door to where the ladies gathered. "If you are looking for Miss Hillier, she has already gone home."

James stopped. "Gone?"

"Did you not get the note from her? His Highness took it on your behalf." The footman edged a step closer to the door.

James stared at him. "No. I didn't get it. When did she send it?"

The footman looked down. "When she asked me to conveying her regards and goodbyes to His Highness."

James glanced over his shoulder at the entrance to the room he'd just left. He had a strong urge to confront the Prince Regent, standing in his drunken fog. No doubt he'd wanted to read just what a private note between himself and Miss Hillier was about. He probably thought it all highly amusing.

The footman clenched and unclenched his white-gloved hands.

"How long ago did she leave?" He tried to keep his voice steady, but the footman blanched.

"Five minutes ago, at most, Your Grace." The man's voice rose a little toward the end.

James turned to the entrance hall, and then swung back. "Why did you mention this to me?"

The footman's gaze moved past him, in the direction of the rowdy reception room. "I was afraid His Highness might be too . . . preoccupied to give it to you." He looked down at his feet. "And Miss Hillier seemed anxious."

James gave a nod and then strode to the front doors.

He couldn't work out whether it was by design or terrible luck, but if someone had hoped to leave Miss Hillier vulnerable tonight, they had succeeded.

Chapter Twenty-three

Phoebe asked the coachman to wait a few minutes, just in case Wittaker was still coming. They sat in silence, bathed in the glow from the brightly-lit windows of Carlton House. Aunt Dorothy yawned and clamped a hand over her mouth in mortification.

"Time to leave." Phoebe couldn't understand what was keeping Wittaker, but it was clear he wasn't coming. She was about to give the word to the driver when a carriage pulled in behind them, the rattle of its wheels on the cobbles vibrating through their sprung carriage.

Someone arriving very late for the dinner. Or perhaps someone who had preferred to skip dinner and go straight for the evening's entertainments.

Thinking of that, she realized almost no mention had been made of Sheldrake this evening. It had been more like a social affair than a memorial. The Prince Regent had raised a glass for absent friends, but he may just as well have meant the living as the dead.

From the driver's seat she heard Rogers call to the driver of the new carriage. He swung down and poked his head through the door. "They want to come past, my lady.

Should we go?"

Phoebe looked toward the door one last time, then nodded. "Yes, let's get home."

They heard Rogers climb back up, the creak of him taking his seat, but before he could urge the horses to move, there was a shout.

Wittaker came stumbling out of Carlton House. He was calling to them, his hand raised although his words were so slurred, they were unintelligible.

She opened the door.

"My lady?" Rogers peered down at her, a worried frown creasing his lined face.

"Wait for him, Rogers. It will be all right."

Rogers hesitated, but gave a brief nod. The driver of the other carriage called something, just as Wittaker reached them and pulled himself inside, and Rogers urged the horses forward before he'd got the door completely shut.

They left with a rumble over the cobbles, down Pall Mall toward Portman Square, their pace slow with the evening traffic.

Wittaker leaned back and breathed out a sigh of relief.

She realized the drunken behavior had been a ploy, and it hurt that he had done that to himself, to his reputation, for her. He shouldn't have to keep blackening his name.

She reached forward and touched his hand, and the look he gave her was startled.

"I'm lucky I caught you in time."

"We waited for a bit. Hoping you would come." She hadn't thought he would, though. But now he was sitting opposite her, looking at her with that clear, steady gaze, she realized she should have had more faith in her instincts.

"Well, that was dramatic." Aunt Dorothy kept looking at Wittaker, just to make sure he really wasn't in his cups. "Why did you pretend to be drunk?"

"To make anyone watching think he's not much of a threat, but still let them know we aren't alone." Phoebe answered for him, and she saw the gleam of Wittaker's eyes in the light of the street lamps as he lifted his head up at her answer.

"Hopefully the rest of your evening was more sedate?" He folded his arms across his chest.

She knew what he was asking, and leant back. "No overt nastiness, except one incident with Mrs. Wentworth. Plenty of subtle signals I am no longer welcome."

"Who is Mrs. Wentworth?" Wittaker looked between them.

"Harold Wentworth's mother. Harold is next in line, so he'll inherit Sheldrake's titles and all the entailed property that goes with it."

"Ah." Wittaker sent her a crooked grin.

"Exactly." Phoebe smiled back, even though a few minutes ago, a smile was the last thing she'd felt like. "It seems I was somehow at fault for not marrying Sheldrake sooner, because if I had, Mrs. Wentworth's Harold would be inheriting as much of my money as was in Sheldrake's control, as well as the titles and houses."

"And Lady Halliford?" Wittaker steepled his fingers and looked at her from under half-closed lids. He looked dangerous and still had that wild, unpredictable air of a drunk, as if he hadn't fully dropped his act.

She shifted on the carriage bench. "She gave me the cut direct, so she couldn't approach me after that. It was quite a relief."

"But surely you don't think us in danger from anyone at dinner tonight?" Aunt Dorothy had relaxed, sitting more fully on her side of the bench.

"I don't know." Wittaker looked out the window as they slowed a little. "Too many variables at play. Tonight could have been the result of malice or a true ploy to get you out of your house and vulnerable. Or something else altogether."

The carriage picked up speed again, and Phoebe leaned toward the window to gauge how far they were from Portman Square. "We're almost home."

Wittaker stirred. He looked half-asleep, his legs stretched across the cab so they brushed the hem of her gown, but she somehow knew that if he wanted to, he could burst into action.

Rogers slowed again, and then pulled up in front of the short path to the door of Home House.

"Ladies, if you'll allow me." Wittaker opened the carriage door and jumped down, and until that moment, Phoebe didn't realize he was going to don the cloak of drunkard again.

He pretended to lose his balance, and then pitched forward, putting out his arms to prevent him from falling through the doors from the waist up.

"If anyone was watching here and at Carlton House, don't want them comparing notes on my amazing abilities of recovery," he murmured to her at the sight of her face.

She gave a nod and he winked at her again, staggered back and held out his hand to Aunt Dorothy. "Madam." He half-bowed as he spoke, and she allowed herself to be helped down.

The front door opened, and Phoebe saw Lewis was standing silhouetted against the hallway light. Aunt Dorothy walked up the path to him, and Wittaker turned back for her.

"Miss Hillier."

She didn't like the way he spoke her name. Slurred and with a leer to it. She knew it was all an act, but something in her recoiled at the sound.

"Hush." He looked at her, serious and concerned, and instead of taking her hand, he reached into the coach, put his hands on her waist and lifted her down, rock-steady.

There was a flash of light from the right and then a bang, and she felt Wittaker flinch. He swore, a word she'd heard many times before on the streets of Manchester, but never from a gentleman's lips in London.

"Go inside." He pushed her in the direction of the front door and then ran toward where the flash had originated.

Straight for trouble yet again.

After what happened in the garden, she shouldn't be surprised, but this time, he was injured. That flinch had not been at the sound of gun fire but the sting of a bullet.

She looked down at her hands and the one that had been on his left shoulder was bloody.

"My lady. Come in." Lewis was halfway down the

path, his face white.

Rogers jumped down from his perch, landing heavily beside her, and she saw he was holding his whip.

She grabbed it from his hand. "Lewis, it will be dangerous, so please don't feel compelled, but if you would like to, follow me."

She ran in the same direction at Wittaker and almost tripped over the whip. She lifted it higher, so it wasn't trailing on the ground and swung her arm back so it was behind her.

Up ahead, Wittaker and their attacker rolled around on the ground, just below the yellow, wavering light of a street lamp. She heard a fist strike flesh and then the gunman rolled to his feet and stumbled back.

He looked set to run, but as Wittaker began to heave himself up, he fumbled in his pocket.

Phoebe's foot kicked something hard and a pistol flew off the pavement and onto the road with a clatter.

She ignored it, keeping up her pace, with Lewis just behind her.

The man at last grabbed hold of the handle of another pistol wedged in his coat pocket and wrestled it out, pointed it in Wittaker's direction.

She cried out. A long, loud scream of rage and frustration, fuelled by years of keeping it in. She raised the whip even higher, running faster than she had ever run before.

The gunman jerked up his head and the look on his face was one of utter astonishment.

She kept coming, and with a curse he spun on his heel

and ran down an unlit side street. The darkness swallowed him up.

Phoebe slowed, chest heaving, eyes on the place where the gunman had disappeared, the whip still raised high.

Lewis ran past her, into the darkness, and the sight of him snapped her out of the strange world she had inhabited for a few moments.

She turned, and found Wittaker getting slowly to his feet, his gaze on her.

"That was . . ." He cleared his throat.

"Loud?" She gave a choking laugh, and lowered her arm.

"How I image Boudica looked when she faced down the Romans." He took a step closer to her. "It was magnificent."

She shook her head, and her gaze snapped back to the side street at the sound of footsteps. "I never realized I could be such a banshee."

Lewis emerged into the light. "Gone," he said.

"Thank you, Lewis." She turned back to Wittaker. "His Grace has been shot. We need to get him into the house."

Wittaker lifted his arm, and winced. "I don't think it's very serious."

She ignored him and slipped an arm around his back.

"Lewis, I kicked one of that rogue's guns into the street. Could you retrieve it?"

As Lewis stepped into the road, searching for it, Wittaker bent his head.

"I can support myself perfectly well." The heat of his breath brushed her ear.

"I know. I just . . ." She drew a deep breath, drawing the scent of him into her lungs, and decided on the truth, for once. "I need to touch you. My brain seems to require it to prove to me that you are alive and mostly fine." She looked away from him, to where Lewis was bending down to pick something up.

Wittaker drew her a little closer. "I'm very happy to oblige. And honored to have your regard."

She looked up at him, startled. "Well, of course you do."

As Lewis walked toward them, a gun dangling from his fingers, Wittaker straightened, but his hand tightened its hold on her shoulder and she thought, for the first time, he relaxed against her.

Chapter Twenty-four

Miss Hillier's butler was a man of many talents, James noted.

He'd gone ahead of them as Miss Hillier helped James back to the house, and by the time she'd ushered him into the library, Lewis was ready with bandages, salve and hot water.

"I've informed your aunt you are well, and will be up to see her shortly." Lewis arranged his medical supplies on a low table by the fire, and James noticed he was careful to keep his eyes from where Miss Hillier stood, with her arm still around him.

He felt the loss of her warmth as mention of her aunt made her pull abruptly away. No doubt exactly the effect Lewis had been going for.

"Aunt Dorothy." Miss Hillier looked upward at the ceiling, as if her aunt might be right above her, watching. "I completely forgot . . ."

"If you would leave us for a few minutes, my lady, perhaps go and reassure your aunt, I will make sure the wound is dressed." Lewis couldn't quite keep the satisfaction from his voice.

She frowned at the butler, as if she heard it, too, and stepped close to James again. Instead of putting her arm around him, though, she peered at his blood-stained sleeve. "I think we need a doctor."

Lewis set the cloth he was holding down. "I promise you I can do it just as well."

They both looked at James for a decision.

He found he very much did not want a doctor. Not only would it stir up even more trouble for Miss Hillier, but a doctor could be followed home and coerced or bribed. He didn't want anyone knowing how slight his injury was.

Better they think him badly hurt and less of a threat.

"You know what you're doing?" he asked Lewis. There was something competent about Miss Hillier's man that James trusted.

"I was a stretcher bearer in the American Revolutionary War, Your Grace. I've treated many shot wounds in my time."

"All right, then."

Miss Hillier looked hard at Lewis. "You'll let me know if it's worse than you think?"

Lewis nodded, and she gave James a last, worried look before she walked from the room, closing the door softly behind her to give them privacy.

Lewis pulled out a footstool for James to sit on, and helped him out of his coat and jacket. They both looked at his left sleeve. It was dark with blood, already hardened almost to black, and the shirt was stuck fast to his skin.

Lewis took a sponge and dribbled warm water over the wound, loosening the fabric until he could lift it from his arm without it pulling.

He eased the ruined shirt over James's shoulders, and James saw the bullet had only grazed him, a shallow groove that ran across his upper arm. It would be painful and annoying, but if treated correctly, it wouldn't slow him down.

"This is the second disturbing incident involving strange attackers at Home House in two days, Your Grace." Lewis kept his gaze on his work as he sponged the blood away. "You wouldn't happen to know anything about it?"

The question was respectfully asked, but James knew Lewis was tense, waiting for some set-down for his impertinence.

"I know a fair bit, actually." He watched Lewis take some salve off the table and stiffened at the sting as he applied it to the open wound.

It would be useful to have an ally here, someone who obviously knew how to handle himself and who would keep a watchful eye.

Not that he planned to leave Miss Hillier to her own devices after tonight's débâcle.

"Lord Sheldrake was involved in something illegal."

Lewis nearly dropped the roll of bandages he was holding. "I knew this would somehow come back to that blackguard."

James leaned back and lifted his arm as Lewis began to bandage him. "You didn't trust him?"

"Looked the place over like a pawnshop owner." Lewis shut his mouth with a click, as if he realized he was walking a dangerous line, talking disrespectfully about a marquess to a duke.

"I can imagine." James kept his tone dry. "I can't tell you what the scheme he was involved in was, but I think some of his associates believe he sent something important to Miss Hillier for safe keeping, or at the least, mentioned some of his illegal plans to her."

"That letter from Sheldrake . . . on Tuesday. The morning you first came calling." Lewis paused, almost done with the bandaging. "Miss Hillier was attacked that very evening."

"Quite." James waited for him to tie the bandage firmly in place and looked down at the neat job. "Thank you, Lewis." He eyed his ruined shirt and decided not to put it on. "Might I ask you to send a footman to my house to fetch me a change of clothes?"

Lewis frowned. "You want to stay here?"

James rose, every muscle aching from his roll on the hard cobbles, and stood beside the fire in just his trousers and boots. "I find I can't leave Miss Hillier alone after what happened this evening. That bullet was aimed at her. If I hadn't swung her down with both hands, if I had helped her out in the usual way . . ." He clenched a hand on the mantlepiece and forced himself back under control. "I could sleep in here. These French doors are the obvious choice if they want to break in."

Lewis gathered up the things he'd brought in on a tray, his posture stiff.

"You don't approve? I won't go anywhere near Miss Hillier's bedroom." James wanted to be annoyed at the man, but found it surprisingly hard.

"It's not for me to say, Your Grace." Lewis's voice was over-polite.

James waited until Lewis was looking at him. "You have a very definite opinion about it. One I respect you enough to hear. Let's have it."

Lewis hesitated, then blew out a breath. "The look of it, Your Grace. Because of the betrothal being broken, there is already so much trouble for her." He set the tray back on the table. "I'll sleep in here. And I'll have one of the footmen sleep on the landing. She'll be protected."

James hesitated. The need to protect Miss Hillier was a compulsion he found difficult to shake. The silence stretched out as Lewis waited for him to answer.

The fire crackled and the scent of apple wood teased his nose. Lewis shifted and the highly polished leather shoes on his feet creaked.

James sighed. "Very well."

Lewis gave a satisfied nod as he walked toward the door, tray in hand. "I'll find a shirt for you to wear home, Your Grace."

James was left in silence, and lulled by the warm glow of the fire he leant against the wall with his good shoulder, suddenly drained.

A noise at the door forced him to look up, and Miss Hillier stood just inside the room. She seemed strangely fixed in place.

James looked down and realized he was still in nothing but his trousers and boots.

"I'm . . ." She cleared her throat. "I should have knocked. My apologies." She spun, hand reaching for the handle.

"Wait."

She stopped. Turned slowly back, her gaze fixed carefully on his boots.

He wanted to break through to her. There was something shimmering in her eyes, something just out of his reach and he wanted to force it out, shake her out of her shell. "What happened to the woman who invited me into her bed chamber in her night shift? The woman who went into my arms this afternoon?"

Her gaze flew up to his. "That was . . . different." She clasped her hands in front of her and brought them up between her breasts. "I didn't know you so well, then."

He gave a low chuckle. "Surely that should have made the invitation less likely, not more so?"

She let her hands fall to her sides. "I trusted . . ." She looked away, a flush building on her cheeks.

He frowned. "You trusted me then, but now you do not?" The pain of that was worse than the stinging groove the bullet had carved into his skin.

She shook her head, looking him in the eye again. "No. Everything you've done since I've met you has increased my trust in you. It is myself I no longer trust."

She stood quite still, head bowed, and he found his feet also cemented in place.

Very slowly she raised her head again. "I *am* that woman who invited you to climb up to her bedroom window. Who pressed herself against you in the garden. And I know . . ." Her eyes were on his chest, and the look in them made him push off the wall.

She took a step back at his sudden movement, and he stilled so as not to startle her again.

She caught his gaze with hers. "I know there are things I haven't experienced. Things I want to explore which I have been unable to. And you will think me most unladylike, but I find, after tonight, I am no longer considered a lady, and I was only grudgingly assigned that designation before. So I will be honest with you, Your Grace. If you would like it . . ." Her voice went down an octave, "I would welcome you as my lover."

He knew he must look like a man hit once too many times in the boxing ring.

He had wanted to break through to her, to uncover the part of herself that he'd sensed was just below the surface, out of his reach. He had never expected an invitation to her inner-most sanctum.

She looked at his body again and blushed. "After you are recovered from your injury, of course. And you have completed your work for the Crown." Her last words tumbled over each other in a rush.

James wanted to laugh at her belated attempt to work in a little time for herself to get used to the idea, or for him to back out of it.

He wanted to tell her how dangerous it was to offer herself to a man with that kind of look in her eyes.

And, Fairbanks was right. He wanted to take her up against the wall.

"My lady?" Lewis stood in the doorway, just behind her, a crisp white shirt in his hand. "Everything all right?"

She seemed to come out of the moment with a blink.

"I think so." She glanced at him nervously and he sent her a slow smile.

"Everything is most definitely all right."

Chapter Twenty-five

Wittaker's chest was now covered in a white shirt Lewis had borrowed from one of the footmen, but even sitting with a man in shirt sleeves was scandalous.

Phoebe shrugged off the thought. What was one more scandalous action in a day of them?

She took a sip of the hot tea Lewis had provided and tried to repress the shiver she felt at being so close to him in such an intimate setting.

"Cold?"

She looked up to find Wittaker watching at her intently from his place by the fire. He had the gun Lewis had retrieved from the street in his hands.

She shook her head, but she did lean closer to the flames. She didn't want him to know how much he could affect her.

She groped for a subject. "If you hadn't swung me out of the coach, if you'd just taken my hand and helped me down, I might be dead."

He moved toward her and sat down in the arm chair opposite, placing the attacker's pistol on the table beside the chair. "I would say it was luck, or chance, but it was neither." He looked down at the tea that had been poured for him and pushed the cup away. "Why did you look that way, in the carriage? Like I had hurt you?"

She forced herself to meet his eyes. She couldn't keep looking away. Hiding herself. "It felt wrong, the way you were acting. It wasn't you, but it was, and it made me upset." She shrugged. "It was silly of me, I know. You were only doing what you had to do. But it wasn't real."

He stared at her for a long time, until eventually she was unable to sit still. She rose up and went to the sideboard, and brought back a crystal decanter of brandy and a glass, instead of the tea he so obviously didn't want.

"It certainly felt that way. For a long time. That nothing was quite real." He spoke quietly as he poured himself a small amount of amber liquid. "But no one noticed, including me."

"What changed?" She leaned back in the chair and watched as he drank the brandy in a single swallow, at the way his throat worked, and the glimpse of skin she could see revealed by his unbuttoned shirt.

"It will sound mad, but I hired a chef." He quirked a smile. He still held the crystal glass in his hand, and he tipped it this way and that, so the light of the fire danced rainbows over the wall. "He forced me to be present. To be honest. And then he came to me for help, and I almost failed him. All because I was so busy pretending to be someone else, I'd forgotten what I was doing it for."

She couldn't tell from his face how the incident he was talking about affected him, but his hand shook a little as he set his glass down.

"So you stopped pretending, and now you're having to force yourself to pretend again?" She was sorry his father was not still alive, so she could flay him for what he'd done to his son.

He shrugged. "I know now I can't do the work any longer, even if there was a need beyond this current affair with the Prime Minister. I don't have the patience for it. And I find I have other . . . interests."

He looked up at her, and for a beat the offer she had made him, and his clear acceptance of that offer, lay in the air between them, sensuous as the feel of silk against skin.

She shifted, not sure whether to run or stay, and he slid from his chair onto his knees and was suddenly in front of her, cupping her face in his hands.

"Shhh." He glanced at the door. "I am going to kiss you. It will not be for as long as I would like because Lewis will only leave us alone for ten minutes at most at a time, self-appointed guard dog that he is." He slid his hands deep into her hair, and tilted her head. "We can taste each other, to begin with." The words were whispered against her lips, and then his mouth was on hers.

She had imagined being kissed.

Even when he could have done so, Sheldrake had not kissed her, and she had been worryingly relieved about it, even though she had yearned for the touch of a man's hands, a man's lips, on her. Had been impatient for it, as she saw her contemporaries married off, some seemingly in loving relationships.

She had known then that her marriage would neither be happy, nor fulfilling.

It had not made the yearning inside her, the wish for something more, any easier to bear. Every year that passed, she felt a growing frustration, a deep-seated need for a physical release she barely understood, but desperately wanted to discover.

But now, under Wittaker's hands, she felt wonder and a warmth blooming inside her, and she arched closer to him, her own hands coming up to rest on the strong column of his neck, to slide up to caress the outer shell of his ears as his tongue tasted her.

She made a sound of delight, and he wrenched back from her, a flush on his cheeks. His hands trembled as he raised them again and brought them up to rest on either side of her face.

"I'm sorry. I have to stop now." His voice was at least an octave lower. He cleared his throat and pushed away, back into his chair.

When he looked at her again, his eyes were burning so hot, she felt their touch on her like a second fire in the room.

And still, she shivered.

"Tomorrow . . ." He cleared his throat again, slid clenched hands along his thighs. "Tomorrow I'll send some of the men who work for me to watch your house."

"What will you be doing?" She took his attempt at distraction gratefully.

"There is only one day left until Bellingham's trial if Gibbs continues on the course he's set, and I learned some things today which I need to pursue."

"I would rather go with you than stay at home." She

saw his face, his almost automatic refusal, but she would *not* be at the mercy of fate any longer. She'd just had her first, heady taste of what it felt like to take control of her own desires, and she loved it.

"Send your men to watch anyway, to see who may try against me again, but if I'm not at home, I'll be even safer. We can surely get me out of the house and into your carriage without being seen tomorrow. I know I might not be able to accompany you to every place you need to go, but I can wait in the carriage where I can't join you, and surely I'll be safer there? You're going to pretend to be recovering from your wounds at home, aren't you? So whoever is watching us will think both of us are at home."

He steepled his fingers. Wavering. "I've taken a look at the pistol Lewis retrieved for us, and it has a gunsmith's mark on it, Beckwith. I'm going to see if he can tell me who bought the gun. That is at least one solid piece of evidence I have connected with this affair. I also need to speak to Bellingham's defense attorney. Get some sense from him of Bellingham's financial situation. And if it turns out he truly is without funds or work, I need to visit someone called Wilson, who apparently owes him twenty pounds, and find out where the money is coming from, and for what. I also need to visit the inn where the tailor who altered his coat used to see him, and speak to the locals. Find out if there is a particular woman he met there."

"A woman?" Phoebe frowned. "What woman?"

Wittaker tapped his fingers together in thought. "There was only one moment when Bellingham lost his calm during the committal proceedings. That was when the Bow

Street officer running the investigation mentioned he had spoken to a woman who had something of Bellingham's in her keeping. He became overwrought, and only calmed when Vickery clarified that it was Bellingham's landlady he was referring to and the item was a promissory note for twenty pounds."

"So that was not the woman and the item that concerned him, you mean?" She leaned forward. "You're wondering who was, and what it is of Bellingham's she has that he's so worried Bow Street will find."

Wittaker nodded. "I think finding her might be the breakthrough we need."

"Sheldrake would never have included me in a conversation like this." She didn't know why the words were suddenly out of her mouth. It was his close proximity, the way the light of the fire lit the planes of his face, and the way his shirt was neither buttoned all the way to the neck nor tucked into his trousers.

The intimacy of it all.

"As I've said before, Sheldrake was a fool."

A log collapsed on the fire, sending up a spray of sparks.

"*Will* you let me come with you tomorrow?" She clasped her hands together, unsure what she would do if he refused. It felt as if more was resting on this than whether she would be safer in one place or another, whether it made sense for her to come with him or not.

He let out a soft sigh. "The idea of you being beside me all day, or at least within close reach, is more temptation than I can pass up."

She was still smiling at him when Lewis tapped softly on the door and walked in.

"Your carriage is here, Your Grace."

He raised his head to Lewis slowly, and kept his eyes on her until the very last moment. "Would you and a footman support me out, as if I am badly wounded?"

"Certainly, Your Grace."

He stood. "Then I will take my leave."

She stood as well, and he took her hand and brought it to his lips. "Good night, Miss Hillier."

Before he let go, she leaned forward and whispered in his ear. "My name is Phoebe."

Chapter Twenty-six

Vickery was on James's front step talking to Harding as his carriage pulled up, and although it was a surprise, James was pleased with the timing.

Everyone made a fuss of getting him from the coach into the house, with Vickery assisting, and James decided if anyone was watching, they would certainly conclude he had been severely hit, and if they bothered to follow Vickery afterward or ask after him, they would also conclude James had made a formal complaint about the attack to Bow Street.

As soon as the front door was closed, he took his own weight, shook off the helping hands and asked Harding to bring Vickery and himself some whisky in the library.

He led the bemused Bow Street officer into the room and gestured to a seat in front of the fire.

"Are you, in fact, wounded?" Vickery peered at the bandage visible under his shirt sleeve, making no comment about James being without a coat.

"A scrape, that's all." James nodded to Harding as he came in, and his butler put the tray on the table and left them alone.

"To do with this affair?" Vickery accepted the crystal

glass James handed him and looked into it, swirling the liquor around.

"I wasn't attacked because of my involvement with this." James was careful with his wording. It was perfectly true. It was Miss Hillier—Phoebe—who was the target of the attack. He hoped her attackers saw him as a nuisance who kept getting in the way, and nothing more.

Vickery eyed him over the glass, and then took a sip. Made a face in surprise.

"Not to your liking?"

"No, not that." Vickery grinned at him suddenly. "Expected more of a bite. This is smooth."

James offered him the decanter again, and Vickery poured himself a hefty splash. "If it's nothing to do with the assassination, what were you playing at out there. All the melodrama getting into the house?"

James lifted a shoulder. "Some men don't like it when I win at cards. Not many, but some, have thought to do away with me before I can call in their IOU." None of this was a lie, just not applicable to the current incident.

But his reputation obviously preceded him. Understanding lit Vickery's face. "You aren't planning a duel, are you?"

James shook his head. "Always handy to pretend to be more injured than you are, though. Just in case." He sent the Bow Street officer a wicked smile, and Vickery shook his head.

"Duelling is illegal, Your Grace."

"I am very aware of that. As I say, I have no plans for one."

Vickery obviously thought he was lying, and James couldn't help the laugh he gave as he swallowed his whisky in a single gulp. "What can I do for you, Mr. Vickery?"

Vickery hesitated. "I've just come from my meeting with the Attorney General." He took a sip from his glass. "Something he said . . ."

The inflection in his tone, and the way he cast a quick look at James made him sure Vinegar Gibbs had heard of James's visit to Bow Street, and had given both the magistrate and Vickery an order not to speak to James again.

Interesting then, that Vickery had come straight here.

He waited the Bow Street officer out.

"He didn't want me talking to you, Your Grace. And definitely didn't want me sharing information with you." Vickery put his glass down, and looked up at James with interested eyes. "I've been an officer of the Bow Street magistrate's office for some time now, and I never saw a man look so guilty, or so afraid. And so I decided I didn't hear him right. I think he must have said I *was* to talk to you."

"I'm sure he must have." James gave a nod. "His voice is so annoying, it's hard to sometimes make out exactly what it is he *is* saying, don't you find?"

Vickery gave a snort of laughter, and then forced himself under control. "I came up with a new witness today. After we saw Mr. Taylor. Someone you would be interested in." He paused, and rubbed a hand along his thigh. "I have two men working for me, and they have been going to every gunsmith in town. Finally tracked the right one down. Beckwith, up at Snow Hill. He confirms he sold the pistols to

Bellingham two or so weeks back."

James tried not to react.

Beckwith.

The name on the gun Lewis had found on the street. The gun James had given to Harding, wrapped in his blood-stained jacket, under Vickery's very nose, not ten minutes ago.

"Why did Bellingham go to him specifically? Do you know?" He busied himself pouring a second glass of whisky he didn't actually want.

Vickery gave a nod. "Specializes in small, concealed firearms, does Beckwith. Has a brisk trade selling pistols to ladies that fit into their reticules and the like." Vickery shuddered, as if the thought of young ladies going about with small guns concealed on their person didn't bear thinking about.

"Expensive?" Some of his excitement faded. Could it be coincidence? Bellingham would have been naturally attracted to a specialist in concealed weapons.

Vickery nodded. "Very expensive, far as I can tell. Bellingham went off to practise shooting them in a park. Even came back to complain it was too difficult to screw the removeable barrel on quickly enough."

"So he went along to Mr. Taylor for a secret pocket that would take the gun with barrel already attached, so he didn't have to." James could see Bellingham's chances of escaping the noose diminishing.

Vickery sighed. "The Attorney General was pleased with the information. He's said there is nothing stopping a Friday trial, now."

James could think of plenty, and obviously so could Vickery, the way his hands clenched and his voice dipped as he spoke of a trial in less than two days' time.

The Bow Street officer left to go home in a dark mood, and James looked into the fire long after he had gone, empty glass in his hand.

Gibbs was pushing the bounds of all decency with this trial date. And the bad news never seemed to end for Bellingham.

He caught a whiff of lavender from his borrowed shirt, and stood slowly. Strange how, despite everything else, he'd personally never felt better.

The look on Phoebe Hillier's face when she had told him if he would like it she would be his lover, would stay with him for a long time.

If he would like it.

He didn't think she truly understood her own appeal. There would have been very few men who would have turned her down.

He could still feel the warm brush of air on his ear as she had whispered her name to him.

But what she didn't know was that he no longer wanted her for a lover.

When they'd met a few days ago, that had been something he'd enjoyed imagining. But now . . . James walked slowly up the stairs to bed. Now he wanted a great deal more.

Chapter Twenty-seven

Thursday, 14 May, 1812

"My lady?"

Lewis stood at the bottom of the staircase as Phoebe made her way down the sweeping golden curve, his upturned face a study in polite attention. His hands betrayed him, though. They were stiff and clenched at his sides.

It was so early, she could hear the birds twittering in the park in front of her house, the sound of the traffic that usually drowned them out noticeable by its absence.

"I'm sorry to disturb the house so early, Lewis, but I have too much going round in my head to sleep." Phoebe kept her own face studiously blank. The thoughts circulating in her head were most definitely private. Very private. "I need to go out."

"Out?" The dismay in Lewis's voice was obvious.

She reached the bottom of the stairs and sighed. "I know. It sounds ridiculous, and I take the threat against me seriously, I truly do. But I forgot to mention to Wittaker last night that I need to visit Sheldrake's staff." All those scandalous declarations and the kissing and his bared chest.

They had wiped her responsibilities from her mind.

She walked hopefully across to the breakfast room, but it was far too early for anything to be set out yet, and she turned back.

"Something I overheard last night made me think they need a little help, and if I don't go now, when will I go? The Wentworths will be moving into Sheldrake's house soon, and once they're in, and have dismissed the staff, it will be very difficult to find them."

Mrs. Wentworth and her son would neither be in the financial position, nor were they careful enough of those depending on them, to help, but they would not tolerate her interference, either. They would see it as an insult.

"Are the Duke's men already watching the house?" She hoped they were, it would make this trip easier to explain to Wittaker if she could take his men with her.

Lewis gave a nod. "The first one came last night soon after His Grace had left, pretending to be a nightsoil man, one who never left our back garden, and this morning a few more came to relieve him, dressed as gardeners. They've introduced themselves. They say there are two more on the street, watching in secret."

"I don't want to cause them trouble with His Grace. I don't want to cause trouble with him, myself." She rubbed her forehead at the thought of what he might say, but he did not command her, and she really had to go now, or Sheldrake's staff would be scattered to the wind.

"Quite." Lewis's tone was thoughtful.

"I meant some days ago to speak to Sheldrake's butler. That's when I thought he'd abandoned them with no salary. But I realized last night his death will be just as great a blow to them. I would have been their mistress in a few short months. I can't leave them without means, and the Wentworths can't afford them."

Lewis was quiet while he fetched her coat from the coat rack under the stairs. "I know Lord Sheldrake's butler. His name is Mr. Jackson, and I think you're right. They will be most uneasy at this turn of events." He held the coat up and helped her into it, making a humming sound at the back of his throat.

"Give me a moment to get my coat, and two of the men from Lord Wittaker, and Rogers and I will bring the carriage round for you. Sheldrake is only five minutes from here at this time of morning. We can be back in less than half an hour."

"I don't want to put the Duke of Wittaker's men at risk." She gnawed at her lip. "I don't want to put anyone at risk, myself included, but certainly not others. You and Rogers, and Wittaker's men, could be caught up in this and hurt."

Lewis had been walking toward the stairs leading down to the kitchens and he stopped. Looked at her with raised brows. "My lady, you could not keep any of us away. I am sure, when I explain what is to happen, that it will be difficult to keep the footmen here at home while Rogers and I adventure off. And the Duke of Wittaker's men will be far less likely to be in trouble with him if they join us, and after a morning destroying the flowerbeds, I'm sure they will be only too eager for some action."

"And Rogers and yourself? If you are hurt . . ."

Lewis took a step closer. "Rogers and I would risk a great deal for you, my lady, and it has nothing to do with the fact that we work for you. Please, accept that we will come freely and gladly, and that none of us plan for anyone to be injured." He bowed, a quick, sharp bend of his upper body and then left her standing, speechless, in the hall.

Five minutes later one of the footmen helped her into her carriage, with Lewis sitting above with Rogers, and two men she didn't know, with her footmen's livery jackets on over mud-stained trousers, standing on the running boards on either side.

They looked tough, and if they were nervous or annoyed at her plans, their faces didn't show it.

The streets were almost empty, as Lewis predicted, and they drew up outside Sheldrake's fashionable town house in under five minutes.

Lewis swung down and knocked on the front door. Wittaker's men dropped to the ground, one going around the back of the house, the other standing beside the carriage. It had the whiff of a military operation to it, and Phoebe didn't know whether to feel reassured or ridiculous.

The door swung open, and Jackson blinked in surprise. "Mr. Lewis, what brings you here?"

She knew the moment he caught sight of her. His mouth snapped shut, and he opened the door wider.

"My lady." He bowed.

"I am sorry to be here so early, and unannounced, Mr. Jackson. But I wanted to speak with you in private."

Jackson drew back, and Lewis waited for her to precede him into the hall. Without thinking, she walked to the library, her favorite room in Sheldrake's house, and Lewis and Jackson followed her.

"If you mean to tell me Lord Sheldrake is dead, Mr. Wentworth has already been by." He looked at the fireplace, and Phoebe noticed a fire had been lit there. Wentworth really must have come here last night, as his mother claimed. She had half-wondered if it had been a lie.

Phoebe drew in a breath. The hard, rough way Jackson spoke could only mean Sheldrake's heir had not been polite, or particularly sensitive. "Does Mr. Wentworth say you will all stay on?"

"No." Jackson looked away, toward the open curtains overlooking the small back garden. "He would keep me, the cook and one maid, but that is all they can afford, I am told."

And Jackson wouldn't stay if he could help it, Phoebe guessed. His tone held open loathing for the Wentworths. "I wanted to offer you and the rest of the staff some aid, Mr. Jackson. If any of you have found another position, Lewis will write you a recommendation on my behalf. And if you would be so kind as to give him the monthly wages for everyone in this house, including yourself, I will make sure you all have three months salary to tide you over while you look for a new place."

Jackson turned from the window to stare at her.

"That's all I came to say. I didn't want you to worry over the situation, not when I could easily make it right. And it would have been . . . awkward to approach you after the Wentworths were already installed in this house."

"You have." Jackson cleared his throat. "Made it right. I thank you."

"If I had married Sheldrake, you would have had no less from me."

"Yes, my lady." He bowed, but unspoken on his lips and in his eyes was the clear fact that she had not married Sheldrake, and therefore had no legal obligation to do this.

"Perhaps I can wait here for a few minutes while you get Lewis those figures?" Phoebe could feel Lewis's nervous energy, the same as her own, to be off home as quickly as possible.

Jackson nodded and led Lewis from the room, and Phoebe walked across to the desk Sheldrake had barely used, except to write his illegible notes.

It was clear of all papers, polished to a gleaming shine, and she could not think he would have left anything of use to Wittaker here. When he left to flee the country, surely he would have taken everything with him that would incriminate him.

"Oh, my lady. I'm sorry. I didn't realized anyone was here."

Phoebe turned and saw a scullery maid already well into the room, eyes wide, coal bucket in hand.

"It's all right. I'm just waiting for Mr. Jackson to come back. Please go about your business."

The maid looked as if she would like to leave, but was already too far in the room to turn and flee.

She couldn't seem to keep her gaze off Phoebe, and in turn, Phoebe watched her.

She was a young girl of around eighteen years old, with long, dark hair pulled back off her face into a loose bun under her white cap. She was quite beautiful, with high cheekbones and long lashes. She had eyes the color of chocolate.

Footsteps sounded across the hallway, and the girl gasped, jerking her gaze from Phoebe to the door.

"Margie?" Jackson frowned as he looked between them. "Everything all right?"

"Yes, Mr. Jackson." The girl ducked her head and turned to the fireplace.

Jackson's look was hard as he watched her kneel before the grate. This girl had done something to displease him. He seemed a fair man, and Lewis liked him, so she wondered what Margie could have done that would provoke such anger.

"We're ready, my lady." Lewis stood by the door, not even coming into the room.

"Thank you." Phoebe nodded to Jackson, and he bowed low to her.

"It is I who thanks you, my lady. Your generosity will make a big difference to everyone in this house." He flicked a look at the maid, who had turned at his words, and was staring at Phoebe again.

Phoebe murmured her goodbyes, and let Lewis lead the way.

Wittaker's men were both by the carriage when they stepped out, and they were on the road, smooth and without a single wasted moment, before Lewis had even closed the carriage door.

She looked out of the window as they drew away from Sheldrake's house, and felt a deep satisfaction that she would never have to go there again.

Chapter Twenty-eight

"So, you are in disguise?" Georges Bisset eyed James curiously.

"Something like that." James fiddled with the scratchy wool of his borrowed jacket sleeve, careful not to move his injured arm too much. His valet had redressed the wound, and aside from being stiff, he had gotten off remarkably easy. "If someone is watching the house, I need a way to get out without being noticed."

Georges shrugged. "You can come with me to the market, and then Thierry can leave a little bit later, and meet up with me. Carry what I buy at the market as he usually does." He handed James two large baskets. "Take those."

James grinned and took them, and followed Georges out of the kitchen door and into the dark of the morning. He had already been given hot, strong coffee and a croissant straight out of the oven, and he felt curiously at peace, even though this was the earliest he'd arisen for as long as he could remember.

When he'd listed the tasks he had to accomplish to Miss Hillier last night, he had left this one out.

On purpose.

Vincent Dowling may be a political reporter for the *Day*, but he was still a journalist, and any hint of Phoebe's involvement would stir his curiosity. James wanted to keep her from him completely.

And he wanted to talk to the man away from listening ears and watching eyes. For Dowling's sake as much as his own. He didn't want to compromise the informer's identity.

"So, you 'ave not said anything about the Prince Regent's dinner. So unremarkable?" Georges could not help the satisfaction in his voice.

"Apparently the Prince Regent only decided to hold the dinner earlier the same day, so I'm sure his chef did the best he could, in the circumstance." James said.

"'Ow many people?" Georges's voice turned from satisfaction to outrage.

"Thirty, perhaps, or a few less."

"*Incroyable*. If I was working for 'im, 'e would 'ave my resignation already."

"Fortunately for me, you don't work for him." James said.

"Yes. For you, and for me, also, it seems." The one thing Georges didn't lack was confidence. "Still, I'm interested in what was served."

"There was white soup to start, nothing like yours, Georges, and sorbet between courses, trout *almandine,* roast quail, some rather good beef, and to tell the truth, I can't remember what we had for dessert."

"Ah. Perhaps not dissimilar to what I would have done under such circumstances. Nothing too complicated. Although, if it were me, you would 'ave remembered the dessert."

James made a grunt of assent and walked beside Georges in companionable silence until they came within sight and sound of the market. The lights and the hum of energy gave the scene a strange air of tension and excitement.

He could see Georges's face sharpen, like a hunter on the scent.

"I'll leave you here," he said, holding the baskets out.

The big chef took them with a slight sniff of disdain, as if carrying the baskets was beneath him. "*Bon chance.*"

James nodded in acknowledgement and walked away into the darkness. The address Dervish had given him for Dowling was close to where the tailor from the day before had his shop. He found a cab around the corner from the market, the driver on his own way home after working around the clubs in St. James until dawn.

He refused to let James pay a fare as he dropped him at the end of the narrow lane where Dowling lived.

"Going home anyways, sir. You keep your money. I made enough out o' the nobs tonight. Forget how much they've given me most o' the time, they're that drunk." He grinned down at James and then lifted his cap before riding away.

James smiled after him. At least his disguise in one of his footmen's clothes was working.

He pocketed the shilling he'd taken out as he walked down a street too narrow for anything but a cart, and climbed the rickety wooden stairs on the outside of Dowling's building, up to a narrow door flush against the wall. There was no knocker, so James rapped hard with his knuckles.

He heard movement within, and then silence, and James knocked again, a little louder.

Eventually he heard the sound of a key turning in the lock, and the door was opened cautiously. The man peering out was in his early thirties, with dark hair receding a little from a high brow, a jacket thrown over a white nightshirt.

His eyes were heavy, as if he'd been wrenched from sleep, but they looked worried, too.

"Yes?" He peered at James a moment, and then his eyes narrowed. As if trying to place where he knew him from.

Another political journalist who recognized him, James realized. "Let me in, Dowling. You don't want this conversation on your doorstep, believe me."

"You alone?" Dowling squinted past him, looking into the gloom, although there was already more light now than five minutes ago, as the sun began to inch over the horizon.

"I'm alone." James found the question curious, but he waited for Dowling to nod, and step back.

James entered a tiny sitting room, with a fireplace to one side, a kettle sitting on the mantlepiece above it. Through a door on the far side of the room he caught a glimpse of an even smaller room with a tousled bed against one wall.

"I know you, don't I?"

"We've never been introduced," James said, hoping he would leave it there.

"And what's this about?" Dowling hesitated a moment, and then waved a hand to the two chairs on either side of the fireplace, which, along with a writing desk and stool against the wall near the front door, comprised the sole furniture in the room.

James sat and after a brief hesitation, Dowling did as well.

"It's early, and I apologise for waking you, but I wanted to speak to you in strict privacy, and thought this was the best way to do it." James watched Dowling as he hunched over himself in his chair, as if still trying to wake up.

The journalist grunted.

"I know you're a Home Office informant, and I know you were present when Spencer Perceval was killed, and I want to know what connection there may be between those two facts."

It was as if he'd applied a hot poker to a sensitive part of Dowling's anatomy. The man visibly flinched in his chair, and stared at James with his mouth open.

"How the devil . . .?" Dowling stood suddenly. "It doesn't matter. Out. Get out." He pointed to the door.

"I'm not going anywhere, Mr. Dowling. Sit down and answer the question. I don't mean any trouble for you." James leaned back in his chair and watched as Dowling tried to get himself under control.

"Who the bloody hell are you?" He lowered himself carefully back into his seat.

"It doesn't matter. I've seen your reports on the radicals and their plans that you submitted to the Home

Office. And I know you helped subdue Bellingham on Monday afternoon. Now, what can you tell me?"

"I've been half-expecting someone, truth to tell." Dowling rubbed a shaking hand down his face. "Thought there'd be more of you, though, come to haul me off."

"Why would that happen?"

"Looking for a scapegoat." The journalist shrugged. "I hoped not, but I've been nervous."

"Why would someone use you as a scapegoat?" James watched as Dowling lifted a candle from the floor, and then fiddled with a tinderbox to get it lit.

"I told the Home Office about Bellingham. In a report. Three weeks ago, I told them someone was asking people in the gallery to point out the prime minister and some of his colleagues. *I* pointed them out to him at least twice. The third time I saw him there, I drew him into conversation, and got his name and where he was from, just in case there was something more than simple curiosity going on. He seemed very calm and certainly not deranged or angry. But now it might look like I didn't attach enough significance to his requests. He was obviously watching his intended victim, identifying Perceval to make sure when he shot him, he would be shooting the right man." With a curse, Dowling spilled the contents of the tinderbox onto the floor, and then stared down at the mess.

"Who did that report go to?" James felt that kick of adrenalin again, that quickening of the heart beat.

"The Home Office Under-secretary, most likely. And then on to the Home Secretary, if he thought it warranted it."

In the gloomy half-light, James and Dowling exchanged a glance.

The incompetence of the Home Secretary was so well-known, neither even remarked on it. Perceval had appointed Richard Ryder to the post because he was a loyal friend, not because he was capable of doing the job. The prime minister wanted someone who would comply with his plans, and as a result, it was widely known that Perceval himself attended to most of Ryder's duties, because the man himself was incapable of doing it.

It had made Perceval Chancellor of the Exchequer, Prime Minister and also the de facto Home Secretary. It had given him full control of government.

"Wouldn't it be ironic if Perceval had received that report himself," James mused. "And ignored it."

Dowling gave a half-laugh, although there was no humour in it. "I've thought the same thing too many times to count in the last few days, but the most likely answer is it is lying in a tottering pile of reports on Ryder's desk."

The scent of the hunt had dulled since Dowling mentioned the Home Secretary. The odds were overwhelming that it had been incompetence, rather than design, that Dowling's report had gone unnoticed.

"What can you tell me about the incident itself?" With the candle still unlit, the only light came from the haphazardly drawn curtains, but even in the slowly lifting gloom, James saw Dowling wince.

"It was a mess." He drew in a deep breath. "I was in the gallery, watching the hearings, and I heard the shot, but really as a background sound, something far away. Then the shouting started and we ran out to see what was happening. Gascoyne was upstairs as well, in another room, and he and I ran down the stairs together. Bellingham had already been identified as the shooter, and we ran up to him, to make sure he couldn't run or shoot again."

"Did that look likely?" James asked.

Dowling shook his head. "He was sitting there, white as chalk, shaking, sweating, not moving at all. The pistol was next to him on the bench. He wasn't a danger to anyone."

"His clothes are torn enough it looked as if he was roughly handled." James said and watched Dowling's reaction.

He pursed his lips. "Emotions were high. People were angry, and Bellingham was right there, unresisting. Gascoyne grabbed his hand so hard, he cried out."

"I see in the hearing transcript Gascoyne says he took the gun from Bellingham to prevent him shooting the prime minister again."

Dowling frowned. "No. The prime minister wasn't there when we got there, he'd been taken into another room and laid on someone's desk while they called a doctor."

James steepled his fingers, tapped them to his lips. "Jerdan told me the same thing."

"I can't imagine why Gascoyne would embellish the truth, but then again, he made a huge production about recognizing Bellingham, too. It was as if he was determined to show himself the hero of the hour."

Could it be that? Or something a little more sinister?

Whatever the case, Dowling had told him all he could.

James stood, and gave a short bow. "Well, thank you for your time, Dowling. You've been most helpful."

Dowling pushed himself out of his chair, and from the look on his face, James had the sinking feeling he'd been recognized.

"You're most welcome," Dowling said. "Your Grace."

James half-shrugged. "No doubt I'll see you around Parliament."

Dowling pursed his lips, but he could not bring himself to question a duke. "No doubt." He opened the door for James and as James walked down the stairs and along the lane, he stood in his pyjamas on his top step, watching all the way.

Chapter Twenty-nine

"Jimmy tells me you went out earlier." James tried to keep his voice level as their coach lurched away from the back entrance of Home House. After all, she had taken his men, and been gone less than fifteen minutes. And the trip had been undertaken at seven o'clock in the morning. Not a time anyone would consider it likely for a jaunt.

Even though it had been a full hour and a half after his own early morning trip.

His men had seen no one around, and they had been watching since the night before. They had also been persuaded by Lewis that the trip was necessary.

All this told him she had not been rash, but he could rationalize it all he liked. He was still angry.

"I forgot to mention it last night, because . . ." She looked up at him from under her lashes and blushed, and he found himself completely immobilised.

He was charmed. And aroused. He could not seem to shake the sensation off.

She cleared her throat delicately. "I took the opportunity to talk to Sheldrake's staff before the Wentworths move in, and offer them some assistance until they find new positions." She lifted her shoulders. "The Wentworths could move in at any time, and although they have no money, they would have refused to allow me to help. I had to act immediately."

"Why?" James tried to unwrap himself from her little finger and get some distance by leaning back against the cracked red leather of the old carriage he had managed to hire for the day. A solid, serviceable, but ancient contraption that would hopefully attract no one's notice as they spent the day following the leads he had gathered yesterday.

She frowned. "Because if I didn't go first thing, I might have missed my chance."

"Why did you want to help them, I mean?"

She didn't answer right away. Like him, she leaned back against the leather and then made a sound of disgust as a sharp edge where the seat had split caught the wool of her coat. She carefully unhooked the thread, her eyes on her task. "It was the right thing to do. And I would have done it, no matter what my relationship with Sheldrake had been, but my urgency, my sense of needing to get it done, in case the Wentworths somehow stood in my way, was because I know I hold some of the blame for the way things were between Sheldrake and myself." She finally worked the coat free, and tried to smooth the thread back into the wool fabric.

"I held myself back from him. I don't suppose it would have made any difference if I had been more open. He may well not have noticed, but I didn't try, even though I'd agreed to marry him." She finally looked up, her blue eyes serious. "I should have refused. No matter the impact it would have had on my relationship with my father, no matter what he would have done as far as my financial well-being was concerned, I should have said no to that marriage. I was persuaded to say yes, and then held myself stiff and cold. I held Sheldrake in contempt. No matter how he behaved to me, that was unworthy of me. I had no business being his betrothed with that sentiment. And helping his staff, doing right by them . . ." She gestured with her hands. "I feel as if I've atoned, somehow. Balanced the scales." She drew her coat tighter around herself, her finger going back to the pulled thread, pressing and smoothing it down. "I feel as if I've fought my way free."

He leaned forward and took her hands. "I like the thought of you free."

The rumble of the carriage wheels and the squeak of the chassis stretched between them, while he kept her hands in his, the feel of them like warm satin between his palms.

When the carriage stopped with a jerk and a call to the horses by the driver, James realized he had no idea how much time had passed.

He looked out the window and saw they had arrived at Snow Hill.

"Do I come with you?" Miss Hillier—Phoebe—asked, leaning close to him to peer out the window as well.

He nodded. "I understand Mr. Beckwith specializes in small guns that can be concealed in reticules and pockets. The majority of his clientèle are women. So today, I will be your adoring husband, looking at pistols for my lovely wife."

She frowned. "We have to pretend to be someone

else? I thought you just wanted to know who he'd sold the gun to."

He shook his head. "I learned last night Beckwith sold Bellingham the pistols he used in the assassination. So we'll be Mr. and Mrs. Lewis, to be safe." He had dressed respectably but not extravagantly for today's outing, and he could be a banker, a lawyer, or a merchant. "There may be a connection between the gunsmith and one of the conspirators. Otherwise it is a real coincidence that Bellingham chose to buy his guns the same gunsmith as our attacker from last night. Whether the gunsmith understands what is going on or not, he may mention our visit, and I would prefer that he didn't know our real names."

She would stand out, bright as a shaft of sunlight, even sensibly dressed as she was in a dark coat and dark wool dress, but there was no helping that.

With luck, she'd dazzle Beckwith, and he would not think anything unusual of their questions.

He got out and held out his hand.

She hesitated, then took it. She was thinking of the moment he'd helped her down last night, he guessed. And he was sorry he had only gotten one single good blow in to their attacker before he'd fled.

"Your arm." She looked down on him from the carriage's top step with big eyes. "Is it all right? I should have asked how it was earlier."

He shook his head as he helped her down. "A little stiff. Lewis did an excellent job, and it really is only a scrape."

She said nothing more as she straightened her skirts,

but she bit her bottom lip in a way he was coming to recognize as distress.

James forced himself to focus on the job at hand, and check on the four footmen travelling with them. Two on top in the driver's seat, one on each side of the carriage, all dressed in street clothes, not their livery.

As he'd ordered, three dropped to the ground and melted into the crowds as soon as he and Miss Hillier stepped down, so the carriage looked exactly as it should, worn and with a single, half-asleep driver nodding off at the top.

The other three would be a moment away, watching for any undue interest.

James left them to it and took stock of the shop in front of them. Beckwith, Esq. Gunsmith was worked in green and gold onto a sign over the door, and the shop looked trim and prosperous.

There was no one behind the counter to greet them when they walked in to the tinkle of the doorbell, and James could smell oil and the acrid, sneeze-inducing smell of gunpowder.

He heard the sound of feet shuffling, and a man in his forties came out from the back, wiping his hands on a grey rag.

"Mr. Beckwith?" James could see black powder ingrained in the man's fingers, and dark smudges on his face and the apron he was wearing over his clothes. Even his grey and brown hair looked faintly stained with black, as if the gunsmith had run his fingers through it.

"Aye. I'm Beckwith."

"You come recommended, sir." James made his voice a little too hearty, and beside him Phoebe stiffened. He caught her gaze and grinned down at her. "I want to get a pistol for my wife to carry around with her."

Beckwith reached under the counter and pulled out a ledger. "What sort of size are you looking for?"

Phoebe lifted her reticule. "To fit in here, please."

"Yes, I have just the design." He flipped through the book and then turned it to face them. It contained a detailed sketch of a small pistol, with the dimensions and the price listed neatly to one side.

"Do you happen to have one with this design?" James asked him, taking the pistol Lewis had found on the road last night from his pocket. "It's a good weapon, and I saw your stamp on it. I thought to get one like it for my wife, only smaller."

Beckwith took it and turned it over in his hands. "Where'd you get this?"

"A friend gave it to me." James leaned against the counter, and watched Beckwith consider his words, his gaze never leaving the pistol in his hands.

"Recently?" He eventually raised his eyes.

"Relatively recently." James smiled.

Beckwith balanced the pistol between the forefingers of each hand and spun it, and James had the sense it was something the gunsmith did often when he was thinking. "This is my work, as you say, but from before I started specializing in smaller weapons. Four or five years back, I made this." He caressed the barrel. "I don't remember who I sold it to."

"Do you keep records? Surely they would tell you?"

Beckwith shook his head. "I do keep records. But this one was part of a set of two, and I made maybe a dozen pairs of these, all identical but for the inlay in the handle. Why are you so interested in who it belonged to originally?"

"My husband likes to know the provenance of things, Mr. Beckwith." Phoebe had been studying the ledger while they spoke, but she intervened smoothly. "He likes to collect things, and know where they came from." She smiled at the gunsmith, and distracted, he smiled back.

"Well, I can't help you, I'm sorry to say. Except to tell you that all those guns were bought by men of standing. They could have been bought and sold a few times since then, but if I recall correctly, every one of those guns went to a nobleman to begin with."

James forced himself to look satisfied. He could feel the heat of Phoebe's body pressed close to his, and he longed to touch the delicate skin on her nape, bent again over the ledger as if she were truly interested in what was on the page.

"How quickly do you want the pistol?" Beckwith only had eyes for Phoebe as well—he was ignoring James completely.

"A week?" James wondered whether the gunsmith would confess he would be busy in the days to come, as a witness in Bellingham's trial.

Beckwith took a step back, and scowled. "Can't do it, I'm afraid. Have something on."

"And what is that, Beckwith?" James made himself sound impatient and annoyed.

Beckwith hesitated. "You'll probably read it in the papers anyway. The man who shot the prime minister on Monday bought his pistols here. I'm to testify to it at his trial and I don't know how long it will last."

Beside him, Phoebe did a good impression of shock and interest. "How terrible for you, Mr. Beckwith. Will it affect your business, people knowing you did business with him?"

Beckwith frowned. "Don't rightly know, but why should it? I take pride in my work an' most pieces is custom made. No ruffians or petty thieves can afford the likes of a Beckwith Original." He gestured at the pistol in his hand in outrage. "Even a gun like this one, though it's not unique, is hand finished. And it cost a pretty penny. I cater to Quality, I do. A few gents like yourself, in the law or business, just like that Bellingham fellow, too, but mostly the Upper Classes. And how was I to know that Bellingham was stark raving, I ask you?"

James lifted his hand to rest on the small of Phoebe's back. "You couldn't, of course."

"Quite right." Beckwith glared at him fiercely, and then seemed to realize James had agreed with him. He huffed out a breath. "Quite right."

"Thank you for your time, Mr. Beckwith." Phoebe smiled. "I would like to order this pistol." She pointed to the drawing on the page. "I've been in a few situations recently where I'd have been happy to have one with me. I can wait until you are able to get to it, though. Shall I send someone around in two weeks to see how far along you are?"

Beckwith had obviously not been expecting a sale,

and he smiled at Phoebe warmly. "I'll be as fast as possible, Mrs. Lewis, but two weeks is fine."

James hid his surprise at her order. He hadn't planned to buy anything here, but there was no doubt Beckwith was pleased by it. He held out his hand for the pistol he had given Beckwith to look at.

"Sorry I couldn't be of more help with this." Beckwith handed it back reluctantly.

And as James took it from him, almost having to pull it from the gunsmith's grasp, he thought he hadn't been the only one lying.

Beckwith was most definitely not sorry.

Chapter Thirty

Phoebe didn't think Wittaker would let her come with him to visit Bellingham's solicitor, Harmer, but he surprised her by getting out the coach and offering her his hand.

"The carriage can't stay here, and I'd rather have you with me," he said when she raised her brows in query, and as she got out she saw he was right. There was no place for a carriage to pull up here, they could only drop their passengers off and move on to find a place further along the road.

They made their way into the building to Harmer's offices, up stairs of dark, lemon-scented wood.

Harmer himself was in the small reception room, giving instructions to his clerk, and Phoebe liked him immediately. He was round and big, but in a way that spoke of a generous country squire rather than a man prone to greed and voracious appetites. His eyes were sharp, too, and intelligent.

"Your Grace." He looked Wittaker over with surprise, and Phoebe realized he must be puzzled at the duke's understated mode of dress. And his reason for being there at all.

Wittaker flicked a look at the clerk. "Can we speak to you in private?"

Harmer nodded, and led the way into a large office off the reception room. It looked out over the street, with four long, thin windows that let in the light and sound of the city below.

"I must admit, I didn't realize you knew me," Wittaker told him as soon as the door was closed.

"You were going to present yourself under a different identity?" Harmer paused with his hand still on the door knob, and stared at them.

Wittaker shrugged. "I wasn't sure. But it doesn't matter. You do know me." He glanced at Phoebe and then back to Harmer. "This is Miss Hillier."

Phoebe exchanged greetings with Harmer and they eventually sat around his desk.

"I don't really know how to proceed, in the circumstances." Harmer looked between them. "Do you have need of my services for something . . . delicate?"

Phoebe looked at him blankly, wondering what on earth he could mean, but Wittaker seemed to have no such confusion.

"Nothing like that. I've been charged with investigating the assassination of the prime minister for . . . someone in Whitehall. And I thought, as Bellingham's defense, you could help me."

Harmer's jaw went slack. "This is about Bellingham?" He looked over at Phoebe, as if trying to fathom her presence.

"What have you found out about him?" Wittaker leant back in his chair, and Phoebe thought she was coming to know him well. He exuded calm and patience, but she knew he was tightly wound as a jack-in-the-box.

"What do you want to know?" The suspicion in Harmer's voice was unmistakeable.

"Where was he getting his money from, for a start?" Wittaker let himself relax even more in his chair.

"I haven't even got that far." Harmer rubbed a plump hand through his sandy hair. "I've only just been appointed to the case, and I'm already hearing the trial is set for tomorrow. I honestly thought it was a joke, but my clerk just came back from Gibbs's office and apparently, that is not so. I'll be on my way over to speak to Gibbs myself. There is no way I can adequately prepare a defense in such a short time."

"No." Wittaker sat a little straighter. "Does anything that you have found point to Bellingham being part of a conspiracy?"

"That's what this is about?" Harmer grimaced. "I can't tell you. I've really only had less than two days to review what little facts I've been given. He claims not. But I don't think he's sane. That will certainly be my defense."

"Have you come across anyone who could help us? Someone who knows him well?" Phoebe wondered what the people who knew him thought of what he'd done.

Harmer looked down at a pile of notes on his desk, and Phoebe had the sense he was delaying while he thought his response through. "Only the obvious, his landlady, Mrs. Robarts. I've sent off to people in Liverpool, but there is no way they will have received any letters from London before this evening, and none will have had time to make it down to London for the trial. Even if they did, I wouldn't know whether they would speak for or against Bellingham by the time the trial begins."

"Where can we find Mrs. Robarts?" Wittaker stood, and pulled back Phoebe's chair for her.

Harmer stood himself, his movements quick and nervous. His gaze flickered between them as he gave them an address. "I'll be honest, Your Grace, I hope this investigation of yours comes to nothing. I don't need any more complications to this case."

Wittaker was already leading them to the door, but he turned back to Harmer. "It'll come to something. Whether it is something that can be brought up in the farce of a trial tomorrow is another matter entirely."

Harmer gave a slow nod. "Whatever happens, the Attorney General is not doing right by the law, neither the letter of it, nor the spirit." He gave Phoebe a polite bow. Wittaker had not explained her presence, and she could see Harmer was curious about her. She smiled and murmured her thanks, and they left him standing, looking thoughtfully after them.

When they came down the stairs, Phoebe saw Wittaker's driver had managed to squeeze the carriage in to a small driveway just a short distance from Harmer's offices. They climbed in, and Wittaker called up the address Harmer had given them.

He had been quiet after they'd visited the gunsmith, and now he was even quieter.

He looked lost in thought, cut off from her, and a wave of longing for a connection like they'd had earlier this morning rose up and broke over her. She leaned forward and brushed her fingers down the side of his cheek.

He grabbed her hand and raised startled eyes to hers. "What is it?"

Her own daring astounded her.

"I . . . You looked unhappy." Embarrassed, she tried to pull her hand from his as she sat back against the uncomfortable seat of hard, cracked leather.

He wouldn't let go.

Instead, he brought her fingers to his lips, and kissed the tips lightly. "It has been some time since anyone cared if I was happy." Only then did he let her go.

There suddenly wasn't enough air in her lungs, and she let the cry of a street seller outside the window distract her from the intensity of his gaze. When she looked back at him, he was watching her, arms across his chest.

"What has you so deep in thought?" Her voice sounded rusty, like a door long locked and only just opened.

"I have a feeling we are chasing our tails."

She nodded. "And yet, what else can we do? We are following the best leads we have."

"If there was something better we could be doing, we'd be doing it. But I don't like feeling like a headless chicken, blundering about."

"We've learned a few things already, and it's only ten in the morning." She wondered whether her aunt had realized she was out yet, or if she was still in bed, recovering from the shock of last night.

He shrugged. "I'll admit the gun from last night is one more connection with Bellingham. But we already knew the people trying to kill you were behind Perceval's assassination. Beckwith was reluctant to say who might have owned that gun, but it was more a guarding of his clients' privacy than anything else, I think. And we knew more than Harmer did about Bellingham."

"You think visiting Mrs. Robarts will be just as useless?"

"I don't know." He tapped his fist on his thigh, his shoulders rigid and stiff. "I suppose she may have known what business he was doing. Or if business associates met him at his lodgings. She would have had day to day contact with him."

"You're worried we don't have enough time. That the trial will start tomorrow and we won't have a chance to find out who was behind this." She spoke quietly, and he met her gaze as he nodded.

"There are so many people who wished Perceval ill. And with Bellingham refusing to name anyone but himself, in the time we have, I have to face that we may not get to the bottom of this."

She kept her gaze on him steady. "You'll get to the bottom of it. Even if you aren't in time to do it before the trial." She had sensed that from him since the moment they met. He was relentless.

He made a face. "What good will that do?"

"Maybe none. But you will do it."

He braced himself as their old carriage came to a rocking halt. "You're right. It's personal for me now, but even if it weren't, I'd follow the trail until I find the culprit."

She waited for him to get out and offer his hand to her before she spoke again. "What will you do with them, when you find them?"

He turned, with her hand still in his, to look at the small house wedged between two others in a pretty street. "I'll turn over their names to the man who asked me to look into this in the first place."

"Will he do anything about it?" She resisted being led forward, suddenly needing to know that this effort, this danger, would not be for nothing.

"As much as he can. I believe that."

It would have to be enough.

A young maid answered the door when Wittaker knocked, and led them into a snug little parlour, where a pretty woman sat, knitting, with a young boy playing with tin soldiers beside her by the fire.

"Mrs. Robarts?" Wittaker bowed, and even though he was not dressed as usual, and might have been any well-to-do gentleman, Mrs. Robarts scrambled to her feet, and nudged her son to do the same.

"You with the newspapers?" She frowned at the thought, but her brow cleared as Wittaker shook his head.

"No. We're not. I hope you take our word that we are inquiring into the matter concerning Mr. Bellingham for the Crown, and cannot reveal too much."

Phoebe didn't think Mrs. Robarts would accept an explanation like that, she certainly wouldn't have, but the woman blushed, and nodded immediately. "Of course, of course."

She invited them to sit, and when they were settled, Phoebe thought the tiny room looked even more cramped with Wittaker taking up so much space in it.

"Mrs. Robarts, I understand you are holding a promissory note for Mr. Bellingham for twenty pounds?" Wittaker shifted on the small armchair he'd chosen, and it gave an ominous creak.

"I already gave it to the Bow Street Runner. Mr. Vickery."

Wittaker nodded. "I know. I just wondered if that was a common thing? For you to hold promissory notes for Bellingham."

Mrs. Robarts nodded her head. "A few times."

"And do you know how Mr. Bellingham earned his money while he was in London?"

Again, she shook her head. "He came to London at the end of December and paid his first week's rent in advance. And I did hear him say he had a shipment of iron or something he brokered, but when that was done, he told me he was staying on, but the money dried up. He owed me almost two months' rent by the end of February, and I was getting worried about it, thinking I would have to ask him to pay up or leave, and him being so polite and congenial, and all, I was loathe to do it. Then suddenly, in the first week of March, he came into some money. Paid me, and bought himself a nice new set of clothes from Mr. Taylor down the way, got those pamphlets of his printed. Started taking us out now and then, to museums and exhibitions." She looked down at her son, who had abandoned his tin soldiers to stare at Wittaker and her with open interest.

"How much was that, in all? Can you guess?" Wittaker tried to put the vulgar talk of actual sums delicately.

Even so, Mrs. Robarts looked uncomfortable. "I think around twenty pounds. Perhaps more."

"You don't know what the money was for?" Wittaker winked at the boy, breaking the tension in the room, and looked back up Mrs. Robarts.

She shook her head. "Mr. Wilson didn't say, and nor did Mr. Bellingham. But the first time Mr. Wilson sent round a memorandum, I asked for an address, in case Mr. Bellingham wanted to contact him. He told me he did business out of the Virgina and Baltick Coffee House, over on Threadneedle Street."

"So it could have been from legitimate business?"

She nodded her head, and then, as suddenly as if a lever had been pulled, she threw herself back in her chair and raised a hand to her forehead as if she had a fever. Phoebe wondered if perhaps she was hoping one would appear, so she could crawl into bed until the whole mess went away. "I never thought. Never, for a single minute, that he had murder on his mind. I would never have let Johnny within a mile of him. And he were polite! A real gent, he was. Why, he took Johnny and myself for an outing on Monday, and then when we were walking back, he excused himself from walking us home, said he had some business to take care of, and what did he do? Went off and shot the prime minister. That was his business. Calm as you please, he said it. Calm as you please! One minute looking at an exhibit, the next, killing a man."

Wittaker looked across at her, and Phoebe gave a tiny nod of her head. They stood as one.

"We are sorry to have overset you, Mrs. Robarts. This must have been a shock to a refined woman like yourself." Phoebe kept her voice low and steady, and Mrs. Robarts took a deep, shuddering breath.

"Thank you." She made the attempt to struggle to her feet.

"Please don't get up, we can see how terrible this must be for you. We'll see ourselves out." Wittaker bowed, an almost impossible feat in the tiny space, and then he took Phoebe's arm and led her from the room.

As the maid closed the door behind them, Phoebe heard Mrs. Robarts start to sob, and winced. She didn't think Bellingham's landlady would be capable of being called as a witness either for or against him at the trial.

"So Bellingham received a sudden injection of funds around the end of February, or the beginning of March." Wittaker held out his arm.

"Without, seemingly, doing any work for it." Phoebe took it, let him lead her to the carriage, and then enjoyed the feel of him behind her, the light touches, as he helped her inside.

She wanted to press back against him, but forced herself to take her seat.

When he'd closed the door, he didn't take his.

Uncaring of his trousers on the filthy floor, he crouched down in front of her and steadied himself with his hands on her shoulders.

"I didn't think it would be so hard not to touch you."

His eyes crinkled in the corners. "I think I'm going to stop trying." He leaned forward and brushed a light kiss over her lips, but before he could deepen it, he was thrown back against his own seat as the ancient coach lurched forward.

Sheldrake would have cursed the driver. He would have had a tantrum that would have embarrassed her to watch, and then humiliated everyone who was associated with his own humiliation.

Wittaker grimaced as the small of his back made contact with the hard bench behind him. He pulled himself up, rubbing his back with a rueful look on his face. "I suppose I was the one who insisted on an old carriage. And the lads would have expected me to be sitting down, not worshipping at your feet." He suddenly smiled at her. "Although I doubt they'd be surprised."

She gaped at him. And in that moment felt the stomach-dropping, heart-pounding sensation of falling. She reached out both hands to the tatty inner walls of the carriage to steady herself.

But it was far too late.

Chapter Thirty-one

The idea there was a woman who held something of Bellingham's that he didn't want anyone to find was one that had stuck stubbornly with James since he'd read the hearing transcript. So it made sense to find out what they could at the tavern Bellingham had frequented, before going on to speak to the mysterious, money-giving Mr. Wilson. Legge's Tavern was less than five minutes from Mrs. Robarts's house.

They pulled up across the road from it, and James watched the customers come and go for a few minutes, getting a feel for the place.

It would have been just the establishment an aspiring and self-conscious man like Bellingham would have been comfortable visiting.

It was clearly prosperous, with the right look for the level of income and standing of the people living nearby, and perfectly acceptable as a place a husband and wife dressed as he and Phoebe were to have a small mid-morning meal.

As he held out his hand to help her from the carriage, James tried to work out what was going through her head.

Something had happened after his attempt to kiss her. She had gone very quiet, and he hoped she wasn't having second thoughts about him. Being kissed in a dirty old carriage may not have been what she had in mind when she had offered to be his lover, but he'd thought she'd pressed back against him for a moment as they'd climbed into the carriage outside Mrs. Robarts's house.

It had pushed him over the edge, and he'd been on his knees in front of her before he'd had a chance to think it through.

Now she put her hand into his, and gripped tight as she held her skirts to one side and negotiated the rickety carriage steps.

There was a blush on her cheeks, and to test her reaction, he did not move back as she took the final step, so she brushed up against him.

She leaned forward and, almost unwillingly, rubbed the soft skin of her cheek against his jaw, and took a deep breath, as if inhaling his scent.

Then she stepped around him, and stood waiting while he tried to move.

The most explicit strip tease at the bawdiest gaming hell he'd ever frequented could not touch the eroticism of the moment.

"You all right, Your Grace?" Jimmy jumped down from the driver's bench, and James managed to pull himself together at the cheeky mischief in his footman's eyes.

He turned without answering and Phoebe regarded him gravely.

"I didn't think you'd let me accompany you to every

place you intended to visit today," she said, and linked her arm through his.

He slid his hand over hers, and felt her tremble. "Our next destination will be tricky. I won't be able to take you with me into the coffee house where Mrs. Robarts said we could find Wilson."

She acknowledged that with a nod. Coffee houses in general didn't allow women, and certainly not ones like the Baltick, where trade and business were conducted.

He led the way forward, making sure his men were correctly in place. His driver sat quiet and half-slumped in his seat and up ahead, Jimmy strolled into the tavern. The other two footmen vanished amongst the crowds.

It was as safe as it could get.

They stepped into a warm, welcoming room that was clean and smelled of simple food made well.

"Apple pie," Phoebe whispered in his ear, and he had to fight the shiver her warm breath caused.

Even though it was only mid-morning, the room was half-full, and a big, aproned man appeared and showed them to a small table near the window.

James saw Jimmy up against a long bar that ran down one side of the room, a mug of ale and a plate of something beside him. He was talking to a rosy-cheeked girl with a tray of ale mugs balanced on her hip.

"What can I get for you?" The publican looked harried.

They gave orders for a light meal and apple pie, and he nodded and turned from them almost immediately and went through a door at the back of the room.

The girl Jimmy had been talking to came over to ask them what they would like to drink.

"You seem more busy that usual today," James said to her with an easy smile, laying the groundwork for questioning her a little later.

She nodded, looking them over a little more carefully, no doubt trying to remember when they might have come in before. "Margie is late, is all. She starts permanent today, but she hasn't come yet." There was a shout for her from the kitchen, and James ordered ale, Phoebe tea, and then she wound her way back between the tables to the bar, collecting empty ale mugs along the way.

There was silence between them for a moment, and then Phoebe began to fidget.

"What did Harmer think we'd come to talk to him about? In the beginning." She asked the question in a rush of words.

James frowned. "Harmer?"

"Something about a delicate situation." She blushed and laid her hands flat on the table, as if to stop them moving too much.

"Ah." He'd forgotten about that. He lifted a finger and stroked across her knuckles. "He probably thought I was there to ask him to draw up a contract, although the women usually aren't invited to that discussion. That's most likely why he was so confused."

"A contract?" She seemed genuinely puzzled.

"Between a man and his mistress. Laying out the terms of the agreement. What she can expect, what will be her due when the liaison is over. What will happen if a child is conceived."

She frowned. "Men draw up contracts like that?"

James nodded. "Some do. It's in the woman's interests, as well, to know what provision will be made for her."

"Have you?"

He shook his head. "I've never taken a mistress." He would have had to keep up the appearance of the dissolute rake with a mistress, more than he was willing to in his private time, because when it was over, he couldn't risk her telling the truth about him.

Phoebe lifted her head suddenly and their gazes clashed. Her cheeks were flushed. "You couldn't let down your guard with them, could you? Until now."

He covered her hand completely with his own. "What we have is not the same thing at all. You have agreed to be my lover, not my mistress." Just thinking of her in those terms, *lover*, made him want to find a quiet room and a bed.

"I hadn't thought of what would happen if I . . ." She forced herself to meet his gaze, and he could see it was an effort for her, delicately raised, polite young woman that she was. "I became with child."

She was rethinking the whole thing. He watched it happen behind her eyes.

"There are ways around that." He kept his voice light. She was too intelligent to be fobbed off, and he would have to make his true intentions known soon, or he risked her rejecting him completely.

She hesitated. "Why is it such a fear then? Why is it written into the contract?"

"Because—"

"Here you go." The girl was back with their tea and ale, and both of them jolted at her sudden intrusion.

James suddenly wanted this side trip over as fast as possible. To have Phoebe alone in the carriage again so he could speak with her in private. "I hear the man who assassinated the prime minster, Bellingham, used to come here often. Did you know him?" He broached the topic earlier than he'd intended.

The girl glanced behind her, then leaned in closer. "Mr. Bob don't like us to say anything 'bout that. Just in case it stirs up trouble. But yes, he were a regular. Took all his meals here. I didn't serve him often, but once or twice I did."

"I think I know who he was. Tall and dark-haired, well-dressed, the papers said? Didn't I see a man like that here talking with one of the serving girls often as not." James took a guess, based on her comment earlier about the missing serving girl. If he were wrong, there would be no harm done. If he were right . . .

The girl nodded. "That'd be Margie. Only part-time, she was then. Just coming to lend a hand during lunch, Mr. Bob said. Right handy it was, having her. But she did take a shine to Bellingham, all right. Always insisted on serving him. Thought she'd find herself a fancy-man, no doubt. Not that that got her far."

There was another call for her from the bar, and she gave them a wink and swung off, hips swaying.

"Sounds like the woman we need to talk to isn't in." Phoebe started to remove her hand from under his, but he gripped it a little tighter.

"Or isn't coming at all, now her part in the plot with Bellingham, whatever that was, is done."

The publican was back, balancing their food with the food from at least one other table. He set the dishes down and James paid him so they could leave when they wanted to.

"I see Margie isn't here today," James said as he started to turn away.

"Oh." The publican, like the serving maid, looked more closely at him, trying to recognise him. "Yes. You a friend?" He looked between them, his eyes taking in their well-cut clothes and rejecting the notion.

"No, just to talk to the few times we've come in here," Phoebe spoke to him for the first time, and it seemed to put him more at ease.

"Well, if she's much later, she won't have no job here at all." He turned away again, and James thought it useless to question him further. He was too busy and annoyed. They would have to leave Jimmy here, have him watch the place, find the mysterious Margie, and follow her home.

They ate the food served to them in silence, while the gentle hum of the tavern swirled around them.

A sense of goodwill and general ease settled over him, and James struggled for a few bites of apple pie to identify it. Despite the circumstances, despite everything, in the end, he decided on contentment.

***

The short walk from the tavern to the carriage felt like one of the longest Phoebe had ever taken.

Wittaker had not tried to speak to her about their

liaison again, or address her concerns about falling pregnant, and she knew he had decided they needed more privacy for such a conversation.

She still didn't know why she had raised the topic. It was as if her mouth was operating without her, in a desperate bid to divert his attention from the way her heart was chaining itself to him, a link at a time.

There was a flurry of activity to their right, and Phoebe noticed one of the footman step out from under the shaded awning of a nearby shop as a woman came hurtling through the crowd toward them.

But she veered toward the door of the tavern after a few steps, and Phoebe realized she must be the missing Margie.

The girl glanced their way before she crossed the street, watching for traffic, and Phoebe gripped Wittaker's hand.

"I know that girl. Margie . . . yes, I think Jackson called her Margie. I never put the two together, but it's her."

Wittaker kept leading them to the carriage, but his head had turned and he watched the girl until she had disappeared through the doors.

"Where do you know her from?" He bent his head close to hers, lowering his voice.

"Sheldrake's. She's his scullery maid. I saw her this morning when I went to speak to the butler about helping them."

Wittaker stopped, brows lifted. "You don't say?"

Sheldrake was so involved in this, he'd been up to his neck, Phoebe realized. No wonder he'd run.

James helped her into the carriage, and waited for his men to join him. "The girl who just ran into the tavern, one of you needs to watch her, follow her when she leaves. But most likely she'll be going back to Lord Sheldrake's residence."

"I wonder about that." Phoebe leaned forward through the partly open door. "She seemed in trouble with the butler this morning, perhaps she'd just handed in her notice to come work here full time. She only has a day or two left at Sheldrake's as it is, with the Wentworths due to move in soon. Jackson said they intended to keep the cook, himself and one maid, and were letting the rest go.

"If they're expecting new masters, butler'd be right miffed if someone upped and left early, so everyone else had more work to do, gettin' the place ready, an' all." Jimmy leaned against the carriage, keeping his eye on the door of the tavern.

"Very likely," Phoebe agreed. "Perhaps that's why she's late. He made her do her share this morning before coming to her new job."

"How did Sheldrake get her the job here in the first place?" James propped a shoulder against the carriage himself.

"Slipped the publican a bob or two, and offered her services for free?" Jimmy said. "Made up some story about watching for a person, or sommat?"

That sounded entirely likely. "And now that she actually needs a paying job, perhaps she asked for one, and because he knows her, Mr. Legge has been happy to give her one."

"Right, well, I doubt we'll get anything out of her now. She's already in trouble and won't thank us for making it worse by taking up her time while she's working. Jimmy, you stay here and watch her, and see if she goes back to Lord Sheldrake's or if she's already found a new place to stay. We'll go on to the Baltick Coffee House."

Jimmy gave a pleased nod, especially when Wittaker handed him money to while away the day in the tavern with, and the other two footmen took up their places as Wittaker pulled himself inside with her.

There was a hum of energy coming off him. Phoebe wanted to smile at it, but she found, when he caught her eye, that she shivered instead.

The carriage pulled away, and for a moment there was only the rumble of the wheels on the cobbles and the high-pitched squeak of the springs as they rattled through the streets.

"So," Wittaker murmured, leaning forward until his knees were almost touching hers. "Where were we?"

Phoebe wanted the floor to open up and consume her, she wanted to go up in the pillar of flames she felt she was already standing in. She couldn't help raising her hands to her hot cheeks and pressing her icy palms against her feverish skin.

"We were talking about . . ." She didn't know how she'd had the nerve to speak about it before—now, she honestly didn't think she had the courage.

"Young ladies aren't supposed to talk about these things, are they?" Wittaker said. He pinched a tiny bit of wool from her skirts between his thumb and forefinger, and rubbed it.

Phoebe tried to look away, but it was fascinating to watch and oddly arousing.

"You're thinking of abandoning your offer of last night because of the embarrassment of this conversation, and your fear of what will happen if you do become pregnant."

That he had read her so clearly shocked her enough that she didn't even nod her head, she simply stared at him.

He gave her a lopsided smile. "You are wise to worry, because I plan to get you into bed as often as I possibly can."

She sucked in a breath, the heat in her cheeks shooting lower, the shock of his words stirring something in her that was quite wild.

"But I will also swear this to you, I can see a way for that to happen without any trouble coming to you." There was something in his eyes, a gleam of satisfaction and amusement.

"And what way is that?" She forced herself to speak, and her voice came out low, and far more sultry than she could ever have imagined.

He took her hand and raised it to his lips as the carriage swung around a corner and they both slid down the benches. As they rocked to a halt, he brushed a kiss along the very tips of her fingers.

"Perhaps that is a conversation for another time." Wittaker angled his head as they heard the footmen jumping down, and the door was opened.

He winked at her as he climbed out, leaving her speechless and unable to do anything but stare.

"You'll have to wait here," he told her. "I won't be long."

Phoebe said nothing as he closed the door, and dodged a cab on his way across the street.

The carriage moved again, jerking her back against her seat, and Phoebe looked desperately for a hand hold.

She wished she could have one for her dealings with Wittaker, as well.

Chapter Thirty-two

The Virginia and Baltick Coffee House in Threadneedle Street was so close to the Bank of England, it felt as if the Old Lady were leaning over it. James turned to watch the carriage stop and start through the traffic to find a place to wait for him, and genuinely regretted that coffee houses did not accept women as customers.

He would feel better with Phoebe with him, even shocked and quiet as she currently was.

He grinned.

A shout from a cartsman that he was blocking the way forced him off the street and through the door of the coffee house, into the warm bustle of tables and men talking with raised voices, and the thick, rich scent of coffee.

Wilson was either a merchant or a broker in the lucrative trade with the Baltic—everyone in this place was—and James again felt the rise of frustration that he may be running in circles, the lucky break identifying Margie notwithstanding.

Bellingham had been a trader and broker in the Baltic, his imprisonment there was what had set him on the tragic path he had taken in the first place. His money could well be legitimately come by and no mystery at all. That his current funds were from Wilson almost assured that.

Except, Bellingham himself had said differently during the committal proceedings. That he'd been brought almost to nothing by his search for justice and compensation.

Twenty pounds would be around four or five months salary to Bellingham. Not nothing at all.

It simply didn't make sense.

James caught the eye of a man behind the counter and moved over to him. The only way to make sense of it was to speak to Wilson.

The proprietor pointed him in the direction of a busy corner of the room, and James made his way to a crowd of men bidding loudly for a shipment of lumber.

A few discreet questions later, and he found Wilson, sitting slightly apart.

"Mr. Wilson?" He hadn't had time to come up with a clever reason to be interested in why Wilson owed Bellingham twenty pounds. The minutes were ticking by, too fast.

Wilson looked up, and eyed him suspiciously. "Yes?"

James lost all patience with lying. "The Duke of Wittaker, pleased to make your acquaintance."

Wilson went still, and then scraped back his chair and bowed. "Your Grace. What can I do for you?"

James sat in the nearest chair and pulled it close when Wilson sat as well, so he could speak without shouting. "I want to know what the twenty pounds you owe to John Bellingham is for."

Wilson didn't just go white, he went a grey-green color. Like he was seasick, or facing a firing squad.

He stared at James with stricken eyes, and then stumbled to his feet and pushed his way through the crowd to lurch out onto the street.

James followed in his wake, his blood pounding in his veins. If he were a wolf, he would have lifted his head to howl as he caught the scent of prey.

He hadn't intended to let Wilson get more than a step or two away from the door but the merchant ducked left and ran.

James chased him down, weaving through the bankers, merchants and clerks in dark suits, and eventually lunged forward and gripped Wilson's upper arm. He'd worked up a light sweat under his coat, but Wilson was panting with fear and exertion.

"You *will* answer me."

Wilson struggled against his grip, but he was out of breath and his whole body shook. He said nothing, his eyes swivelling around, looking for some escape.

James suddenly had enough. He had far more interesting things to do. Like a woman to seduce and propose to.

He gripped Wilson's other arm, and forced him backwards a few steps into a gloomy side alley. As soon as they were out of sight of the street, he slammed Wilson into the wall, pinning him against it, lifting him bodily so his feet barely touched the ground.

Wilson gaped. Took a long, shuddering breath. "I don't know what the money is for. I'll often take in money from one person, pay it out on their behalf to another."

James jerked him against the wall again to show just how lacking in patience he was. "And who is it that you took the money from in this case, originally?"

Wilson shook his head. "I don't know!"

There was something in his eyes. A desperation, and such a deep fear, James had the sense no threat he made would be enough to budge him. Not unless he was prepared to torture the man, which he was not.

But Wilson was lying. James was sure of it.

He stepped back, hands up to show Wilson he no longer had plans to hurt him. "I know you've given Bellingham money more than once. And I would say you had better get your story straight, because the next person to ask you the question may be the Attorney-General. And you won't have the luxury of claiming you don't know."

Wilson stepped away from him, taking out a handkerchief and wiping his brow. He made a sound, a choking, croaking noise at the back of his throat, and then ran back to the street.

James followed him, quiet as he could. He hoped Wilson ran straight to his source. He was panicked enough for it. He was almost beside himself with fear.

Wilson stood outside the coffee house, trying to hail a hansom, and James spotted his own carriage making a slow trundle past.

They most likely couldn't find a place to pull in near enough, and had decided to circle the block instead.

With Wilson's attention on an approaching hackney, James ran across and pulled himself up beside his footman.

"Slow down," he called up to his driver. He looked back and saw Wilson shake his fist as the hackney refused to stop.

Wilson peered over his shoulder at the alleyway where James had questioned him, and then began to walk away, head swivelling as if looking to see where James had gone.

James dropped to the ground. "Keep going. Take Miss Hillier to my house. Through the back door, in case someone is watching. I'll make my way home when I'm done."

The footman looked longing after Wilson. "Sure you don't need my 'elp, Your Grace?"

James shook his head. "With Jimmy gone, I'll feel better if all three of you are watching her and keeping her safe."

He was sorry he couldn't explain to Phoebe himself what was happening, but Wilson was almost around the first corner, and he ran after him.

The merchant had obviously given up watching for anyone. He had his head down, like a man in deep and troubled thought, and James slipped easily into the crowds behind him.

If he'd played his cards right in the alley and shaken Wilson up enough, hopefully he was about to lead him to the man who'd put him in his current situation.

The man who'd funded the prime minister's assassin.

***

Phoebe saw Wittaker run across to them, leap onto the moving carriage and then drop down again and disappear into the crowd.

She envied him his ability to take action.

A footman opened the carriage door a little way and stuck his head in. "We're taking you to His Grace's town house, my lady. He'll meet us back there." He withdrew immediately, and Phoebe was left staring at a closed carriage door.

Wittaker may have been in a hurry, but there seemed no question that she would obey his command along with his men. She didn't know whether to be annoyed or not.

The force of the turn as the carriage swung back towards the quiet enclaves of Mayfair made her slide down her seat. While she carefully undid the damage the ripped seat had done to her coat again, she decided it would be interesting to see Wittaker's house.

Did men take their lovers to their homes?

She thought not. They snuck into their lovers' rooms late at night, or met at weekend parties in the country. She'd heard enough gossip in the corners of ballrooms to think she had that right.

This might be her only opportunity to see where he lived.

When the carriage at last began to slow, she peered out the small window set into its door. They pulled into the large circular drive of an elegant mansion beside Green Park.

But they didn't pull up in front of the door, the driver continued around to the back, and drew up beside a low set of stairs leading to the kitchens.

"His Grace asked us to come round the back in case someone was watching the house." The footman opened the door for her.

She'd guessed that for herself, and as she stepped down, she noticed another carriage already waiting nearby. It could be Wittaker's official carriage, but it didn't carry his crest and there was a driver standing by the horses, as if waiting for someone.

Nerves fluttered up suddenly inside her at the thought of going through the back of the Duke of Wittaker's house.

How would she explain her presence?

If the footman noticed her discomfort, he ignored it, bounding up the stairs and opening the door. "I'll leave you in the library, if that's to your liking, my lady?"

He held the door for her and she forced herself not to hesitate as she stepped into a well-lit and beautifully equipped kitchen.

Most of the staff merely glanced across and continued with their work, but as the footman led her between tables of activity, she found the way blocked by what had to be Wittaker's chef, and a young woman of around her own age wearing half-mourning.

"And who is this, Tom?" Wittaker's chef turned to face her, and she had the impression of a fierce personality and a great deal of passion.

"This is Miss Hillier, Mister Bisset." Tom gave the chef a cocky grin and explained no further.

"*Enchanté*." Bisset bent over her hand, and Phoebe had no choice but to curtsey in return. She could feel the heat of embarrassment rising up her neck to her cheeks. Even if society thought her ruined, she couldn't help the feeling of exposure at being caught breaking the rules.

"The back door again. His Grace has something very mysterious going on." Bisset looked at her thoughtfully, but there was no judgement in his eyes.

Phoebe pretended not to hear that. "My pleasure to meet you."

"This is my dear friend, Miss Barrington." Bisset indicated the woman standing at his side, and Phoebe looked up in shock.

"Miss Barrington." She nodded her head, trying to pretend she didn't know who the woman was. Which of course was ridiculous, because a month ago the whole of London was talking of Miss Barrington's engagement to Lord Aldridge.

"Will His Grace be joining us?" Miss Barrington asked her.

"Not for some time." Phoebe thought wistfully of his race across London after whoever it was he had found of interest in the coffee house. She would love to be with him, rather than trapped in this situation that was becoming more embarrassing by the moment.

What was Lord Aldridge's fiancé doing in the Duke of Wittaker's kitchens?

"I can see you are as at sea about my presence here as we are about yours, Miss Hillier." Miss Barrington suddenly smiled at her, and it turned what was a beautiful face into an enchanting one. "Georges, I'll take Miss Hillier to the library, and you can bring us some tea and cake."

"*Bien*." Bisset looked at Miss Barrington with affection and with a sweep of his arm, indicated they proceed.

Phoebe had taken only a few steps before Georges called out to them.

"Wait. Miss Hillier. Did you attend the Prince Regent's dinner last night?"

Phoebe turned, struggling to keep her face neutral. Had they heard the gossip from the dinner already?

She nodded cautiously.

"Can you remember what was served for dessert?"

Phoebe was so surprised, she opened her mouth, closed it again, and then frowned. "I'm sorry, Mr. Bisset, but I can't remember, which is strange. Dessert is my favorite part of the meal."

"It is nothing." Bisset gave a forgiving flourish of his hand, but he was smirking. "I had heard from His Grace it wasn't very memorable. Not everyone can be Georges Bisset, *n'est pas*?"

Phoebe let herself be led out of the kitchen and through a long hallway to a library that must be at least twice the size of her own.

A man appeared in the doorway after they'd entered. He looked forbidding, but Miss Barrington merely smiled at him.

"Good morning, Harding, or is it afternoon yet? Miss Hillier and I will take some tea here."

Tom had accompanied them in, but now he bowed and walked out of the room, forcing the butler to give way and then follow him out with his mouth in a thin, disapproving line. She wondered what explanation Tom was giving him.

"Harding is all right. Just a little stuck in his ways.

Things haven't been the same in this house since Georges was hired and I think he's still recovering." Miss Barrington was watching her with interest, but it wasn't the unfriendly, aggressive stares she was used to at the balls she usually attended, and she relaxed a little.

Since society's new darling was being so forthright, and since she no longer had much to lose, Phoebe decided to be forthright herself.

"May I ask how you know so much about this household?" She didn't believe Miss Barrington was Wittaker's lover. He would never have sent her to his house if he thought there was any chance they would meet, and she didn't think he would have taken her up on her offer if he had a woman like Miss Barrington in his life already. There was something about her that said she would take up every corner of a person's life and fill it completely.

Miss Barrington gave a small smile. "I don't have many friends, especially not in London, but Georges Bisset is one of them. I visit him often, and in the process, I have learned a great deal about this household. About Wittaker, I know considerably less."

Phoebe tried to align what she knew about Miss Barrington with the information that her best friend was a chef. "Your fiancé doesn't mind your visits?"

Miss Barrington gave a low chuckle. "He does mind. But he's wise enough to keep that to himself. And that's most likely because he knows any objection he has has its basis in unfounded jealousy, and is therefore ridiculous."

She had led them to a comfortable arrangement of chairs, but Phoebe turned away from it and walked to the shelves lining two whole walls of the room to look at the books.

"Would you consider telling me your story?" Miss Barrington asked from behind her. "I have to say that I have had a very soft spot for the Duke of Wittaker since I met him earlier this year. He was a great help to me, and I wish to see him happy."

Phoebe turned at her words. "I wish to see him happy, too. So we are aligned in that."

Miss Barrington gave a nod, and walked over to join her. "Are you the Miss Hillier who is engaged to Lord Sheldrake? I suppose you must be, if you received an invitation to dine with the Prince Regent last night."

Phoebe should have known she would not be completely unknown. Gossip and ill-will had followed her ever since she had come out in society when her father had become a baronet. "I was betrothed to him." She thought of merely saying he was now dead, but something rose up in her, a refusal to deny what had happened. "He broke off the betrothal on Sunday evening. He was killed on Tuesday."

Miss Barrington's gaze snapped to hers in shock. "I'm sorry to hear that." She touched Phoebe's arm lightly. "I imagine this is a hard time for you."

The door opened and Harding brought in a tray with tea and piled high with cakes on an intricate, three tiered cake stand.

They both murmured their thanks and then realized Harding was going to stand there until they took their seats, so they gave in to the inevitable.

"We'll pour for ourselves, thank you, Harding," Miss

Barrington told him, and he left reluctantly. Phoebe wondered if he thought they were going to steal the silver spoons.

When he was gone, Miss Barrington fussed with the teapot. "I'm usually a better companion. I'm sorry I didn't know about Sheldrake and no doubt caused you pain asking after him."

Phoebe hunched a little in her chair. "It is the high topic of conversation at the moment in the ton."

"I'm sure it is." The way Miss Barrington spoke, Phoebe had the impression of dry sarcasm, and relaxed a little more.

"I'm surprised we haven't met already," Phoebe waited until she had a cup of tea before she spoke again. "We must surely have been at some of the same balls."

Miss Barrington shook her head. "My father died in February, and I've been in mourning. I haven't socialized since I returned to England, except for some private dinners."

"Oh." Phoebe frowned. "But haven't you recently become betrothed to Lord Aldridge?"

Miss Barrington looked down at her cup. "Lord Aldridge lives a few doors from me, and his family and mine have known each other since before I was born."

There must be considerably more to it than that, judging from the way she spoke, but Phoebe did not pry any further. She had already overstepped the bounds of politeness with her questions.

"What will you do now," Miss Barrington asked after a moment of silence, and Phoebe knew she meant now that

Sheldrake had ruined her.

She shrugged. "I have a few plans. After last night's dinner, I'm quite aware none of them should include being part of the ton any longer."

"That bad?"

She shrugged again. "I'm more lucky than most. I don't need money. I didn't even like the demands of the Season, if I'm honest, so no longer attending the balls and parties will be a relief. But it feels like I don't fit anywhere. My mother's family is mostly gone. My grandfather sold his manufacturing works when he retired, because my mother was his only grandchild. And I'm untouchable now amongst my father's circle. If I get a proposal of marriage from that quarter, it will be for my money, and I'll be expected to be grateful. I'd rather forgo that altogether."

She hadn't sounded bitter. To her relief, she realized she didn't feel it, either. She'd sounded matter-of-fact. But she hadn't meant to reveal so much.

"I think you will like a friend of mine. Lady Durnham." Miss Barrington fiddled with a tiny petit four iced in brilliant green, with gold-leaf on top. It looked too beautiful to eat. "She dislikes the Season as well, and her husband positively abhors it. I think it would be a most pleasant evening if I invited you and His Grace to dinner, with Lord and Lady Durnham, and Lord Aldridge." She popped the petit four in her mouth and frowned. "He's done something to this. I can't quite . . ." Her eyes sparked. "Cardamom. Delicious."

Phoebe stared at her and she laughed.

"Don't mind me, Miss Hillier, Georges is always outdoing himself, is all." She stood. "My carriage is waiting for me, and I have to be off. But I will send you an invitation within the next few days."

Phoebe stood as well. "Thank you. It was a pleasure to meet you."

"And will I see you again here?" Miss Barrington asked, curiosity in the tilt of her head.

Phoebe shook her head. "I don't think so. His Grace and I are involved in . . . something. My visit today is unusual."

"You are mixed up in the investigation into Perceval's death?" Miss Barrington had gone still. "I knew Wittaker had been drawn into it, Jonathan told me he was, but you're in it as well."

Phoebe didn't know how to respond.

Miss Barrington shook her head. "Don't worry. I know all about keeping quiet. I'm sure you can't discuss it. But . . . how interesting!" She gave Phoebe another of her blinding smiles. "Well, good luck, Miss Hillier, and what a pleasure to have met you."

She left the room on a wave of subtle perfume and a swish of silk skirts, and Phoebe sank slowly down into her chair.

Then she reached out, and took a brilliant green petit four with a gold-leaf flower on it from the tray.

Chapter Thirty-three

Wilson began to get twitchy again somewhere near Mayfair. James guessed he must be getting close to his destination.

He found it handy that the merchant was heading in the direction of his own home, but the deeper they got into the most exclusive, expensive enclave of London, the more dread weighed him down.

This was not going to end well.

He wondered which of his acquaintances had plotted to kill the prime minister.

Wilson took a final, furtive look over his shoulder and ran up some stairs to a black door set between two Grecian columns in a well-proportioned town house. He was granted access after a minute of waiting on the doorstep, fidgeting as he cooled his heels and looking up and down the street.

James waited until Wilson was admitted, and then walked up the narrow access lane between the house and its neighbor to the back door.

He could find out later from Dervish who this house belonged to, but if he could find out now, so much the better. He had little to lose while he waited for Wilson to re-emerge.

The kitchen door was down a narrow, slightly slimy set of stairs on the basement level, and it was propped open with a half-brick.

"Hello?" He knocked and poked his head in.

A girl was sitting at a table peeling carrots, and she jumped up and came towards him.

"Yes?" Her fingers were stained orange from her task, and she rubbed them against the gray apron she wore over her skirts. She looked thin, and very young.

"I'm from the papers," James said. The clothes he'd worn today would cover journalist well enough. "Got a guinea or two for some information on what happened when the prime minister was shot." He pulled out two coins and extended his palm. At worst, she could tell him she didn't know what he was talking about and he could pretend to have come to the wrong house.

The girl looked at the guineas longingly. "What would the papers want with questioning the staff? You don't know I've got anything to say."

James winked. "My boss is interested in anything he can get. Good or bad. Whatever you're comfortable saying. You'll go down as an anonymous source." He proffered the money to her, and she covered his palm with her own, and slid the coins off. She crouched and forced them into the hem of her skirt. "In case Mr. Hartley searches my pockets," she said, and gave him a cheeky grin. "He could come in at any time."

He gave a nod.

She lowered her voice. "All I heard was that General

Gascoyne were a right hero. Saved the day. And from that mad man that came round here a couple months back."

"Bellingham came here?" James had read in the transcript that Bellingham had met with Gascoyne, that's how the MP had recognized him at the scene of the crime, but he'd thought it was to his offices in Liverpool, or London, not his home.

"Aye, I served the tea." She looked warily behind her. "Mr. Hartley couldn't help exclaim when he saw his name in the papers. He announced the man to the general, and recognized it right away. But I would have guessed it, meself, wot with the papers publishing parts of his pamphlet. Mad, he was, that day. Talking jus' like in the bits from his pamphlet. Going on about being betrayed, being owed money. All the years he'd spent in prison in some terrible Russian jail." She lowered her voice further. "Not that I didn't believe him, mind. He were convincing, the little I heard. I'm quite sure he was wrongly accused and the British ambassador didn't help him as he should, but why he thought that lot would lift a finger, or admit fault and pay him some compensation? Absolutely bonkers."

"Can you remember when this meeting was, exactly?"

"'Twere after New Year, but before Valentine's Day. Third week of January, around about." She looked suddenly uncomfortable, as if she'd forgotten herself, and who she was talking to. "Best be off with you now. Mr. Hartley'll be back any minute when the general's visitor is gone."

James tipped his hat, and reversed out the doorway.

As he approached the end of the lane where it opened into the street at the front of Gascoyne's house, he paused, just in time to see Wilson leaving, shoulders still hunched, going back the way he'd come. He waited another few minutes for the merchant to pass him by, and to his surprise, saw Gascoyne himself come out.

He was dressed for walking, with a hat, boots, and coat, and he set off purposefully in the opposite direction Wilson had taken.

Intrigued, James fell in behind him. It was harder to go unnoticed in Mayfair, there were so few people on the streets, but Gascoyne didn't look around, or seem to notice he was being followed. He walked stridently, anger in the over-hard stamp of his soles on the cobbles and the stiff line of his shoulders.

They got closer and closer to James's own house, and it was no surprise when they reached the massive gates of Park Place and Gascoyne marched up the drive, his boots crunching with every step he took on the gravel.

Why Gascoyne would confront him directly, he couldn't understand, but he would take the opportunity happily. He felt he'd been working in the dark until now, guessing but never knowing, and at last, a little light had been shed.

The only problem would be making sure Gascoyne didn't get so much as a glimpse of Phoebe.

He slipped through the gates himself, walking as quietly on the gravel as he could until he reached the lawn, where he broke into a run.

He raced around the side of the house.

The carriage he'd rented for the day sat, sad and dilapidated, to one side, and James passed it and slipped through the kitchen door.

There was no one about but a maid washing dishes in the small washroom off the main kitchen, and so he managed to get through to the hall without having to explain what he was doing entering by the back door of his own house at a dead run.

Harding was standing in the hall, most likely already aware that Gascoyne was approaching the front door, and waiting to open it the moment he knocked.

"Delay him while I change, Harding."

Harding's eyes widened at the sight of him.

"And under no circumstances whatsoever is he to see Miss Hillier. Where is she?"

"In the library, Your Grace."

"Send Gascoyne to the drawing room, then, and stay with him. I'll be right there." He was running up the stairs as he spoke, and Towers, his valet, stepped out from his dressing room at the sound. "Just a quick change," James told him, already shedding his black jacket as he went.

When he came back downstairs, in dark blue superfine and a stark white waistcoat, only five minutes had passed. Harding stood just within the drawing room doorway, his color high, and Gascoyne glowered in the middle of the room.

"Good day, General." James nodded to Harding, and the man left with a stiff back and a great deal of dignity. James eyed Gascoyne with interest.

"Wittaker." Now that they were face-to-face, James could see Gascoyne trying to rein himself in. Make this a reasonable and measured response. "I have just had a disturbing meeting with one of my constituents. He claims you threatened him."

James actually laughed. He couldn't help it. "I see. Do you have so little to do that you follow up on every complaint by a constituent immediately?"

Gascoyne's eyes widened as his temper flared again. "Not at all. I happened to be walking this way, and thought I'd find out what it was all about."

"Is that so?" James was still standing near the door and leaned back against the doorframe, his arms crossed over his chest. "It seemed to me, the way you stormed out of your house after Wilson left you, that you were headed straight here, with no other destination in mind."

The implications of what James had just said slowly filtered through, and Gascoyne gasped. "You cur! You were following me."

James raised his brows, and Gascoyne suddenly launched himself at him, fists out.

It was so unexpected, James was caught unawares for a brief moment. But it had been many years, countless roast dinners, and surely crates of port since Gascoyne had actively served in the Coldstream Guards.

James neatly sidestepped him, his arm coming up to block one of the blows. He held it there, so he stood with arm raised, looking straight into Gascoyne's eyes. "Interesting that this is such a touchy subject for you."

"Damn you. You've been nothing but a nuisance . . ." Gascoyne shifted, as if to strike again, and then James watched his brain catch up with his mouth, watched the rage and fear fade from his face to be replaced by worry as he put a hand out against the wall to catch his breath. At last he seemed to realize he was giving the game away.

"I . . ." He wouldn't look at James, his eyes darting around the room. "I'm not sure what came over me, Wittaker. Though it was most ungentlemanly to follow a fellow. Most ungentlemanly."

James smiled. Time to shake the tree. "What you really wanted to do was rail at me for threatening your co-conspirator, Mr. Wilson. Tell me to mind my own business, perhaps? Ask me what the devil I thought I was up to? Why I keep being on hand every time one of your lackeys takes a shot at Miss Hillier? Ex-army men who served under you, are they?"

The red of anger and exertion faded to dead white as Gascoyne staggered back in shock. "I have no idea what you mean." The words were wooden.

"Why did you think I followed Wilson to you in the first place? I wanted to shake him up, so he'd lead me to whoever had got him to pay that money to Bellingham."

Gascoyne moved away from him, back to the center of the room, shaking his head.

"Strange you didn't mention you were giving Bellingham large sums of money when you made a meal out of identifying him as a constituent of yours after he'd shot Perceval. Did it slip your mind while you were saving the prime minister from a second shot?" He said the last with a sneer to his voice, and Gascoyne looked away, bright red seeping up his neck again.

"Your problem is you tried too hard to insert yourself into the affair on the side of the rescuers. I wouldn't have originally looked your way at all if you hadn't lied about the business of taking Bellingham's gun. There are too many witness who know the truth. But you couldn't help inflate your role, could you?" James watched Gascoyne try to pull himself back together. To take back control of the conversation.

"What's your interest in this anyway, Wittaker?" Gascoyne spoke with a tremor in his voice. "You're just a wastrel rake, as far as I can work out. Why would you 'look my way' at all?"

James shrugged. "One keeps oneself amused as best one can." He smiled. "You had to find some way to give Bellingham money that wouldn't lead directly to you, because he couldn't have stayed in London if you didn't. He'd have had to go home to Liverpool, and that would mean he couldn't be worked on and persuaded to kill Perceval."

"No!" Gascoyne's gaze snapped to his face. "I gave him the money through Wilson because I felt sorry for him, but I didn't want to create a precedent. If he knew I was giving it to him, with my position in the government, it might have emboldened him further in asking for compensation. He is mad on this issue. He cannot let it go. Cannot put it behind him."

"And you used that, didn't you?" The smooth, practiced way Gascoyne trotted out his excuse for funneling money to Bellingham stuck in James's throat. The lie of it was in the defiance of Gascoyne's glare and the contempt on his face. There was no charity involved in these payments, but it would be very difficult to prove otherwise. Or at all.

"Dash it, man. I'm sorry for my reaction earlier," Gascoyne blinked, and tried to look contrite. "I knew how it would look if this came out. I panicked, is all. Wilson will back me up. He was only doing me a favor, helping me help that poor wretch."

If James were to guess, Wilson was probably getting on a boat at the docks at that very moment, to spend some time in the Baltics, or at the very least, on his way to Liverpool.

"You know, the one thing that interests me the most is the effort you've put into getting that first petition Bellingham sent to the Prince Regent's office. You killed Sheldrake for it, you've tried to kill Miss Hillier twice. What is it about that document that has you so frightened?"

Gascoyne gripped the back of the nearest chair. James thought he might crumple to the floor, and pushed even harder.

"If I were you, I'd get co-conspirators like Halliford to stop interfering so much; sending his wife around to Miss Hillier, arranging dinners to force her out of the house. They are giving me a very clear trail to follow."

Gascoyne glared at him, contrite forgotten as baleful and resentful took its place. "I have no idea what you're talking about. All I'm hearing is guesses, and ones in poor taste, at that. Perceval was a fine man, and while we may not have seen eye to eye on the slave trade, or the economic impact of his Orders in Council on the trade in Liverpool, to suggest I had something to do with his death because of my Christian charity towards one of my more unfortunate constituents is abominable." Gascoyne pulled down his waistcoat with a sharp tug. He marched toward the door.

James blocked the way longer than was polite, and then stepped aside. "I'll find some way to hold you to account for this, Gascoyne. And I don't want you to so much as look in Miss Hillier's direction ever again."

Gascoyne bared his teeth. "I have no interest in Miss Hillier. And as for the other, Bellingham pulled the trigger, that is a fact. My giving him money, Wilson helping me, whatever else you find out, nothing more than men helping a fellow human being, not realizing the terrible deed he had planned."

Gascoyne jerked his shoulder away from James as he marched out the room and down the hall.

As his ramrod straight back disappeared into the front hall, James had the sinking feeling the general was right.

Chapter Thirty-four

Phoebe heard the sound of a raised voice, put down the book she was reading and got to her feet. There was a violence to the shouting, a feral edge that had every instinct urging her to stand.

She watched the door and jumped when it opened. Harding slipped in and closed it firmly behind him.

They stared at each other for a beat, and Phoebe thought he looked as rattled as she felt.

"Who is making all that noise?" she asked at last.

"His Grace is just in a . . . meeting . . . with a gentleman, and he asked me to make sure you aren't seen by his visitor." Harding's voice was clipped, but as the voice rose even louder, his words trailed off, and he turned to look at the closed door.

Given the tone Wittaker's visitor was taking, Phoebe wasn't surprised he wanted her out of sight. Not to mention it would be difficult to explain to anyone what she was doing unchaperoned in the Duke of Wittaker's house, let alone someone as hostile to Wittaker as this man seemed to be.

The shouting stopped suddenly, and the silence that

followed was disconcerting. She couldn't bring herself to sit down again.

"Are you comfortable, my lady?" Harding had turned back to her and stood to attention, but in such a way he looked as if his shoes were pinching or his cravat was too tight. His gaze fell on the tea tray, and she almost heard him sigh with relief at something to do.

He came forward, tsking to himself. "A fresh pot?"

"That would be lovely, thank you. And some more of those green petits fours, if Monsieur Bisset has any. They are quite extraordinary."

Harding gathered everything together, and then stopped short at the door as they both heard someone storm past, and then the front door slam.

The library door swung open, and Wittaker stepped aside to allow Harding out. "Coffee for me, Harding. Hot and strong."

She wasn't sure why her heart gave a little jerk of fear and anticipation when he shut the door after Harding disappeared, and they were alone in the room.

"Who was that shouting?"

Wittaker's lips quirked up. "I found out who was paying Bellingham through Wilson. The Member of Parliament for Liverpool, General Gascoyne. He was unhappy that I uncovered his secret."

"You think he encouraged Bellingham to kill Perceval because Perceval's policies were hurting Liverpool too much?" Phoebe had heard about the mass unemployment and stagnation of the shipping trade in Liverpool since Perceval's Orders in Council and his support for banning the slave trade.

But something didn't make sense.

Two men had tried to kill her for the document Sheldrake had sent her before he was murdered. "Where does the petition to the Prince Regent come into it, then?"

"Yes. They made a mistake there. If they'd ignored it, we would have had to ignore it, too, because it doesn't make sense. And we don't know what it points to. But given their desperation to lay their hands on it . . ." Wittaker joined her at the little arrangement of chairs and his gaze flicked to her side of the low table.

He waited for her to sit, and then took up a place opposite her. It was a polite dance, when she could see in his eyes he had no wish to be polite. He wished to be most impolite, indeed.

"Sheldrake would have cared nothing for Liverpool, anyway." Phoebe forced herself to look away from him, to concentrate on the conversation. "When he spoke to me that last time, he made out as if his involvement had been heroic, somehow. That he'd been doing something brave. He wouldn't have felt that way if the goal had been to increase trade in Liverpool."

Wittaker gave a slow nod. "I originally thought whoever is behind this may have found out about Bellingham from the petition, that it was the thing that brought him to their attention and gave them the idea to use him. But I spoke to one of Gascoyne's servants, and apparently Bellingham visited him personally to lay down his grievances at least at the same time as he submitted that first petition."

"But if that's so, why does the petition come into it at all? Unless . . ." Phoebe tried hard to think why Sheldrake would keep it and risk his life to safeguard it. It was the one thing that tied him to the crime.

"We have to be missing the significance. They must think it points a finger at another of the conspirators. If we could find out who works in the Prince Regent's office—" Wittaker stopped short and Phoebe lifted her head.

What she saw in his eyes made her stomach plummet, like a slow tumble down the stairs. "No," she said. "No."

Wittaker was looking a little less surprised than she at the suggestion they were making. He sighed and rubbed a hand over his face. "Do you know the story of Thomas Becket?"

Phoebe gave a tight nod. "I received an excellent education, thanks to the retired Oxford don my mother hired to tutor me. The story goes that King Henry II was angry with Becket, and asked who would rid him of the troublesome priest. Four of his knights took that to mean he wanted Becket dead and killed him."

"Who will rid me of this troublesome prime minister?" Wittaker kept his voice low.

She felt weak, and a little sick. She was suddenly sorry she'd had two petits four. "We're talking about the Prince Regent." She said it in a whisper.

"He certainly had motive." Wittaker's voice rose to its normal pitch, but it sounded far too loud to Phoebe. "When the Prince Regent tried to accuse his wife of adultery a number of years ago, Perceval threw himself into the princess's defence. When he was done, he compiled a report of all the Prince Regent's wrong-doings, and had five thousand copies of it printed as pamphlets. He blackmailed the Prince Regent into accepting Princess Caroline back, by threatening to put them up for sale. Only when the Prince Regent allowed Princess Caroline back at court did he burn the lot of them."

Wittaker rubbed the side of his temple. "Then there's the Regency Bill, which Perceval used to curb the Prince Regent's powers. And finally, when the Prince Regent tried to force a change of government when the Regency Bill was up for renewal, to put men in place who were open to scrapping it, not only did he fail, but Perceval made him make a public announcement to say what a good job he thought Perceval was doing."

"Rubbing salt in the wound." Phoebe winced.

"When Perceval forced him to take his wife back and renounce his accusations, I heard it said he shouted and swore and said he'd like to jump on Perceval until he was dead." Wittaker shook his head. "I can only imagine what he wanted to do to him when he forced him to tell the world how wonderful he thought Perceval was." He paused. "And that happened in late February."

"When Bellingham came into some money?" Phoebe wished they were not travelling down this path. It was already smacking of treason.

"Perhaps the Prince Regent got the petition around the same time as Perceval humiliated him." Wittaker tapped a long, blunt finger against his lips.

"If he mentioned it, and Gascoyne was in the group, the general may have said something about Bellingham being mad when it came to the subject. That he couldn't be reasonable about it." Phoebe forced herself to say it. She thought it, after all, and they were already deep into dangerous territory.

"It might not even have been as direct as that. Gascoyne could have brought it up afterwards to the Prince's friends, when the Prince Regent was no longer in the room. My guess is, they would want to shield the Prince from any hint of wrongdoing."

"You think the Prince Regent has no idea what they've done?" Phoebe could hear the over-eagerness in her voice and grimaced.

Wittaker paused. She waited for him to speak, but he didn't.

"You think he *knew*?" She tried to swallow. It felt as if a stone was lodged in her throat.

"He knows something. Or he suspects. I picked that much up when I went to cadge an invitation off him to that dinner. Someone there, one of his cronies, quoted the Thomas Becket line, and the Prince Regent's reaction was vicious. I couldn't decide if it meant anything or if was just that everyone was drunk and in a foul temper." Wittaker went quiet as Harding entered with a tray, and the fragrant scent of coffee filled the room.

Phoebe let him pour her some tea, and was not surprised when her hand shook as she lifted the cup to her lips. He placed a plate piled high with green petits fours in front of her, the little gold-leaf flowers on top winking in the early afternoon sun.

When Harding left, he didn't close the door behind

him, and with a wry smile, Wittaker got up and closed it again.

This time, she had no doubt it was to keep their conversation private, rather than anything . . . else.

She cleared her throat. "That's what Sheldrake meant when he said no matter what, he and his friends would be hung out to dry if they were caught. They'd never bring the Prince Regent's name into disrepute."

"It goes deeper than that." Wittaker took a swallow of coffee. "I don't think they anticipated the public's reaction to Perceval's death. They thought the prime minister was the problem. That everyone would be happy he was gone, and that would be the end of it. But the crowd has been calling for the Prince Regent's head as well. I don't think any of them understood how deeply unpopular the Prince is. That Perceval's death would result in a call for the Prince Regent to go the same way."

"They probably thought any hint the Prince Regent might be behind Perceval's death would sign his death warrant with the radicals. Or would tip the public into more open defiance. They panicked." She thought of the way they'd thrown two men armed with guns at her, and realized that was the only word for it.

Wittaker nodded. "They panicked. And it's exposed them."

"What do we do? This is all just guesswork, really." She realized she was wringing her hands, and forced them into her lap.

"I'll go speak to Bellingham, see if I can get him to admit any of this. No matter the consequences to the Prince

Regent and his friends, Bellingham's neck is on the line, and he should have to opportunity to speak the truth."

"Will he, though?"

Wittaker hesitated, then shook his head. "I think he's convinced he did this all himself. That the money was from a generous benefactor helping him with his cause, but it was his cause, no one else's. I would like to know how he came up with his absurd legal argument that he can't be held guilty because he didn't kill the prime minister with malice aforethought. The very fact that he planned the murder negates that defense, and Bow Street has ample evidence he did plan it."

"Margie, perhaps?" She wondered how Margie fit into this.

"Yes." He stretched the word out, stretching out his legs at the same time. "I'd forgotten her for the moment, but I'd be very interested in speaking to her about what happened between her and Bellingham, before I speak to him. I'd love to know what Sheldrake put her up to."

"And what she has of Bellingham's that he's so afraid someone will find."

He smiled at her. It was the first smile she'd seen that wasn't either wry or self-deprecating.

It was dazzling.

"We'll have to speak to her, now we know so much more. It's urgent enough we can't wait for her work day to end, we'll have to go back to the tavern and confront her." He held out his hand to her as he stood.

She took it, but absently, her eyes on him. That he included her so naturally, had worked this out with her with no posturing or ego, was the most precious gift a man had ever given her.

"What is it?" His voice had gone husky.

"You see me," she said. She had to blink back the tears that stung her eyes. "You really see me."

"I will go and fetch the carriage," he said, quietly, withdrawing his hand, "before I start thinking of walls too much."

He was out the door before she could ask him what he meant.

Chapter Thirty-five

They arrived at the tavern just in time to see Jimmy running down the street. Wittaker leaned out and called to the driver to follow him, but he turned off the main road, down a narrow, crowded lane, and the carriage had to stop.

"Wait here." Wittaker glanced at Phoebe as he jumped out and then he slammed the door and disappeared into the crowd with Tom and the other footman.

It was probably less than a minute later, although it felt longer than that, when the carriage moved a little way forward and pulled in to the side.

Phoebe crouched down by the window to follow Wittaker and his men's progress, and then gasped when she saw Margie step out from the shadows of a deep-set doorway, and watch them, as well.

Jimmy must have been chasing her, and she'd known it.

When Wittaker and Jimmy were far enough away to make Margie feel comfortable coming out of her hiding place, she started walking again, but she was only on the lane for a few steps before she turned down a small side alley.

Phoebe's heart kicked up, and before she could think about it too much, she eased out of the carriage.

Wittaker's driver wouldn't leave her to follow Margie if she asked him. She didn't think he'd come with her, either, and leave the carriage.

She started after the girl, hoping the driver didn't notice her and call out, and perhaps alert Margie that she hadn't completely shaken her watchers off.

She felt the thrill of the chase, the sensation she'd envied Wittaker earlier when he'd taken off after Wilson outside the Baltick Coffee House.

It was exhilarating.

The passage Margie had taken was narrow and dim, the buildings on either side blocking out the sky. The cobbles lining the lane were slick, and above her head, Phoebe could hear the laundry which was strung between the houses flapping in the wind, the sound muffling her footsteps.

The way twisted and turned, burrowing deeper and deeper into a labyrinth Phoebe hoped she could find her way out of. Margie stepped around a sharp corner, and when Phoebe reached the same place, she was gone.

But she couldn't be gone. There was nowhere to go. Phoebe ran forward, and almost fell down the stairs at her feet.

She peered down the dark stairwell, angling her body to let in as much light as possible, and Margie looked back up at her, pressed back against an old, battered door.

"You." She spoke part in relief, part in confusion.

"What are you doing here?"

Phoebe stepped back. "Will you come up?"

Margie weighed the question. "Will you come down?"

Phoebe didn't want to. She could be trapped down there. Margie stared up at her, silent and calm, and she gave a tight nod and forced herself to step on the first step.

"Wait." Margie stepped more into the light. "I'll come up."

Phoebe said nothing at her change of heart, she was just relieved. She waited for Margie to emerge.

Margie took the last few steps slowly, and they watched each other until she was finally back on street level.

"You think Lord Sheldrake was having it off with me?"

The question was so unexpected, Phoebe gaped. "No. Is that why you think I chased you down?" She frowned. "Were you?"

Margie shook her head. "Mr. Jackson thinks I were. That that's where I would go every lunch time. He thought his lordship and I were meeting somewhere to have it away."

Phoebe was speechless for a moment. "I know what you were doing every lunch time."

Margie looked up sharply. "*You* were the one asking after me at lunch? Jane told me a man and a woman were."

Phoebe nodded. "You were befriending Bellingham."

Margie crossed her arms. "What's it to you? Why are you so interested?"

"Lord Sheldrake sent me something, some evidence

he had, and now the people who killed him are trying to kill me. I'm trying to find out who they are, and stop them."

The young woman narrowed her eyes. "How did you get on to me?"

"We were trying to find out who Bellingham spoke with when he was at the tavern, and you arrived just as we were leaving. I recognized you from this morning. It could hardly be a coincidence, you working at the tavern and for Lord Sheldrake."

Margie looked away. "Didn't really know why his lordship asked me to do it. That I swear. He paid me well and I didn't ask no questions. All I had to do was talk to Bellingham, and then tell him legal things, pretending my brother were a law clerk. His lordship told me stories, like what a law clerk would know, working on cases, and I was to tell them to Bellingham, like something interesting to pass the time of day, like."

"I'm surprised Sheldrake thought it would work."

"Bellingham was very interested." She looked up again. "Asked me questions to ask my 'brother'. I knew he were thinking about killing someone in the end. Can't say I didn't, not with the questions he were coming up with. And I knew his lordship were encouraging it with the answers he gave me to pass back."

She closed her eyes, and tipped her head back, as if trying to catch some of the light filtering down on them.

"He couldn't get past his imprisonment, Bellingham. I think he were innocent of what they said he'd done in Russia, and that the British ambassador didn't help him as he should. I heard the story from him often enough, and I'm sure he's telling the truth. He simply couldn't put it behind him. Being in prison was so far from his idea of what his life should be—losing everything he'd worked for. He couldn't cope. He liked his life ordered and tidy." She bit her lip, and a tear ran down her cheek. "No one helped him. He told me all the places he tried to get help. Redress, he called it. He was getting desperate. I think it was his last push, you see. I spent so many weeks with him, seeing him every day, and he knew if he couldn't get a resolution soon, he'd never get one. And he couldn't accept that."

"And that's when he started getting interested in legal defenses?"

Margie nodded. "Was he right? Will he get away with it if it was without malice aforethought."

Phoebe couldn't hide her shock that Margie had believed it herself. She shook her head. "Without malice aforethought is only applicable in the case of accidental death. Mr. Bellingham planned the murder of Mr. Perceval. He bought the guns, he practised shooting them, he even had a secret pocket sewn into his jacket to hide his weapon. That defense will never hold up."

Margie stared at her, and her gaze had turned from pleading to anger. "So they used me to trick him? Trick him into killing the prime minister?"

Phoebe nodded.

"Just a bunch of nobs, needing a working man to do their dirty work for them, like usual." She spoke with a sneer. "And a working woman, too, at that."

Phoebe nodded again.

"You know, the only good to come out o' this is my

job at the tavern. This might not look too fancy to you," she gestured down the stairs, "but it's an old basement room. The rent is cheap and it's mine. No one can come looking through my things, and there'll be no more lecherous lords feeling me up when I walk past, and I can't say a word about it."

"Sheldrake did that?" Phoebe couldn't imagine it, but as this last week had shown, she didn't know Sheldrake at all.

Margie shook her head. "Mr. Wentworth. Wanted me to stay on as the one maid they could afford, how about that? Another thing Mr. Jackson was angry about. What was he going to tell Mr. Wentworth if I didn't stay?" Margie tossed her head. "I told him what he could say when I walked out this morning, after doing everything Mr. Jackson gave me to finish before he'd let me go with that money you gave us." She took a deep breath. "And thanks for that, by the way. Paid me deposit on this room, it did. Got me my freedom, so I owe you one for that."

"You don't owe me anything." The sky above darkened, and Phoebe looked up and saw through the narrow gap that storm clouds were gathering. "But can you tell me, what did Bellingham give to you?"

"Give to me?" Margie frowned. "Oh, the list? The one I gave to Lord Sheldrake?"

"What list?"

"He were nervous about something. Asked me to give my brother a list, check it to see if it would hold up in court."

"What did it say?" Phoebe shivered as the wind blew

a little harder.

Margie shrugged. "I can't read. I gave it to his lordship, and he were right angry. Threw it straight in the fire, and said Bellingham were coming apart at the seams, and that it was all going to hell. Told me to tell him it would definitely hold up."

"When was this?"

Margie looked at her; a long, steady look.

"It was Saturday or Sunday last week, wasn't it?"

She nodded. "Saturday afternoon." She turned away. "I saw him one last time, Sunday afternoon."

"I'm sorry." Phoebe could see the girl had come to like Bellingham. Her hands were clasped together, and her shoulders were hunched. "It was wrong of Sheldrake to use you." She shook her head. "Everything about this was wrong."

Margie looked back at her. "That chap following me? Was he with you?"

Phoebe gave a nod. "I'll call him off. Get them to leave you alone. If the list went in the fire, there's no proof of any of this."

"There were a man. Not a nob, though, someone else, like a lawyer or a merchant or sommat. I think Lord Sheldrake was payin' him, too." Margie lowered her voice. "He sometimes came round the tavern, talked to Mr. Bellingham. Encouraging him, like, to not let it go. Assuring him he were in the right, sort of thing. It weren't just me danglin' some bait. They were eggin' him on."

Phoebe gave a nod, but like everything else, it was nebulous, hard to pin down the wrong of it. She turned to go back, then stopped. "If you need help, or lose your position, you can come to me."

"Ta, but I'll do fine all on me own." Margie climbed partway down the stairs. "I'm done with getting mixed up with nobs."

As Phoebe walked away, she thought it ironic she was done with it, too. Except for one. She was deliberately getting mixed up with him.

The rain started long before she reached the street where the carriage was waiting, and the shouts and calls of housewives pulling in their washing overhead made her smile.

She'd never been given a choice in who she associated with before.

She did now.

And she'd make her choice count.

Chapter Thirty-six

Everything had gone to hell.

Jimmy, just ahead of them in the crowd, slowed, and then stopped, spinning a full circle, looking for the girl.

"She was right ahead of me." He spun again, as if a second time would reveal what he was searching for.

"Keep looking. Tom, stay with him and help, George and I will go back to the carriage." James had a sudden sinking feeling about having left Phoebe alone with only the driver to keep watch.

No one could know they were here. They were still using the old battered coach he'd hired for today's investigations, but he was jogging by the time he reached it.

The carriage was pulled up on the left of the street, but the way was narrow enough that his driver kept being harangued by passing carts, and the man looked hot and bothered, despite the cooling breeze and the darkening skies.

James could see his relief when he spotted them.

He opened the carriage door, and stared at the empty interior.

"Where is Miss Hillier?" He tried not to shout, not to

panic, as he called up to the man.

The driver frowned. "Inside."

But she wasn't.

He turned, the movement reminding him painfully of Jimmy, not minutes ago, looking up and down the street.

Why would she leave, and without attracting the driver's attention?

He couldn't understand it.

She hadn't gone the same way as he and his men, he would have seen her on the way back. So the alternatives were the way they'd come or . . . there was a narrow lane almost directly opposite the carriage, and something about it had him stepping in its direction. "George, you trace our way back towards the tavern. We all meet back here at the carriage."

His footman disappeared into the crowds, and James crossed the street at a run, dodging wheelbarrows and people, and stepped into the narrow access way. It was colder here—there was a relentless wind blowing between the buildings, and the dark sky meant it was even gloomier than in the wider street.

Rain started to fall, and it blinded him as he strode as fast as he could on the slippery cobbles through the twists and turns the lane made between the high buildings, accommodating a kink here and a jutting corner there.

Then he stepped around a sharp turn and ran straight into Phoebe, walking with her head down against the stinging needles of rain.

"Oh." She was in his arms before she even knew he was there, and he held her, his chest tight and his breath short at the relief of finding her.

"Thank God." He shuddered in a breath and reluctantly loosened one arm to push wet tendrils of hair off her forehead. "Where did you go?"

She looked up at him with wide eyes, and he realized he was holding her as if he would never let her go. He couldn't help himself.

He could feel an uncomfortable sting where his injured arm protested at the strain he was putting on it, but he didn't care.

"I saw Margie come this way, so I followed her." She tipped her head back and gave a rueful grin. "I knew your driver wouldn't leave me and go after her himself, and anyway, what would he have done with her, grabbed her against her will? I didn't think he'd leave the carriage and come with me, either, so I did it on my own. We would never have found her once she'd disappeared down here, not until she came back to work at the tavern tomorrow, and with the trial starting in the morning, that would be too late."

"You're . . . right." He forced himself to admit it. It was strange to have someone help him, someone who understood all the stakes, intelligent enough to put the pieces together without being told, and who wasn't afraid to take action.

He didn't think Gascoyne would come after her again, not after this afternoon's confrontation. He must realize now how much James knew, how little killing Phoebe would achieve, but he may not have had time to pull off his dogs yet. She was still at risk, and the thought of her down this dark, narrow lane alone made his heart pound.

He tried to hide his fear, although he still couldn't loosen his arms. "Did you discover anything?"

She nodded, and miraculously didn't try to struggle free, seemingly content to stand in the rain pressed up against him. "I spoke to her. Sheldrake had her pretend she had a brother who was a law clerk. She related tales from this fictional brother to Bellingham, feeding him various defense strategies. They also sent a man in to befriend him, casually, it sounds like. He'd let Bellingham go on about his troubles over a pint and encouraged him to keep going."

"Did you find out what it was Bellingham gave her?"

She leaned forward, and rubbed her forehead against his coat to wipe away some of the rain, as if she, too, couldn't bear to let go of him. "A list. She can't read, but from what Bellingham told her, it sounded like a list of how he planned to carry out the assassination, and then the defense he intended to use. Everyone he could turn to for compensation had refused him, some of them multiple times. He had to find another way to bring the issue to the public's attention, something so violent and shocking, no one could ignore him, and he wanted Margie's 'brother' to tell him if his defense would hold up in court."

"What did Sheldrake do with the document?" James didn't wonder Bellingham had panicked during his hearing at the thought of his list of steps to kill the prime minister ending up in Bow Street's hands.

"He threw it straight in the fire, and told Margie to tell Bellingham the defense would hold. That was the last time she saw Bellingham before he killed Perceval. My guess is Sheldrake panicked. If one list existed, who else had Bellingham told or given a list to? That's why he ran. He didn't know Bellingham had finally decided to kill the prime minister, he just knew that they'd wound him up too tight and Sheldrake decided not to take any chances."

James shifted as a fresh wave of icy rain came in from above, trying to protect Phoebe from the worst of it. He still couldn't move. Couldn't find any motivation to walk her back to the street, to the relative comfort of the carriage. It was as if they were in a cocoon, and he held on to it for a little longer.

"If Sheldrake destroyed it, then we have nothing. Nothing to tie this to Sheldrake, anyway. Margie is a young serving woman, and the prosecution could easily discredit what she has to say, not to mention it's her word against a dead peer of the realm. No one will touch that. And there's just as little tying it to Gascoyne." He had known this was likely, almost from the beginning, but knowing it for sure was worse than he'd imagined. Draining, and suddenly depressing. As sharp and cold as the rain trickling down the back of his neck.

"Unless we can get another of the Prince Regent's men to confess, no." She wedged herself even more tightly in his arms, and lifted her hands, smoothing her fingers over his cheeks to brush away the raindrops.

"I still plan to see Bellingham today. And with everything Margie told you, perhaps I can get him to admit some of it. At least force the court to give Harmer more time to mount a defense."

She made a hum of agreement and then leaned

forward and brushed a kiss on his jaw.

He shuddered, and tipped her head back. Rain had plastered her hair to her scalp, and she looked stripped to her essence, looking back at him with eyes that spoke of hunger and heat and . . . happiness.

"We need to get back." He whispered it close to her ear, letting his lips brush her cheek, and her temple.

She snuggled deeper. "I know."

"You know I spoke of a way to free you from any worry of becoming with child?"

She went still and raised her head, languid and so desirable his legs almost couldn't support him. "Yes?"

"I won't deny the idea of being your lover was something I enjoyed thinking about since I met you, but every day I've been in your company I've become more and more sure I want something more."

She frowned. "More?"

He clasped her even tighter, tried to find the most eloquent way to say it. "For the rest of my life."

She stared at him.

He held her gaze. "I know we've only known each other less than a week, and I'll climb up the wall to your bedroom in secret for as long as you need to decide, but understand that whatever relationship we enter into when this thing with Bellingham is done, I don't just want you for a lover. I want you for my wife."

Chapter Thirty-seven

She stared at him in shock. "We've only known each other since Tuesday."

"Enough time for you to decide to take me as a lover," he said, and there was satisfaction in his voice. "And in these last three days, we've spent more time alone together than most courting couples get over the whole of a Season."

That was true. She knew he had shown her more of himself than he might ever have done if they had not met under the extraordinary circumstances they had. Still, why would he—

"You don't have to decide right now." He bent his head and rested his forehead on hers. "I just wanted you to know, for me, there is no going back. You have me completely captivated. I have no plan to end our liaison. And I would make it permanent as soon as you give me your answer."

"I'd take him up on that, luv."

Phoebe looked up, blinking back the rain, and saw three women hanging out of their windows, mindless of the soaking they were getting, watching them with smiles on their faces.

"He looks like a nob in that fancy coat, even though he's soaked through an' all. And he likes to cuddle you close. That's always a good sign."

Phoebe couldn't help the laugh that spilled from her. She lifted a hand and waved. "I think you're probably right."

She looked back at Wittaker, and the sudden joy in her shifted to searing desire at the look on his face. He bent and kissed her, to the cheers and cat calls from above, until they both pulled away, breathless.

He stepped to one side, with his left arm still firmly around her shoulders, and bowed to their audience. "Much though we've enjoyed ourselves, it's time to go."

"Don't go on our account," one of the woman called. "Been most entertainin'."

She loved the way he grinned at that. Sheldrake would never have been holding her close in a dark alley to begin with, but even if he had, he'd have reacted with affront and bluster if they'd been caught out.

She gave a final wave as they turned the corner and she realized she was still smiling like a love-struck fool by the time they'd reached the street.

She tried to school her features, but Jimmy gave her such a strange look as they approached the carriage, she decided she probably hadn't done a very good job.

"All right, my lady?" he asked.

"Yes." She could feel a flush of heat at how long they'd been gone. "Margie realized you were following her. She went down that lane, and I went after her."

"Oh." His chagrin was evident.

"No harm done." Wittaker gave her a sidelong look that was part amusement, part leer, and she found herself laughing again.

"I have to speak to Bellingham, and Newgate is close enough to here for me to walk," Wittaker said as he helped her up into the cab. She was gratified to see it was as hard for him to release her hands as it was for her to let go. "Would you go to my house again?"

She shook her head. "My aunt will have spent the day packing to leave London tomorrow. I need to spend some time with her."

"If it helps, I don't think Gascoyne will send any more men after you. She should be safe enough."

Phoebe pursed her lips. "I think she's unsettled more by the reaction to my betrothal ending than anything else. And there is no escaping that."

"Yes, there is." He took her hand again and kissed it. "Because you are now betrothed to me."

She hadn't thought of it in those terms. She'd been thinking about being with the man himself, now she remembered he was also a duke.

"Do *not* do that." Wittaker pulled himself into the carriage after her and closed the door.

"Do what?"

"Withdraw." He didn't take his seat, he crouched in front of her. "I can see it happening behind your eyes."

She closed them, then took a deep breath and looked at him. "This sounds stupid, but I forgot, in the alley, that you're a duke. That all those people at the Prince Regent's dinner . . ."

"They'll behave as if that never happened when you're happy for us to announce you're to be the next Duchess of Wittaker. And they'll hope and pray you do the same. That you don't give *them* the cut direct for their behavior." He leaned back on his heels. "I've been playing this game for a long time, and I can promise you that the less you care, the more they do."

She gave a wry laugh. "I was starting to like the idea of no more balls and soirées."

"Phoebe," he almost purred her name, "you do as you like from now on. You would have anyway, I suspect, whether you'd met me or not. As Miss Hillier, or the Duchess of Wittaker, you can ignore every single invitation you ever get, or attend them all, it makes no difference to me. Although the more you ignore, the more desperate the hostesses of London will be for you to accept."

She gave a slow nod.

"No more building up the barricades against me?"

She shook her head, and he leaned forward and nuzzled her neck before pulling back.

"And just to make sure I understand completely, your reaction in the alley was a yes to my proposal?"

She hesitated. "It wasn't a no." She dropped her voice to a whisper so no one but he could hear her. "I want to be with you as often as possible. I crave your company. But I'm not sure I'm ready to be the center of a scandal. And accepting your proposal now, on the heels of Sheldrake's rejection and death, that's exactly where I'll be. But if you're happy to do it, I would like you to climb up to my bedroom as often as you can." The thought of them together, with no watchful eyes on them, completely free to do as they liked, made her heart leap into her throat.

She was twenty-four years old and she had felt something extremely important was missing from her life for at least the last four. She had the sense Wittaker would show her exactly what that important thing was.

"I'll see you later, then." His hand shook a little as he reached for the carriage door.

"You're thinking of walls again?" she asked suddenly.

For a moment, he looked absolutely shocked.

"You plan to climb up to my bedroom? Or will you come in the front door?" She suddenly felt uncertain, as if she'd misunderstood him.

He smiled. A long, wicked smile that made her heart beat faster.

"It depends how late I am. But you're quite right, I was thinking of walls."

***

It was a struggle to get his head straight as he walked the ten minutes it took to Newgate Prison. The rain had eased off, but his shirt and jacket still stuck to his skin uncomfortably, and he was almost glad of the distraction.

As the shadow of Newgate fell over him, though, and the insidious stink of human waste and despair blew at him on the cold wind, he managed to push thoughts of having Phoebe alone with no possibility of an interruption to the back of his mind.

Newman, Bellingham's jailer, leapt to his feet with alacrity when he saw him, no doubt remembering the generous tip James had given him for information last time.

"He just has a visitor in there at the moment, Your Grace, although I can turn her out, if it's urgent?" Newman bobbed like a grey-feathered robin.

"Her?" James frowned. "Who's in there?"

"Miss Mary Stevens, Your Grace. Seems she lives with Bellingham and his wife in Liverpool. Bellingham's wife and Miss Stevens run a dressmaking shop or some such." Newman fiddled with the buttons on his jacket. "Thought there could be no 'arm in letting her talk to him. Letting him give her a message to take back to his wife, given tomorrow . . ."

James gave a nod. "I would be most grateful if you would ask her to wait for me when I go in to speak to him. I'd like to see her for a moment. I won't be long with Bellingham."

Newman gave a nod, and then disappeared into the small passage near his desk. When he came out, a young woman was with him. In her late twenties, he would guess. She had dark hair and was neatly dressed, although the clothes she had on were worn, and her face held a tight, worried look.

She curtseyed awkwardly. "You wish to speak with me, Your Grace?"

"If you don't mind waiting, Miss Stevens. I won't be long, and I won't keep you."

She gave a reluctant nod, and James made his way to Bellingham's cell.

The man was standing, watching the door, and he smiled when James was let in by the guard. "Good afternoon again, sir. Did you find my papers?"

"Not yet, Mr. Bellingham." James had forgotten all about the blasted papers, and wondered if Harmer was looking for them. "At the very least, they will be presented at your trial, and you can ask for them, then."

Bellingham gave a sigh, as if this failure was one he was used to dealing with.

"You told me the other day that no one helped you, but that isn't true, is it?" James leaned back against the bars. There would be no sitting as if visiting a friend today.

Bellingham did not look concerned. He shook his head. "No one helped me. Not a single soul."

"Margie did. And her brother, through her." He would not tell Bellingham the brother didn't exist yet.

Bellingham looked up, the movement like an animal suddenly sensing danger. "All Margie did was tell me stories of her brother's employers. That wasn't help."

"What about the list you gave her for him to look at. That wasn't help?"

Bellingham looked at him through wide eyes. "You have the list?"

James shook his head. He wasn't going to lie to Bellingham, he was here to help him, not terrify him. "It has been destroyed."

Bellingham sagged, half-falling into his chair. "I knew that was a mistake, but . . ." He ran shaking fingers through his dark hair. "Destroyed, you say?"

James nodded. "And the money you were getting from Mr. Wilson? That wasn't help? What about the help in finding the gunsmith?"

Bellingham blinked and shook his head. "I haven't

had any help. I've answered that question enough times. The money . . . well, if Mr. Wilson said I was owed the money by one of his clients, I was owed the money. It didn't surprise me at all that someone had forgotten to pay me during the time I was in jail. He's a businessman, he doesn't give money out unless it's owed."

"Why didn't you use it to help your wife and family, instead of printing pamphlets and buying guns? That money could have kept your family for a year or more."

For the first time, Bellingham became truly agitated. He wrung his hands and lifted out of his chair to pace. "It was my last chance to get a settlement. I need to provide for my family. Not just get them through the year, but have enough for a good future for them. I had that before, and then injustice took it away from me. The money Mr. Wilson gave me meant I could finally do everything I needed to to have the matter resolved."

He finally caught James's eye and James could see the determination and the self-pity there. A strange mix.

"I will tell you as often as you like to hear it. I have been trying to solve this since I returned from Russia many years ago. I didn't have help from anyone. And I've finally had to help myself. I've taken matters into my own hands and crafted justice for myself, and no one tomorrow will deny me my rights. How can they?"

James gave a reluctant nod. Bellingham was determined not to see the hands that helped him, and to be fair, they had intended that to be the case. Gascoyne was only known to him as his Member of Parliament; Sheldrake, not at all. There would be no recanting of his story.

He waved to the guard to let him out and took his leave of Bellingham.

The roof seemed to be lowering down on him by the time he stepped into Newman's office and he couldn't bear to stay here another moment.

"Would you like to walk out with me while we talk, Miss Stevens?" he asked the woman waiting for him.

She gave a relieved nod, and James slipped Newman another coin as they let themselves out.

"Do you mind my asking the financial situation Mr. Bellingham and his family are in?" It was a little late for this question, given he knew Gascoyne had been behind Bellingham's payments, but as someone who lived with them, Miss Stevens would surely know the truth.

She gave a bitter laugh. "They are so poor, Mrs. Bellingham had to take their son out of school, because they couldn't afford the fees, just after Christmas. But there is a hundred pounds in Mr. Bellingham's box in his cell. I just saw it now, while he was looking for something in there while I was visiting."

"He wasn't doing any work that could earn him that kind of money?"

She shook her head. "He was doing the books for our business. That was the sum of his life since he returned from Russia, until he came down to London. He told us he was coming to sort out a mix-up one of our suppliers made, sending us too much ribbon, and that he had a small part in an iron sale, where he'd earn a little money. Then he didn't come back. Mrs. Bellingham wept when he finally wrote and admitted he was caught up in the madness of that Russian business again. Wept as if her heart would break."

She was silent until they had descended the stairs of the prison and stood on Newgate Street. "What happened to them in Russia has haunted their lives. And Bellingham won't let it go, even though he promised her he would. It eats at him like a sickness, and when he's in its grip, it's like a fever comes down on him, and he's insensible to everything."

"You think he's mad?"

Miss Stevens looked up at him, and then nodded. "When it comes to this one thing, yes. He's a good father, I would swear to that, and when he's busy working as our bookkeeper, he is a good accountant and husband, too. But mention Russian, mention his time in jail, and he cannot be reasonable. He simply cannot."

"Will I see you tomorrow at the trial?" James lifted a hand to call her a hansom.

She shook her head. "I'm going back to Liverpool tonight. I stayed on an extra few days when I heard what he'd done . . . But I cannot leave the shop so long."

"Did he give you a letter to his wife?" James hadn't seen anything in her hand when she'd left Bellingham's cell, and wondered at that, now.

She shook her head, and then gave a sad smile. "No. He says he will be able to tell her of his success himself. That he simply cannot be found guilty, and they will at last be compensated. That justice will finally be served."

There was nothing to say to that.

"I saw him on Sunday afternoon, you know. The day before he . . ." She rubbed her forehead. "He took me and the friend I'm staying with on an outing, and he told me he had been putting something off, avoiding it, but that he would finally put it to rest on Monday, and be home shortly." She shook her head. "I was just glad he would be coming back soon. I had no idea . . ."

A hansom pulled up, the horses dancing beneath their reins.

"Have a good journey, Miss Stevens." James helped her up to the cab, and then paid the driver her fare.

"It's all such a waste," Mary Stevens said, as she settled herself in her seat.

James looked back at Newgate, dark and forbidding, and as the hansom disappeared down the street, thought the same.

Chapter Thirty-eight

James's club was quiet. It was a good hour before dinner, and only a few stalwarts occupied the deep armchairs scattered around the main room.

Dervish was in his usual place, and James saw he had called in Durnham and Aldridge as well.

He took a seat, and there was silence for a beat, while the murmur of voices and the clink of crystal glasses lulled them all.

"You have something?" Dervish asked at last.

He looked exhausted, and James guessed he had had almost no sleep since Perceval was murdered. He would have been getting as much intelligence as he could about how close England was to revolution.

James gave a nod. "You will not like it."

Dervish closed his eyes and leaned back his head. "I've understood that since the moment I heard of the assassination."

"Much as Henry II's advisors would have felt, when they heard of the assassination of Thomas Becket, I imagine."

There was absolute silence now. None of the men

sitting in the small, private alcove so much as moved.

Dervish's eyes had snapped open, and he was looking at James with such horror, James might as well have told him he'd murdered his mother.

“If it helps,” he said, “there is no way to prove it definitively. Harmer won't be able to find anything to use in the trial tomorrow.”

“My God.” Dervish exploded from his seat, turned to the door, and took a few steps towards it. Then he stopped, turned back and sat again, hands gripping the arms of his chair. “Tell me.”

James looked at each man in turn, and saw he had their undivided attention. “A horrible coincidence happened sometime in February. The Prince Regent received a petition from John Bellingham, a seemingly ridiculous petition, and mentioned it to his friends. One of those friends happened to be General Gascoyne, who, as the Member of Parliament for Liverpool, where Bellingham lived, had received a personal visit from Bellingham around the same time. Something about Bellingham made him think the man was close to a very fine edge.

“This would have been just after Perceval had publicly humiliated the Prince Regent when he tried to remove Perceval from power. Words were most likely spoken in the Prince Regent's private chambers, threats of violence against Perceval made. And suddenly, Gascoyne and a few of the Prince's friends, including Sheldrake, Halliford and Bartlett, decided to help their friend be rid of the man who had been nothing but a thorn in the Prince's side since he came into government.”

"And it didn't hurt that it would be in their own interests, as well," Durnham said. "Especially Gascoyne's. Getting rid of Perceval would be a good way to get rid of the Orders in Council. The very thing that is ruining trade in Liverpool."

"You say it will be hard to prove?" Durnham spoke as if his voice was rusty.

"Gascoyne admits to giving Bellingham money through an iron merchant who often acted as an informal bank, but pretends it was a charitable act, not a calculated move to make it possible for Bellingham to continue to stay in London. And I think Wilson, the iron merchant, will be long gone by now. Also, Sheldrake used one of his maids to befriend Bellingham, and pass him ridiculous legal advice that made it seem as if the law would be on his side if he took justice into his own hands. Sheldrake also hired a man to befriend Bellingham and encourage him.

"But in the end, it's the maid's word against a dead peer of the realm. Gascoyne won't give himself away. He's frightened, but he won't lose his nerve, I don't think.

"The only evidence we have is the original petition, which the Prince Regent must have left in his rooms after he'd laughed over it with his friends, and which Sheldrake must have stolen, just in case things didn't go as planned. There was also a written list on how best to kill Perceval, but that was written by Bellingham himself and will only make the case against him stronger, if it existed, which it no longer does. Sheldrake burned it before he ran for the coast."

"We're forgetting the trial," Aldridge spoke softly. "There is something wrong there, too."

"Sir Vicary used to be the Prince Regent's legal council, before he was made Attorney-General." James steepled his fingers. "Someone has pressured him into getting this matter settled as fast as possible. Whether he thinks it's to secure national peace, and get the threat of a radical revolution off the cards, or whether he thinks he's shielding the Prince Regent from even a whiff of suspicion, is anyone's guess."

"No matter what the reason, he's an accomplished enough lawyer to know he's committing a travesty of justice." Dervish's voice was grim.

"And Bellingham is going to sail into that courtroom tomorrow, convinced he's going to not only be found not guilty, but finally receive the compensation he's been after since he returned from Russia."

"You've spoken to him?" Durnham stretched out his legs, but he didn't look relaxed, he looked furious.

James nodded. "I couldn't question him too openly about what he knew with a guard right there, but he is in a delusional world when it comes to this. He sees everything that happened to him to keep him here in London as from his own efforts or luck. He is convinced he did this on his own."

"And the Prince Regent?" Dervish looked like he wanted to leap out of his chair again, but managed to control the impulse. "How much of this does he know about, do you think?"

"He knows something. Enough that he's nervous. Probably not the details, is my guess, but the general gist of it? Yes."

"And he's most likely nervous because it didn't go the way they planned. They hoped the crowds would be pleased Perceval was gone, but the crowds didn't stop there. They called for the Prince Regent to be next. It's brought the whole country very close to revolution." Aldridge's smile was savagely satisfied.

James nodded. "He honestly didn't realize how unpopular he was."

"He can have no illusions about it, now." Dervish finally stood, but carefully. "I'm going home."

They all rose from their chairs.

"I'm sorry there isn't anything more substantial to bring you." James said.

Dervish gave a bitter laugh. "I'm not. What would I do with it?" He rubbed a hand over his head, so his hair was sticking up at all angles when he was done. "And even if you did, no matter that they manipulated a man obsessed, he did pull the trigger himself."

James inclined his head in silence. He felt he had let Bellingham down. "He wouldn't have done it, you know, if they hadn't given him money, given him terms like 'without malice aforethought' and encouraged him. From what witnesses said of his behavior after the event, he was in shock, and he dragged his heels over the deed, putting it off time and again. Sheldrake panicked because he thought he wouldn't do it, but would start talking of it, and implicate them all. If it weren't for them, Bellingham would have gone home."

They were all quiet for a moment.

"Well then, when I've gotten some rest, and my

temper under more control, I think I'll just mention some of this to the Prince Regent." Dervish's eyes were as cold as his voice.

He bowed to them all and left, and James felt a small measure of satisfaction. Dervish would use this to rein the Prince Regent in a little.

It was better than nothing.

Chapter Thirty-nine

Friday, 15 May, 1812

Phoebe woke slowly, as the light of dawn spilled through the one uncovered window in her room. She lay staring across at it, wondering why the sound of the birds calling in her garden below was so much louder than usual, and then remembered she had left the window open.

She sat up abruptly.

She was still on top of the covers, just as she'd been when she'd lain down after dinner last night to wait for Wittaker. She was in her night shift and a gown, but someone had pulled a blanket over her.

There was a scent in the room, that green, spicy scent of Wittaker after he'd climbed the ivy to her window, and she saw ivy was trailing, in a whimsical drape, across the end of her bed.

There were roses and daisies threaded through it, and as she leaned forward to brush a finger across a velvet rose petal, she wondered if he'd brought them up the first time, or if, finding her fast asleep, he had gone back down into her garden for them and climbed back up to place them here for her.

She lifted her hand, and found it was trembling, and that she suddenly had tears pricking the back of her eyes, as an emotion so big, so vast it felt as if her body couldn't contain it, swelled up inside her.

She slid off the bed, and the movement dislodged a note on her bedside table. It fluttered to the floor, and she picked it up: *I will fetch you at nine tomorrow to attend the trial, if you would like to go. James.*

James. She had given him her name, but men, and especially men with titles, were different. She knew her aunt never referred to her uncle by his first name. If fact, Phoebe didn't even know what it was. Her mother, from her more middle class background, had wanted to call her father by his first name, but he had always discouraged it.

A warmth trickled through her, and she had the idiotic urge to kiss the note.

Like a schoolgirl.

She gave a derisive snort and put it in a drawer, unkissed.

She had already eaten breakfast and was ready to go when her aunt joined her, earlier than usual because she was leaving just after nine o'clock herself, back to her sprawling house in the country.

"You looked exhausted last night, but you seem much better now. Positively glowing," she said as she kissed Phoebe's cheek. She eyed her carriage outfit. "You're going out?"

Phoebe nodded. "To Bellingham's trial."

Her aunt's eyes widened. "How are you getting in? I read in the papers yesterday evening it's by ticket only. One guinea a ticket!"

"The Duke of Wittaker has arranged it. He is to accompany me."

"But Phoebe, you never mentioned this last night." Her aunt clasped her hands together, so distressed she did not even notice that Lewis had poured her tea.

"I received a note from him this morning."

Phoebe caught Lewis's sharp look. He would know no note had been officially delivered, but Phoebe ignored him.

"What has you so upset?" She took her aunt's hands. "The worst has happened. They can't do more to me than they have already."

"You would be surprised," her aunt sniffed. "It is just that I don't want you ensnared. At the moment, you're ruined but on speculation alone, based only on what you and Sheldrake *might* have done together as a betrothed couple, but there are many who would give you the benefit of the doubt.

"If you travel down this path with Wittaker, I fear you will be branded a demi-rep, or his mistress, and there will be no respectable offer of marriage." Her aunt lifted a hand and stroked her cheek. "I saw the anger in you at the Prince Regent's dinner, the rejection of everything they are, but I don't want you to throw away a chance at a family and a happy life to spite people who shouldn't matter anyway. However exciting a handsome rake like Wittaker might seem."

She drew her aunt into a hug as the doorbell rang, and felt her aunt stiffen beneath her embrace.

"Wittaker?"

"I'm sure it is, yes." Phoebe kept her arm about her. "Show him in, please, Lewis."

When James entered the room, her heart leapt, and it was all she could do not to walk into his arms.

"Ladies." He bowed, and unable to help herself, Phoebe stepped away from her aunt and held out her hands to him.

"Thank you for the flowers." She blushed as the words spilled from her mouth.

The flicker of surprise on his face at her mention of his midnight antics was gone in a moment. He took her hands, and lifted her fingers to his lips. "I enjoyed getting them. And it is a pleasure to see you looking so well, Miss Hillier."

Her aunt made a sound, and they both turned to her. "There is something . . ." She was staring at Wittaker.

"You are no doubt talking about the love-sick look I get on my face when I am in your niece's company. I am quite sure it is sickening to watch, but I'm afraid I can't help it." There was laughter in his eyes.

Her aunt gave a slow nod. "I see you have things in hand, Phoebe." She stepped forward and kissed her cheek again. "I will have a good breakfast and then be on my way. You best be off if you are going to the trial, there is no doubt it will be a crush."

James held out his arm for her to take and Phoebe looked back to give a final wave as they walked away.

Her aunt was staring after them, a wide smile on her face and tears on her cheeks.

She raised a hand to her lips and blew Phoebe a kiss.

***

It *was* a crush.

When they arrived at Old Bailey, the crowds were so thick, they struggled to gain entry.

Phoebe noticed more than one bribe exchanging hands as people bartered to get inside, and once they were in, it was unadulterated chaos.

"It looks as if it's every man and women for themselves," Wittaker murmured in her ear, finding them a place near the back so they could leave easily. "I see more than one Member of Parliament having to actually rub shoulders with their constituents." There was laughter in his voice, and she grinned back at him.

She noticed a number of affronted men in stately dress, forced to find a place amongst the throng.

The smell was terrible. The odour of unwashed bodies mingled with the dank air wafting up from the tunnels to Newgate Prison, the stench strong enough to make her lift her handkerchief to her nose to breathe through.

Someone had made an effort to combat the smell by placing herbs along the judges' bench and on the dock, but they looked wilted and ineffectual.

"Is that the Lord Mayor of London up on the bench with the judges?" she whispered.

He gave a nod. "The Lord Mayor of London and the Lord Chief Justice. I'm surprised they are so eager to be here. There is no way this trial can ever be remembered well."

Bellingham was brought in, his hair neat, his face

clean, but his clothes very much the worse for wear: ripped and torn, as if he had been set upon by a crowd.

Phoebe supposed he had been.

It was the first time she'd seen him, and he looked calm and alert. His long face was serious but showed no signs of nervousness.

The talk in the court dropped off as he was ushered to his stand, but then rose again, even louder.

She recognized Harmer, Bellingham's solicitor, from their meeting the day before. There were a few men with him, his colleagues, she guessed, who would form the defense team.

"Vinegar Gibbs, the Attorney-General," James whispered to her, pointing to the sharp-faced man standing across from Harmer.

The Lord Chief Justice called the court to order, and Phoebe could sense the duality of the crowd around her; outrage and approval swirled through the throng as every request by Harmer and his team for more time was denied.

Gibbs accused Harmer and his colleague, Alley, of contriving to delay the administration of justice.

Bellingham was forced to plead, and as he stood and launched into his own defense, the papers he'd requested clasped tightly in his hands, she had the terrible feeling she was watching a farce.

"He isn't even looking at them," James murmured in her ear. "He was desperate for those papers, but he hasn't glanced at them once."

"Perhaps they make him feel more secure." Phoebe watched the accused as he talked about his terrible experiences in Russia, and had the sense of a childlike desperation, a naivety that obscured all the realities of his situation.

A crushing sense of helplessness weighed her down as she looked from his serious, earnest expression, to the cold, closed looks on the faces of the men lined up to judge him.

She had thrown the shackles of helplessness off as much as possible this week and she could not bear to watch this.

She leaned in to Wittaker. "Do you mind taking me out? I cannot stay. It feels as though I am watching a carriage bearing down on a child in the street, and I cannot do anything to prevent what is going to happen next."

James gave a nod and then they were up, and he was pushing through the crowd with his broad shoulders, her hand tight in his, until they were on the street.

It was a London street, she knew it couldn't smell fresh and sweet, but it seemed to, after the packed courtroom.

"Thank you." She stood close to him, his hand still clasped in hers. "I'm sorry if you wanted to stay. If you'd like to go back in—"

He shook his head. Then frowned as a man gave a final, indignant shout to a bailiff. He climbed into a coach, and his travel companion leaned across him and shook his fist at the bailiff, anger in every movement they made as they drove off.

The bailiff watched them leave stoically, arms crossed.

"What was that about?" James towed her behind him as he approached the portly man.

He frowned. "Who's asking?"

"The Duke of Wittaker."

She hadn't heard that tone from him before. It was icy and precise, like the sharpest knife, and the bailiff straightened up.

"Two gentlemen wot came from Liverpool to speak as witnesses on the Bellingham matter, Your Grace."

"For the accused or against?"

"Don't rightly know." The man doffed his cap.

"Why weren't they allowed in? They must have ridden the fastest possible way to get here so soon." James looked after them, but the carriage had already disappeared.

"The Attorney-General was told they were here, Your Grace, he said to turn them away." The man shuffled back.

She tightened her grip on James's hand. "Surely Gibbs isn't allowed—"

James's eyes were hot enough to set the court building alight. "Whether there is a loophole or a clause that allows it or not, as a human being, he should have let them in. This, more than anything, makes me think he knows what is truly going on here."

She tipped back her head to watch him. He looked down the street again, and ran his free hand through his hair.

His gaze rested on her for a moment. "I will take you home, and come to you tonight if I can. But I need to see Gibbs about this."

She nodded. "What will you do?"

He gave a shrug. “I'll have to wait until the session is over. I would like to thrash him, but short of that, I don't know. Whatever I can.”

He tucked her in close under his arm and ran his thumb across her knuckles.

“Strange,” he whispered into her hair. “Even though I have seldom felt so angry, having you with me helps. Gibbs should be grateful for your very existence.”

Chapter Forty

The church bells rang seven in the evening. They were edging towards summer, though, and the sun was not yet completely set.

James saw one of the lights shining from Gibbs's office extinguished, and quickened his step across the street.

The clerk he had sparred with on Tuesday was about to extinguish a second lamp when he walked in. He stared blankly at James as he gave a nod and walked past him, straight toward Gibbs's private office.

James didn't bother knocking, he simply walked in.

Gibbs was sitting at his desk with a glass of brandy in his hand, staring at a pile of papers.

He looked up sharply. "Wittaker. What the devil do you mean, barging in here?"

"I came to give you a message." James didn't take a seat, he walked up to the desk and leaned his hip against it, arms crossed, looming over Gibbs.

Gibbs pushed his chair back to stand.

"Sit."

Phoebe had calmed him earlier, had centered him, but she wasn't here now, and the sight of Gibbs stirred the rage of this afternoon all over again, hot and deadly.

Gibbs sank back in his chair so suddenly, it rocked a little. James could see the confusion and the hint of fear on his face.

"What is this about?"

"I've come to tell you to resign." He watched Gibbs take that in, and frown.

"Resign, on what grounds?"

"Corruption. Dereliction of duty. Failure to uphold the law. You can take your pick."

Gibbs gaped at him.

"Bellingham is to be hanged on Monday, I understand, and the jury took less than fourteen minutes to find him guilty."

"I'm not the jury—"

"You set the trial date less than four days after the crime took place. And I know why." James did not try to hide the contempt he felt for Gibbs. For all of them. "You can pass this message on to the Prince Regent. We know. And if anyone has the bright idea to try something like this again, should there be another politician in future His Majesty doesn't like, we will make sure the papers have the full story, no matter how little proof we can produce."

Gibbs let his glass slip from his hand. It hit the desk and through some miracle did not tip over. He was turning purple again, but Wittaker honestly didn't care if he had an apoplexy this time or not.

"We?" He wheezed the word out.

"Lord Dervish, myself and a number of other interested parties."

Gibbs slumped back in his chair, his mouth working.

"I expect to hear of your resignation in the next few weeks." James turned and started for the door.

"Wittaker." Gibbs almost gasped out his name.

James turned.

"Didn't know . . . was told . . ."

"Here's the thing." James paused in the doorway, watching Gibbs take a hard slug from his brandy glass with a hand that shook. "I don't care if you knew exactly what had happened or not. You deliberately set out to deny Bellingham a fair trial. That is not acceptable to me, and I will ruin you if you do not step down with immediate effect. The thought of you continuing in the justice system offends me."

He kept eye contact with Gibbs for a long, drawn-out beat, and then turned and walked out.

The clerk stood in the middle of the front office, eyes wide, mouth open. James strode past him without a word, and as he started down the stairs, he heard the crystal glass Gibbs had been holding shatter against the wall.

The sound satisfied him more than he liked to admit.

***

She was in her private garden, walking quietly among the rows. A soft breeze stirred through the hedge and ruffled the herbs, sending the fragrance of lavender, rosemary and fennel swirling about her.

The sun was almost completely set, and the last stains of orange melted out of the sky.

There was a scrabble of leather on stone, and she took a few long steps away from the wall, her eyes straining in the twilight to see who would come over the top.

Wittaker peered down at her. Then he grinned and jumped to the ground. "This is almost like old times."

She smiled back and stepped into his arms, then gasped as he lifted her and swung her up against the wall, holding her in place with his body.

"Almost," she murmured, lifting her hands to pull his head down close to hers. "But not quite."

Author's Note

Spencer Perceval, the only British prime minister ever to be assassinated, was killed in May 1812 by John Bellingham. It was the JFK assassination of its day and it sent a ripple of shock through Britain.

All the evidence relating to Bellingham's part in the crime that I mention in this book, from where he stayed, who he bought the pistols from, the secret pocket he had sewn into his coat, the events that transpired through the shooting itself, as well as for Bellingham's stated reason for the crime are true.

In most cases, I've used the names of the real people involved, like the Attorney-General, Sir Vicary Gibbs, Mr. Harmer, Bellingham's defense council, Vickery the Bow Street Runner and a number of others.

Perceval and the Prince Regent did hate each other, for the reasons I give in the book, but the idea that some of the Prince Regent's friends could have used Bellingham to kill the prime minister on his behalf, or as a service to him, is from my imagination.

There have been conspiracy theories around for a long time over why Bellingham killed Perceval, and who was helping him.

What is very true is that Bellingham really did have no money, yet mysteriously continued to live, and live well, in London for months after his money ran out. The promissory note for twenty pounds from Wilson really existed, and Wilson did use the Baltick Coffee House as his place of business.

Also true is that Bellingham's first submission to the Prince Regent was mislaid, and he had to resubmit it.

Gascoyne's testimony at the hearing was contrary to other known facts and that, along with the mysterious money, and Bellingham's real panic during his hearing when he heard Bow Street had spoken to a woman who had something of his, helped build my plot.

So many people had an axe to grind with Perceval. The sheer number of people who would have been happy to see him dead has meant it's been hard narrowing down the field of who, if anyone, used Bellingham, in his madness and obsessive drive, to do away with the prime minister.

Andro Linklater's book *Why Spencer Perceval Had to Die* documents much of the evidence that lays the case open for genuine grounds to believe a conspiracy was at work, although Linklater prefers American traders and businessmen, operating out of an office in Liverpool and desperate to stop a war between England and America, as the culprits.

If someone had wanted an end to the Orders in Council, which Perceval was using to disrupt American shipping and which was playing havoc with British trade, killing Perceval certainly worked. They went away almost straight after his death.

However, the communications of the time were slow, and America had already declared war by the time news of the retraction of the Orders in Council reached them. Even though the Orders had been dealt with before war was declared, the Americans had already begun mobilising, and it was too late to stop.

Ironically, if Bellingham could have got his nerve up a little earlier and killed Perceval even a week before he did, he might have prevented England and America going to war.

It may have seemed to anyone who wanted the Orders in Council done away with that removing Perceval was the only way to do it. Prime ministers could be in office for fifteen years or more and Perceval had such a grip on government, it may have seemed impossible that he would be ousted by normal means.

Mollie Gillen's book *The Assassination of the Prime Minister* is not only the best book available on the facts of the case, Gillen also provides diary entries and newspaper clippings from the time so we get a view on what a wide range of people thought about Perceval and his murder. Gillen is careful to present the facts only, and not to speculate on whether Bellingham was a dupe or the 'lone gunman' he appeared to be.

The truth is, if Bellingham was someone's dupe, he was perfect. He really was convinced he would get away with Perceval's murder. He could have run from the scene, and no one would have stopped him, or likely caught him afterward, but he didn't. He intended to take the blame, in the name of obtaining justice and compensation for the injustice done to him, and if someone wanted Perceval dead, and no one official looking in their direction to find a suspect, they couldn't have invented a better candidate than

Bellingham.

Bellingham's trial was widely regarded at the time, and since, as a travesty. There were at least two sets of witnesses who raced down from Liverpool to attend the trial, against all odds and surely at huge expense, and yet it seems they were turned away by the court officials, presumably under the orders of Sir Vicary Gibbs, the Attorney-General. Gibbs did resign after the trial, citing other reasons, but it was suggested by contemporaries at the time that the lynch-mob mentality of his prosecution had ended his career.

Bellingham's wife received a large sum of money from a collection of people who were thrilled her husband had shot the prime minister and who felt sorry for her for what both she and her husband had endured through their trials in Russia.

Knowing the extremely bad blood between the Prince Regent and Perceval, as well as stumbling upon mention of the odd behavior of Gascoyne, I couldn't help but develop the conspiracy theory that I did, although as I mentioned earlier, there really was no shortage of suspects for me to choose from.

The facts of the matter will probably never come to light, but it was extremely interesting delving into this incident and this time in British history.

Michelle Diener

Praise for Michelle Diener's other books:

Luxury Reading: Diener has set a standard for what good historical fiction ought to be . . .

Chicago Tribune : With its richly detailed historical setting and intrigue-filled plot, "In a Treacherous Court" is simply irresistible.

Affaire de Coeur Magazine: Awesome! History woven flawlessly into riveting fiction.

RT Magazine, August 2011 issue: Just when readers think there is nothing new to be learned about Henry VIII, debut author Diener delivers a taut suspense . . . that will keep you turning the pages.

Readers Entertainment: Diener's writing style is beautiful, to the point, vivid and exciting. The characters are going to hook you first, and the intrigue will keep you turning the pages.

Publishers Weekly: Diener (Keeper of the King's Secrets) delivers a rousing read …

ABOUT THE AUTHOR

Michelle Diener was born in London, grew up in South African and now lives in Australia with her family. She was bitten by the travel bug at a young age and has managed to feed her addiction with numerous trips to exciting places all over the world. She writes historical fiction and fantasy, and loves traveling to other times as well as places through the pages of a good book. You can contact Michelle through her website or sign up to receive notification when she has a new book out at www.michellediener.com.

Made in the USA
Lexington, KY
30 November 2015